Mad Dog & Englishman

Mad Dog & Englishman

J. M. Hayes

Poisoned Pen Press

Copyright © 2000 by J.M. Hayes

First Edition 2000

10 9 8 7 6 5 4 3 2 1

Library of Congress Catalog Card Number: 00-103988

ISBN: 1-890208-49-3

Poisoned Pen Press
6962 E. First Ave. Ste 103
Scottsdale, AZ 85251
www.poisonedpenpress.com
info@poisonedpenpress.com

Printed in the United States of America

For Barbara,

and for the fearsome Partridge Quails of '62
when we were young and the earth was verifiably flat
and all the universe orbited around Kansas.

Mad dogs and Englishmen
go out in the mid-day sun...
　　　　—Noel Coward
　　　　Mad Dogs and Englishmen

An artificial intercontinental flight vehicle does not
impress someone whose *hematasooma* (soul) is capable
of superluminal intergalactic space travel.
　　　　—Karl H. Schlesier
　　　　The Wolves of Heaven:
　　　　Cheyenne Shamanism, Ceremonies,
　　　　and Prehistoric Origins

Oh, you can't go back to Kansas,
It just up and blew away...
...you can't go back to Kansas,
'cause that was yesterday.
　　　　—John Stewart
　　　　"Kansas," *The Phoenix Concerts*

Summer in Benteen County, Kansas, is a season possessed of all the gentle subtlety of an act of war. Winter, of course, is no better, but the memory of frosts and blizzards and winds that begin to suck away your life before you walk a dozen steps had grown faint by the early hours of that Sunday morning in late June. A week ago, the thermometer had risen past the unbearable mark for the first time in the summer of 1997, and, in automatic response, the humidity rushed after it—to a level technically described as obscene.

The sheriff lay in the sultry darkness, wondering how to extricate his arm from under the woman sleeping soundly beside him. He wanted to leave, but he didn't want to wake her. The situation reminded him of the definition of "coyote ugly" someone had once told him. When you discover the woman you picked up the night before is so disgusting you're willing to chew your arm off rather than wake her to get free—that's coyote ugly. He wasn't that desperate, and Judy certainly didn't deserve the label. Judy was, in fact, a knockout.

He tried shifting a little to see if improved leverage might make the difference. It didn't. Judy was solidly atop his arm and it was numb and tingling for lack of circulation. Waking her would be easy, she'd probably just roll over and go back to sleep. But she might not. That possibility was enough to keep the sheriff from disturbing her with his efforts.

He had married and divorced Judy in July, the end coming a few days after the eighth anniversary of their beginning. About six months later, they'd started sleeping together again. Benteen County was the kind of place where everyone knew everybody else's business and, since TV reception without a satellite dish was erratic, gossip was still a favorite pastime. Neither the sheriff nor his ex-wife were the sort who would have cared, if their jobs hadn't depended on the community's perception of their morals. He was in his third term, and wanted to serve more. Judy taught at Buffalo Springs High School. For both jobs, an absence of obvious moral turpitude was required. Six months of enforced celibacy had proved to be all either of them could stand. Without the availability of acceptable outlets, they'd taken to filling each other's needs on an irregular basis. Plenty of people might suspect, but this man and his ex-wife did have a good excuse to see each other regularly, an excuse named Heather. She would turn thirteen over Labor Day weekend.

It was sex, and it was release, something both of them had found difficult to do without, but they weren't considering remarriage. The problems that led to their divorce hadn't dissipated. Their skill at the little gibes that hurt was now of Olympic caliber.

That was why the sheriff didn't want to awaken her. They'd sparred from the moment he came through the door last night. After Heather went to bed it got a little ugly. The sex had an angry tint to it as well. They were both so mad by the time they got around to it that it took on a sort of frenzied quality in which pleasure was something to be inflicted, not given, and a shared climax was both a victory and a defeat.

He tried a different approach. He snuggled closer to her, letting their combined body heat mount. Sweat begin to bead and drip, despite the efforts of the air conditioner in the window across the room, humming in frustration at the impossible task of keeping the night's heat and humidity at bay. After a few minutes, his strategy worked. Judy rolled away, searching for a cooler spot, and as she rolled he managed to draw his arm from under her nearly perfect form.

He sat on the edge of the bed for a moment, letting the air conditioner dry him while he massaged feeling back into the limb. Then he gathered his clothes, separating them from hers, searching through the dark for where they'd been wildly tossed. He remembered, with an odd mix of lust and shame, how, earlier, they'd nearly torn them off each other. He shook his head at the absurdity of it, and, barefoot, padded softly out of her room and down the hall to the bathroom to dress.

It was a woman's bath now, complete with curling irons, hair dryers, dozens of mysterious oils, lotions, and scents. Even the toilet paper was floral. The sheriff found that a little silly.

He pulled on his jeans and ran the sink full of water, borrowing a washcloth, to sponge off his face and upper body, and some of Judy's least fragrant deodorant. He would have showered, but the noise might rouse her. He considered the brief loan of one of her razors but his beard grew slow and thin and he knew he could get by without it, especially as an alternative to the lecture he'd get if she suspected he'd used it.

He examined his face closely in the mirror to be sure and was surprised at the age of the visage that peered back. His short hair was still black, no grey anywhere, but his forehead was higher than he remembered and the lines around his eyes and mouth had turned from crinkles into crevices from too many years squinting into the Kansas sun, too much exposure to the wind that rushed up from the Gulf of Mexico in the summer, or plummeted from the pole in winter, with no more than a couple of trees in Nebraska or Oklahoma to slow its passage.

He had high cheekbones and a Roman nose. But for the surprise of the pale-blue eyes that peered out of his dark face, he looked more like a full-blooded Cheyenne than the quarter he was supposed to be. He wondered what genetic happenstance had left him with such an Indian face and such Anglo eyes, especially when his former mate's genealogical researches suggested that quarter Cheyenne actually subdivided into one part Cheyenne, one part Sans Arc, one part Buffalo Soldier, and one part Mexican.

He put on everything but his boots. In socks, then, instead of bare feet, he went to the bedroom at the other end of the hall to check on his daughter. It was amazing to think something so wonderful could have resulted from the disaster of his relationship with Judy. Her bed was empty. He turned and just kept from running down the steps to the first floor living room where lights still blazed and the TV made noises for the benefit of neighbors who might be able to imagine parents sitting up into the wee hours to discuss their daughter's future.

Heather was curled up on the couch where she'd fallen asleep in front of the TV. She was wearing one of the t-shirts he'd given her, an extra-large purple with a snarling Kansas State Wildcat. It was big enough to serve her as an oversize nightie, even though she was turning lanky and coltish in her adolescence. He had the urge to find a blanket to tuck her in, but it was, if anything, still uncomfortably warm in the living room. He satisfied himself with turning off the TV, slipping quietly into his boots, and tiptoeing to the door.

"Dad?" she said, sleepily, just as he put his hand on the knob.

He turned and watched her sit up and rub her eyes. "What time is it?" she asked around a yawn, stretching and shaking her tousled hair back into place.

"Four-twelve." Before digital watches he'd never cared, nor differentiated, beyond the nearest quarter, how many minutes before or after the hour it was. Times change, he thought, on the face of his watch and on the face in the mirror.

"You should be in bed," he scolded, mildly.

"Couldn't sleep, what with all the noise you guys were making, especially those sounds Mom makes right near the end."

If he'd had a lighter skin he would have blushed. Instead, he just stood there, unable to think of something appropriate to say.

"I don't understand," she continued. "You guys bicker and fight and then you fuck. Is that the way it's supposed to be? Is it good for either of you?"

He decided this was one of those times when you ignored the f-word. Though that was probably part of this particular testing of the available parent, it wasn't the critical part. "No," he said, honestly.

"No?"

"No, it's not the way it's supposed to be and no, it's probably not good for either of us. Obviously it's not good for you either."

"Then why?"

"Old habits, I suppose. It's hard to explain and you're still a little young to understand."

"That's bullshit, Dad! I started menstruating months ago. Did you know that? Did you ask? Did you care? I've seen animals do the deed. I've known about fucking for years. I've even had offers."

One thing she seemed to have inherited from her mother was an intuitive sense of what to say to really get to him. With every inner reserve stressed to the max, he refrained from asking who had made those offers. Maybe the appropriate thing would have been to turn on the outraged parent act and pack her off to bed and himself out the door. He didn't know. He was as lost at parenting as he had been at husbanding. Since an adult might understand, if not forgive, he gambled and decided to treat her as such.

"This is a small community, old-fashioned with old-fashioned values. People can have extramarital relationships or cheat on their spouses, but only if they're willing for everyone in the county to know about it and treat them accordingly. Your mother and I are public figures. We can't fool around and keep our jobs—unless, maybe, we fool around with each other. That doesn't make it right, especially since, sometimes, we don't seem to like each other very much. But sometimes we still care for each other a lot. And, we're human. Like everybody else we've got weaknesses. I guess we thought we were getting away with it, fooling the community and fooling you too, with nobody, except maybe the two of us, getting hurt. It looks like we were wrong and I'm sorry. I'm sorry, too, that I didn't know you'd started menstruating. You're growing up so fast...and don't ever let your mother hear you say the f-word or mention the noises she makes or you're not likely to live long enough to grow up the rest of the way. OK?"

She sat with her elbows on her knees and her chin in her hands and he could see that there was, indeed, an incipient adult in that child/woman's body. That adult would be here, full-time, a lot sooner than he was ready for.

"I don't know, Dad," she admitted. "It's not that I want you to stop being with Mom. I just don't want to see you guys hurt each other. But thanks for trying to answer. I didn't think you'd bother."

He walked back over from the door and she rose from the couch and came into his arms. Her hug told him the world might be worth living in after all.

Boris, the German Shepherd, met him at the back door after he sent Heather to bed and let himself out. Boris wagged his tail and let the sheriff scratch his ears, but kept turning to look back toward downtown Buffalo Springs, whining in a way that sounded like an effort to communicate. He seemed a little more frustrated than usual at the sheriff's inability to decipher *lingua canis*. The dog stood on the porch as the sheriff went down the walk and out the gate to where his new Chevy truck had been pulled off the street and into the drive. He hadn't really been worried about traffic, but it was more than twenty years since his last, and only other, new vehicle. He had no intention of letting this one start to collect dents any sooner than necessary.

The Reverend Peter Simms was a Benteen County native. He knew better than to expect anything beyond an occasional, teasing respite from unbearable heat or humidity before September, if then. He also knew, since neither his home nor his church possessed air conditioning, that Job must temporarily stand aside to make room for Peter Simms.

For everything—turn, turn, turn—there is a season—toss, turn, squirm—and a cause for every insomniac under heaven. The cause for Reverend Simms' restless inability to sleep, despite the very early Sunday hour, was a combination of heat and humidity, both in the high eighties, and a fuse that, for some inexplicable reason, kept unscrewing itself just enough to shut down his ineffective evaporative cooler and the rotating fan he'd bought to assist it. Operating together, they made his bedroom almost bearable, but every time he started to get comfortable enough to drift off, they would drift off too and he would have to find his slippers and flashlight and go twist the infernal fuse back into contact.

After four trips, Peter Simms gave up the fight. He disentangled himself from his sweat-soaked sheets and sat miserably on the edge of his bed, staring at the digital alarm clock beside him. It was set for much later. Thy will, Oh Lord, he thought, but there was a hint of peevish self-pity in it as if he were affixing blame instead of shouldering a necessary burden.

He rolled out of bed and shut off the alarm, stuffed his toes into his slippers again, padded wearily down the hall to the back door, across the porch and into the yard. At the corner of the house, he opened the electrical box and screwed the offending fuse back into position. The motor in the evaporative cooler in his window immediately began to hum. The faint glow of a night light illuminated his way back to his bedroom. He turned the cooler and fan off in case they were the problem. He removed his slippers, shucked out of his striped pajamas, and waddled flat-footed into the bathroom to place his doughy body beneath a stream of cold water from the shower. It came out tepid and the power went off again while he was soaping himself. It didn't surprise him. He'd propped the flashlight in the sink just in case. When he emerged, he felt cleaner, and, if not eager to face the day, at least capable of it. With the good sense of a cautious man, he applied a double dose of antiperspirant before setting off to church to rewrite his morning's sermon. A bit of scripture praising air conditioning was what he had in mind, but anything that even hinted there was nothing immoral about keeping one's pastor comfortable would do.

The eastern horizon, flat and distant, flashed with hints of a storm—too far to hear it grumble, let alone feel its breath, cooling or otherwise. The lightning glowed the color of bruised, over-ripe fruit through an atmosphere burdened with dust, humidity and pollution. Sunrise would be spectacular. The Reverend Simms gave the storm a myopic glance as he stepped down from his back porch. He judged the flickerings along the horizon as among the Lord's less enthusiastic efforts, then ignored them. He made his way across the back yard, down the alley, and south toward the Buffalo Springs Non-Denominational Community Church. Despite his liberal use of antiperspirant, he was sweating before he got to his back gate. He didn't notice the shadow that detached itself from his lilac bushes and floated silently in his wake.

Buffalo Springs was the Benteen County seat. Veteran's Memorial Park adorned the square just east of the courthouse and north of Simms' church. The county had never been very populous and so had few veterans to memorialize. A generic hero in bronze stood atop a concrete pedestal from which the plaque listing names and conflicts had long since been stolen, probably a prank by kids from a neighboring town. Since it was no longer certain whom the place honored, and since the citizenry providing the tax base for projects like park maintenance and beautification had been steadily shrinking for decades, the park had been allowed to return to something approaching natural prairie. Of course it was home to too many trees. No matter how often the town was visited by Dutch Elm disease, a few always managed to survive, usually near where the park's fountain used to be. The valve to the fountain had been turned off long ago, shortly after the fountain, like the plaque, had vanished. Old valves have a way of seeping, and the lush state of the grasses, saplings, and weeds made that end of the park Eden-like in comparison to any part of Benteen County not adjacent to the North Fork of the Kansaw or one of its tributaries, or land which was regularly irrigated. And then there were the evergreens that must have been imported from some especially desolate climate, since they were surviving quite nicely in fitful clusters throughout the park, their spacing ideal as a windbreak for winter storms behind which massive drifts of snow could build to block the street at the south side of the square.

Peter Simms normally skirted the park and its hazards unless he was in a hurry. Fantasies of moving several large fans from the church auditorium back into his small office and testing their potential to turn the sweat that was already drenching him into the evaporative cooling system nature designed prompted him to the direct approach. Oblivious to the seeds and burrs that began attaching themselves to his pants legs, he entered the park on what had once been the north promenade. There was a path of sorts that led toward his church.

He heard the jogger before he'd gone more than a few steps. There weren't many joggers in Buffalo Springs, and fewer, to the best of his knowledge, who chose such an early hour to test the treacherous footing of Veteran's Memorial Park. Reverend Simms peered curiously behind him. The runner was following the same route he'd chosen so he stepped aside to avoid blocking the narrow track.

It was very dark among the saplings and evergreens. The moon did little more than turn some distant clouds opalescent around the edges and the heavy atmosphere blocked out all but the most determined starlight. Street lights didn't help much. The county had given up replacing the bulbs that were regularly shot out by customers leaving The Bisonte Bar or The Road House after exchanging bets about their respective marksmanship with the rifles that hung in the window racks of their pickups. County revenues were off—so were most of the lights.

The jogger was a trim figure moving with an easy rhythm that Simms envied. As the runner approached, the Reverend tried to guess who it could be.

"Good morning," he said. The jogger just reached out, slapped Simms lightly on the cheek, and disappeared into a thick copse of trees.

"One," a voice whispered from where the jogger had gone.

Peter Simms was taken aback. "Who is that?" he demanded of the darkness, ready to join the joke that was being played on him as soon as he understood it.

Just a little afraid, he stepped back out on the path and peeked around the trees. A hand flashed out of nowhere and slapped him lightly on the other cheek.

"Two," the soft voice said.

"Two what?" Simms inquired in a voice a couple of ranges higher and tighter than normal. No answer. No sound.

Peter Simms decided to leave the park, get back out in the open where his tormenter would be more visible, where it was just possible the sheriff or one of his deputies might drive by on some mysterious nightly errand. Back on the street, logic and reason might again prevail, and, if not, there were houses nearby where he could seek help.

He only managed a couple of steps before the night runner passed him again, this time swatting him hard on the seat of his trousers.

"That's three," the jogger said.

"What are you doing?" Simms asked, his voice leaking hysteria.

To his surprise, this time he got an answer. "Counting."

The sound seemed to come from somewhere behind Simms even though the darkly clad figure had just disappeared into the shadows ahead.

"Counting what?" Simms voice was a little more under control this time, now that the joke was apparently moving to its climax.

"Counting coup," came the reply, just over his shoulder. He turned and saw something flash out of the night and felt it flick the back of his left arm. It wasn't a hand this time. The touch was cool and almost unnoticeable, but Peter Simms felt a sudden flow of moisture. He reached with his other hand and touched the spot. It came away dark and damp and he realized he was bleeding.

"Oh my God," he whispered. He jerked his head left and right, looking for the blade wielder, looking for a place to run or hide. Surely this was only a nightmare. At any moment he must wake up in his bed to the beep of his alarm. Something bit him on the other arm and he saw that his sleeve had been slashed and his shirt was acquiring a dark wet stripe that lengthened and widened as he watched.

"Oh Jesus!" he screamed. "Don't hurt me!" It was as fervent as any prayer he'd ever uttered.

A deputy sat behind a desk in the old county courthouse about a hundred yards away, reading a commentary from the preceding day's Wichita *Eagle-Beacon* that argued the Dow could never sustain its inflated value at seven thousand and listening to the static that occasionally crackled from his departmental radio. He was undisturbed by the Reverend's plea.

Boris, in his yard at the east edge of town, heard. He barked a couple of times, and, when the sound changed, tried to match the agony of that distant howl. A few canines responded, but no humans. They soon ceased, as had the voice they echoed. Boris silently patrolled his territory, troubled by the presence of a danger he sensed but was unable to challenge.

He looked more like Jason, or Freddy Krueger—or some other not-quite-human murderer in one of those dead-teenager movies—than a man. Since his hair had been way too short to braid in the foreseeable future, he'd shaved it off. He wore a thin strip of leather as a head band, one he'd dyed black with shoe polish, and, in the band at the back of his skull, a single raven feather—well, actually crow, but it would take an ornithologist to know. His body was clad only in a pair of black Speedo swim trunks, since he hadn't been able to come up with satisfactory makings for a breech cloth, and he'd covered himself from head to toe with black, licorice-flavored body paint he'd bought in a sex paraphernalia shop in Wichita. There were ragged white strokes of vanilla lightning artfully arcing down each arm and leg and across each of his cheeks. He'd managed to incorporate the Speedo logo into the stroke on his right leg. He was just setting out the leather bags of painted sand and the cow skull that would have to make do in place of a buffalo skull when a pickup came down the street on the south side of Veteran's Memorial Park and pulled up where the curb would have been if one of those bond elections had passed.

"What the hell are you doing, Mad Dog?" a familiar voice asked over the strains of a John Stewart CD turned up high enough to test the truck's sound system.

Mad Dog was disappointed. He hadn't thought anyone would recognize him in his elaborate costume, not even his half-brother, the sheriff.

"That your new truck?" He walked up to the window, careful not to touch anything in case his body paint might stain the Chevy. "See you got a good stereo with it. Nice."

Without the body paint, Mad Dog looked a lot more Anglo than his brother, even though they shared their equal but slim claim to Cheyenneness through their common mother. His hair wasn't a very dark brown and it tended to sun streak and curl as it lengthened, two of the reasons he hadn't managed to let it grow long enough for braids before getting disgusted and chopping it off.

Mad Dog was his real name. He'd been born Harvey Edward Maddox. His father ran off shortly after his conception, and, fueled by his long held disgust at distantly related Lester Maddox's unheroic rise to racist infamy, Harvey Edward had legally adopted the nickname he'd earned as a high school football star in Buffalo Springs. It had more to do with emerging ethnic pride than nostalgia for lost youth, though. Somewhere about the time he began to contemplate his own mortality, Harvey Edward Maddox became Harvey Edward Mad Dog, born-again Cheyenne.

"How'd you know it was me?" Mad Dog asked the shadow in the truck's cab.

"Who else would do something this silly? Besides, I recognized your Saab parked down at the corner. Which brings me back to my original question. What the hell are you doing?"

"Vision quest."

"Say what?"

"Vision quest. You got a problem with that? This is a public park and I'm a member of the public. You gonna tell me I need a permit to sit here and fast and pray for a vision?"

John Stewart finished explaining why you can't go back to Kansas and the sheriff thought he had a point as he reached over and turned the CD off. The only sounds that remained were the smooth idle of the pickup's 350 cubic inch V-8 and the stirring of gentler than usual morning breezes through the park's trees.

"No. Especially not until somebody complains, which they may well do when they start arriving for services at the church just across the street here. I'm not gonna give a damn what you do in this park. You know me, Mad Dog. I've got a strong commitment to individual liberties, so long as they don't interfere with anybody else's."

"Well then, Englishman, you'll excuse me if I get back to setting up my stuff. I want to get started long before sunrise."

The sheriff hated being called Englishman, which was one of the reasons Mad Dog so consistently used the nickname. Given his own name, English, and his relationship to Mad Dog, it was a natural. Folks all over Benteen County knew who you were talking about if you mentioned Englishman.

"Mad Dog, you are about the contrariest person I ever knew."

The sheriff didn't see the big smile that lit his older brother's face. The Cheyenne were known for their Contraries. They were the fiercest warriors, men who chose the difficult task of living their lives backwards, doing the opposite of what they were asked, always fighting alone on the flanks of battle and taking the biggest risks. Being a Contrary was an awesome responsibility and a tremendous honor. Mad Dog was delighted with his little brother's comment, regardless of how he'd meant it.

"Vision quest," the sheriff muttered as he reached over to punch John Stewart's *Phoenix Concerts* back into stereophonic life. He put the truck in gear and headed down the street toward the Benteen County Courthouse.

A magnificent sunrise was followed, shortly, by the arrival of a goodly portion of the citizens of greater Buffalo Springs. Parking was haphazard around the town square, there being no marked spaces. Some folks preferred parallel, others pulled in straight, but most favored an angle related to the direction from which they'd arrived or in which they intended to depart.

The area in front of the Buffalo Springs Non-Denominational Community Church, and, across the street, bordering the Veteran's Memorial Park in which Mad Dog was conducting his first annual summer vision quest, drew a heavy crowd—thanks to Mad Dog, one heavier than usual. At the opposite end of the square, the immediate vicinity of Bertha's Diner drew a slightly larger multitude, evidence that feeding the soul ranked behind feeding the body in Benteen County.

Mad Dog's modified lotus position behind the cow skull drew the curious, but he maintained his solemn and unresponsive vigil, despite a disconcerting tendency for residents to recognize him in what he had expected would be, if not a disguise, at least major camouflage. He drew a larger crowd than he might have since the Reverend Simms failed to show for services, but, as the sun began to beat the dusty square instead of merely illuminate it and the usual stiff breeze failed to materialize, the Reverend's contingent headed either for home or Bertha's. By late morning, Mad Dog was alone with the universal forces from whom he sought enlightenment.

Mad Dog had left his watch in the Saab, feeling that a digital Japanese time piece was out of place with the rest of his costume as well as with the timelessness of his intent. Still, from the shadows, the ever thickening crowds at the diner, and the way he was sweating, he guessed it must be after eleven. It might be a little early for him to expect a vision, especially since he'd cheated a bit on the fasting when he started out that morning, helping himself to a couple of cups of coffee and a pair of cream-filled cupcakes that proved almost as tasteless as they'd looked. Still, relatively fresh calories were being processed by his digestive system so he was surprised when he noticed a blurring of his vision and a humming in his ears. He'd been staring vacantly at the out-of-order Veteran's Memorial Park restroom. It was a small structure that, in its day, had discriminated against users neither for race, creed, nor even sex, since it contained plumbing to accommodate only one visitor at a time. The door, which should have been padlocked, seemed to be ajar. Just in front of it the air was filled with dancing spots, almost as if someone was about to beam down to the park from the Starship *Enterprise*. All this was accompanied by a faint buzzing in Mad Dog's ears. He sat there, patiently waiting for the vision to solidify into something recognizable or for the sound to take on meaning. Neither happened. Nothing, in fact happened, except the morning's coffee worked its way through Mad Dog's kidneys to his bladder, making concentrating on the impending vision increasingly difficult. This wasn't something he'd planned for. He'd expected the sun to sweat the coffee out of him—it was certainly sweating something out of him—but the coffee had taken its normal course and expected to exit by the usual route.

Mad Dog let himself glance around at the street. He was surprised that the blurring swirl of spots didn't remain in the center of his vision. When he looked away from the restroom his sight was clear. Whatever the phenomenon, it was located in space and time and not just in the inner workings of his mind behind his nearly coal black eyes.

The adjacent street was abandoned. There was a collection of cars down at Bertha's, but no faces peered his way through her front window. Mad Dog decided to examine the phenomenon more closely and perhaps relieve himself of the coffee behind the structure or in some of the park's thicker bushes.

The humming was louder as he approached the building. The spots grew clearer. A pungent odor became increasingly noticeable as he drew near. The spots, he was surprised to discover, were flies, a swarm of them so thick as to explain the hum and the apparent distortion of the atmosphere in the door to the restroom. He'd seen swarms like that around dead things, usually ones that were well past ripe, but the smell that steadily grew more offensive wasn't decay. There was a coppery tinge to it with fecal overtones. The door to the facility was still padlocked, but lock and chain hung from the hasp, dangling where they'd been pried free of their attachment to the wall. Fresh scars on the surface gave evidence of the force used to separate them.

Mad Dog took a deep breath of relatively fresh air, swiped wildly at the flies, and stepped to the door, pushing it further open to see what was interesting the flies. What he discovered made him address a deity other than the ones he'd been concerned with contacting. He lurched away from the restroom and fell to one knee, vomiting cupcakes onto the dry grass. His stomach continued to heave long after it was empty.

What remained of the Reverend Simms, lying face down in the abandoned toilet, took no offense at Mad Dog's reaction. The flies didn't complain either. They were delighted to have an option.

◇◇◇

Doc Jones had the sad, sagging face of a bloodhound. His big ears stood out from the side of his nearly bald head and his jowls drooped so heavily that they pulled down the corners of his mouth in the perpetual frown of disapproval he brought to any occasion that required his presence.

The sheriff met him at the door to his ten-year-old Buick station wagon, which sometimes doubled as hearse or ambulance, as the doctor parked beside the even older Benteen County Sheriff's black and white. The patrol car's light bar broadcast an invitation to anyone who hadn't yet joined the throng milling about the edge of Veteran's Memorial Park. Its driver, Deputy Wynn, known to friends and enemies as "Wynn some, lose some," was the only person in full uniform. He was making an effort at crowd control, keeping people back from the restroom by providing grisly descriptions of what was still lying there to those who would listen. Most citizens would, and were.

"This for real, Sheriff?" Doc waved at the crowd as he pulled his house-call bag out of the vehicle. "You really got a homicide here?"

"That, or the most determined suicide I ever heard of."

"Be damned," the doctor muttered as the sheriff led him toward the facility. "Been coroner in Benteen County seventeen years and this is my first homicide. Thought I was going to have to retire before I got one."

"Guess you lucked out, Doc."

"Don't get sarcastic on me. I'm not glad somebody got themselves murdered. I'm just interested in the challenge. Want to see if I'm up to finding a cause of death, narrowing down the time, giving you the clues you need to bag the killer. It'll be a hell of a lot more interesting than flu or VD or hemorrhoids, or sewing up some drunk who picked wrong from among the several roads he was seeing as he drove home. Where is it?"

The sheriff pointed at the door, still ajar and filled with flies.

"Who puked in the weeds?" Doc advanced as eagerly as a teenager shopping for his first car.

"Mad Dog. Mine's over behind those trees."

"Yours? Sheriff, I'm surprised at you. You've pulled more than one kid out of a hot rod that needed kingpins instead of twin carbs." He paused before the door. "Mad Dog didn't do this." The way he said it made it about half statement and half question.

"Don't think so," the sheriff said. "He found the body and came and got me after he stopped heaving his guts out. But he was here before dawn, probably about the time this happened. I haven't ruled anybody out yet. Hell, I'm not even sure who's in there."

"Good," Doc Jones stated. "The mystery is what makes this challenging. Not much fun in just corroborating a confession. You or Mad Dog touch anything?"

"Just the door…at least me. Unless Mad Dog did it, I don't think he touched anything else either."

Doc smiled, straightening out the crescent of his mouth. He slipped through the curtain of flies, then came right back out again, several shades paler. "Jesus Christ!" he said, imploring the same deity addressed earlier by Reverend Simms, then by Mad Dog. Doc Jones did manage to avoid losing his breakfast, however. The arrival of a premature baby had kept him from eating it. Doc braced himself against the door frame, mouth hanging open, inviting flies.

The sheriff refrained from making a wisecrack. What lay in there in a pool of congealing blood and excrement remained too vivid in his mind. "Any idea who he is?"

"Shit, all that cutting, I'm not even sure it's a he yet." Jones shook his head and swatted at the flies, regaining self-control. "You want to take some pictures of the crime scene, get it done. I'm going to take the deceased's temperature and check for rigor. Maybe look for lividity too, though with all that blood loss I may not find much, Then we'll move the corpse over to Klausen's funeral parlor. I need some place cool that doesn't smell like an abattoir where I can work on cleaning this cadaver up and figure out who or what it was."

The sheriff hadn't gotten over the shock enough to think about pictures and he certainly didn't want any. He wouldn't need them to remember, and he didn't want to look again. But Doc Jones was right. If anyone was charged, if this went to trial, there would have to be pictures.

"Could it be Peter Simms? I hear he didn't show for church this morning. I can't think of anything much short of this that would keep him from delivering a sermon."

Doc waved at the flies again. "I don't know. Body's about the right size but it's so mutilated and covered with dried blood.... Course, in a place like Buffalo Springs, it seems pretty likely if you've got a spare corpse and a missing person, they're going to turn out to be one and the same. Go get your camera. Soon as we finish I'm going to need help getting it into a body bag and over to Klausen's."

"OK."

"Get a shovel or a dust pan or something too," Doc shouted at the sheriff's back. "Damned if I want to pick up all those entrails by hand."

The sheriff paced back and forth across the antique white octagonal tiles that covered the floor of the mortician's lab in the back of Klausen's Funeral Home. He was trying just to listen to what Doc was saying and ignore the wet, sucking noises that resulted whenever Doc probed at the ruin that had once been human. The sheriff had a notebook and a pencil to take down any pertinent facts Doc might mention. There was a dark mark in one corner of the exposed page where he'd started to write something, only to break the lead because of the force with which he'd tried to write it. He thought about excusing himself to look for a pencil sharpener, but there was a ball point in his pocket. Doc had brought in a little portable cassette recorder and the sheriff didn't think he'd ever forget one second of this day anyway. Besides, once he got out of the back room at Klausen's, it would be hard to get him back in except as a customer.

"It's Peter Simms all right," Doc was saying, sponging the last of the dried blood off the corpse's face. "Funny, he's been mutilated so much, but the killer hardly touched his face at all. Kind of like he didn't want us to have a problem making an identification."

"You got a cause of death yet, Doc?"

Jones laughed, a sound with just a touch of hysteria to it. "Take your pick," he said, stepping away from the stainless steel tray and waving at the bloody remains with its contrastingly pale, cherubic features. "Off hand, I'd say he bled out—cardiac arrest as a result of loss of blood. There's any number of these wounds that would have killed him eventually. I mean, Jesus, he's had half his fingers cut off, his guts split open and spilled all over the place, his nuts hacked off, and slashes made all over his body—most of those minor, really, though some of them go clean to the bone—and he's been scalped. If the Reverend was lucky, the killer got to a major artery real quick and he was dead before the worst of this happened. Or he had a heart attack and died of fright. But he could have survived quite awhile, through most of this, and my guess is whoever did it would have wanted him to be as aware as possible, else why bother. I'll be able to tell you better after I open him up."

The sheriff wanted to look away, but he couldn't. Simms' face was as peaceful as might be expected after the mortician was through. He was even smiling, a knowing smile that seemed to indicate he'd recognized the joke after all and was enjoying the discomfort of those who had yet to fathom it.

"*Risus sardonicus*," Doc explained. "Death's grin. Some of the facial muscles contract during rigor mortis. It's a natural phenomena but I can never help thinking they're laughing at me.

"You don't look so good, Sheriff. You've got what you need from me for now. Why not go start solving this. I don't need you here anymore. God knows, I sure wouldn't stay for the rest of this if I didn't have to." He reached down and picked up a pair of bone shears and worked their gleaming jaws to demonstrate. "Soon as I get cause and narrow down time, I'll let you know. Go on, get."

"Thanks Doc," the sheriff was more relieved than he cared to admit. "You sure you don't need help."

"None you can provide. Besides, I just got my wish. I think this might be proof of that ancient Chinese curse. 'May you get what you wish for.' Well, what the Reverend here got was worse. Go grill your brother or track down a killer. I've got a chest to crack."

The sheriff went.

The Benteen County Courthouse occupied most of the block at the west end of the square, just across the street from the park. It was a red-brick, two-storied structure with attic rooms, a central tower above its sloped roof, a plethora of chimneys, and metal gingerbread along its eves. It was a handsome building, a reminder of thousands of courthouses built just before the end of the nineteenth century and, for the most part since, replaced by structures less pleasant to the eye, less evocative of justice than expedience, but easier to heat and cool and maintain.

The sheriff swung his truck carefully into the parking lot behind the building. Actually, it was more a vacant lot than a parking lot and its exact boundaries remained a matter of dispute with Lanny York who lived next door. Lanny continually mounted an advance of fresh rose bushes that departmental deputies and other county employees as regularly ran over with their vehicles or the county's only black and white. The bill for replacing those roses currently totaled $384.59, not including interest, but the county board of commissioners had denied the claim on the basis of the location of York's property line and the entire matter was moving ponderously trialward. The sheriff, concerned both with the narrow margin by which he'd last been elected and what rose thorns could do to his new truck's paint, carefully avoided York's latest thrust into no man's land and parked in the corner of the lot farthest from any other vehicles. He locked the doors, though it had been three months since even a purse left in an open vehicle had gone missing in the county. He climbed the steps to the courthouse's back door and let himself in.

The "ground floor" was almost six feet above the surrounding prairie, not much of a pedestal upon which to set county law and government, but in land this flat, any elevation tended to be noticed. He threaded his way past vacant offices and out into the main foyer where a massive staircase led up to the courtrooms, only one of which remained presentable enough for use. His office was across the hall where frumpy, ageless Mrs. Kraus sat at the reception desk in front of a wall so covered with trails of moisture through decades of dust that, at first glance, it looked to be a contour map of someplace with more rugged topography than Benteen County.

"Where's Wynn?" the sheriff asked.

"Don't know," Mrs. Kraus growled. Her voice tested the limits to which whiskey and heavy smoking could carry human tones. She was supposed to have been pretty once, a hot number who sent Mr. Kraus, exhausted but satiated, to an early grave. "Wynn can't seem to remember how to work his radio. Ain't heard from him since you sent him over to Reverend Simms' place to look around."

The sheriff walked over to her desk and picked up the handset out of its charger. Half a dozen rechargeable walkie-talkies were all the county could afford for its deputies. Since the county was so flat, they could occasionally make themselves heard for twenty, thirty miles, but if you wanted to contact a deputy over in Crawford or Cottonwood Corners, both within Benteen's borders, you picked up a phone.

"Five-oh-one to five-one-one" The sheriff said to the radio. The radio lay in his hand and didn't reply. "Five-oh-one to five-one-one," he repeated.

"Told you," Mrs. Kraus rasped. "I even tried calling the Reverend's house a few minutes ago. No answer. Can't raise anybody else either. Billy French's wife says he had to go over to help his sister jump start her car so the family can drive back to his place for Sunday dinner. She's gonna have him call soon as he gets back. He's the only deputy you got's supposed to be on call today. Hank and John took Hank's boat over to Cheney Reservoir. Said they were going fishing, but most likely seeing which of them can drink the most beer or pick up anything remotely resembling a girl. Neither one's due back till their shift starts tomorrow night. And Burke's on vacation. I'm your only employee who's both findable and willing to come in on a day off."

"And I thank you for that," the sheriff told her. He was grateful, but he knew the time-and-a-half she was earning, and the chance to become the source of inside information that the local gossips would be chattering over for months, were ample recompense. "And Mad Dog?"

She nodded toward the back of the building. "Been waiting back in the jail since I came in. He do it? Wondering about that worried me a little." She pulled open the top drawer of her desk and showed the sheriff the Glock semi-automatic she kept for personal protection. "But not too much."

"That's what we're trying to find out." The sheriff turned. "Let me know if you raise Wynn and tell French to get his ass in here when he calls. I'm going to have a fraternal chat with our guest."

"Want me to get you a rubber hose?" Mrs. Kraus asked as he went back into the foyer, slipped behind the main staircase, and started down the corridor that led to the jail. Her laughter echoed hollowly, a croaking sound not unlike an asthmatic's cough, and, no more mirthful.

The Jail was behind an iron door that still swung open and closed with remarkable smoothness. There was a jailer's room on the right guarding three tiers of cells that climbed toward a distant ceiling. They were depressingly primitive, eight-by-eight-by-eight cubes with inch-thick iron bars half a foot apart, bolted into iron plate floors and iron plate ceilings. Nothing more than slop buckets and metal bunks with thin mattresses and blankets had been installed to make them habitable. The upper tier of cells was abandoned now. The roof had leaked up there too often and rust had made the attachment of bars to ceiling more a matter of faith than fact. Half the cells in the middle tier were no better and even a couple on the bottom level were out of play, locked with their keys broken or missing. The cells that remained could only be secured by chains and padlocks and were seldom occupied by anyone other than the occasional drunk. Mad Dog sat in the cell in the back corner, his body paint striped with sweat so that he blended, chameleon-like, with his surroundings. The cell door hung open. There wasn't even a chain and padlock on that one.

The sheriff grabbed a chair out of the stack next to the door to the jailer's office and carried it back into the musty darkness. He put it on the floor just outside the bars in the space where Mad Dog's vacant stare was most nearly focused.

"OK Mad Dog. Tell me about it."

"Wynn some, lose some" was living up to the latter half of his nickname while Mrs. Kraus and the sheriff were trying to raise him on the radio and by phone. He'd been ordered to check on Reverend Simms' house while the sheriff and Doc Jones manhandled the body bag into the back of Doc's Buick. Wynn had cleared the last of the spectators from the park and hopped in the black and white to go do just that. He was a very conscientious deputy, but his intentions had a way of outweighing his performances. He was carrying his radio, volume carefully turned up so he'd be sure to hear any signals over the patrol car's noisy exhaust. Unfortunately, he'd mixed up the squelch and volume controls again and accidentally switched to a channel other than the one used by Benteen County Law Enforcement.

Wynn was not what you'd call an imaginative man. That helped make it easier for him to deal with the glimpse he'd caught of the body in the Veteran's Memorial Park restroom. The moment he heard the Reverend hadn't shown for morning services, Wynn decided that the body was Peter Simms. Being an officer of the law, Wynn immediately set his deductive processes to discovering the killer. The things that had been done to Simms—Wynn remained blissfully ignorant about most of them—led him to believe the killer must have hated Simms passionately, or was some sort of psycho. Benteen County was not without its eccentric citizens, but Wynn just couldn't picture any of them being capable of that kind of butchery. It would take a legitimately crazy person—and he paused here to give Mad Dog a bit of additional consideration—to perform a deed like that.

Mad Dog had loved to badger the Reverend, posing mind-twisting theological contradictions for Simms' explanation, none of which Wynn could remember. They were too perplexing and they troubled his soul when he pondered them. Even so, Wynn couldn't picture Mad Dog chopping away at Peter Simms like some local Lizzie Borden in body paint.

The Reverend hadn't been close to his family, none of whom shared his evangelical passion. Old Man Simms, whose farm was nearby, was too infirm for something like this, whatever he might have felt about his youngest son. Peter Simms' older brother ran a custom wheat-cutting operation out of Crawford on the far side of the County and didn't have much to do with either his brother or his father. Besides, he was probably somewhere in North Texas or Oklahoma about now. Wynn thought he remembered hearing that Simms had a little sister who'd been shipped off to school somewhere years ago. Wynn hadn't heard about her being in the county since. As far as Wynn knew, none of them, nor anybody else, loathed the Reverend enough to explain what had happened in the park. And so, he decided, with sudden intuition, the killer had to be an outsider.

Those thoughts occupied Wynn as he cruised down Peach Street toward where the Reverend's simple frame house sat three doors from where the street dead ended. That was when he saw the black man.

The black man was walking along Peach near the corner of Adams. He was a slender figure in a pair of worn hiking boots, faded jeans, and a dusty polo shirt. He turned to watch Wynn pass with a sort of guilty stoop that made Wynn check his face carefully. It wasn't one Wynn recognized. With only three black families in Buffalo Springs, and probably no more than a dozen in the entire county, it sparked a blazing leap of conviction within Wynn's normally placid imagination. He'd found the killer!

He hit the brakes, twirled the wheel, and spun the cruiser to a broadside stop in the middle of Peach Street. The black man's eyes got noticeably larger and he crouched a little at the sight of a police car making such a violent turn. Wynn reached down and flipped the switches that would turn on the lights and siren. The siren didn't obey, the little yellow wire that had a tendency to slip off its connector under the dash apparently having done so again, but the lights made an impressive display. Flashes of red and blue and amber strobed the street as Wynn put the throttle to the floor and the back tires threw up a pair of rooster tails of dust that obscured the houses on the south side of the street. As the patrol car began fishtailing wildly in his direction, the black man turned and ran.

He didn't stay on the street. If he had, Wynn might have run him down on the excuse he was exercising necessary force to stop a fleeing felon. The man hopped a hedge instead, trampled through a flower bed, and ducked around the Thorn's house, hurdling a succession of little Jimmy Thorn's toys as he disappeared from Wynn's view.

Wynn locked up the brakes again and slid dramatically over the Thorn's hedge and halfway across their lawn. He threw open his door and bolted out of the vehicle, drawing his .357 magnum as he ran. When he got to the Thorn's back yard, the fugitive was nowhere to be seen. It had been a dry spring coming hard on the heels of a dry winter, and since little Jimmy had a penchant for digging up anything that grew or was any shade of green, there was plenty of dust to show Wynn clear evidence of the man's trail.

It led towards Reverend Simms' place by way of a succession of back yards.

The second one over had a four-foot wooden fence, designed to keep three- and four-year-olds from wandering when their mother was occupied with their younger siblings. Wynn was about halfway to the fence when his prey vaulted its twin on the other side of the yard. Wynn tried to draw down on him, but the man was out of sight before he could do it. Wynn ran to the fence and started climbing. The man hopped a third fence further down. Wynn shouted the dramatic, "Stop or I'll shoot!" phrase while he struggled to find solid purchase from which to aim, but the man slid out of sight again. Wynn resumed his climb, and once more, the man cleared another fence, this time into what should be Simms' back yard. Again, he had chosen the very moment when Wynn was least able to maintain his balance and aim his pistol. He had also gained a couple of back yards while the deputy was trying to negotiate his first fence.

Wynn fired a wild shot in frustration and killed a stuffed teddy bear someone had left lying in the dust as he tumbled, ass over magnum, into the dirt. This wasn't working. Wynn rushed to the next fence, careful not to examine how his slug had eviscerated the bear. The black man was nowhere to be seen. Wynn turned on his heel, raced back to the black and white, and began a mobile patrol of the neighborhood. As he drove past Simms' house, he could hear a phone ringing inside. Mrs. Kraus was still trying to locate him. The possibility never occurred to Wynn. The killer was out there and he was, by God, going to get his man. The patrol car, light bar colorfully competing with the sun, cruised streets and rolled down alleys, cut across yards. Wynn's .357 trained from the driver's window at every corner, every shrub, every hiding place until it proved clear. The murderer stubbornly refused to surrender, or even be sighted.

"Hey Mad Dog!" the sheriff said it louder after his first effort failed to produce a reaction. Mad Dog's eyes seemed to be focused on something far away. Was he tripping on the remains of some bad acid he'd dropped back when he was a flower child in the '60s? The sheriff waved a hand in front of him, wondering for just a second if maybe....

Mad Dog blinked, shook his head the way a dog shakes itself free of water. "Englishman," he said in a tone of pleased recognition.

The sheriff nodded. Maybe this was a time to be gentle.

"It was Simms, right?" Mad Dog asked. "And everyone thinks I'm the one who killed him, don't they?" Mad Dog's eyes were alert now, searching his brother's face.

"Some folks, maybe. Most just wonder what you were doing out there in war paint and not much else."

Mad Dog leaned his massive shoulders back against the bars, a couple of which gave a little. He was a big man, what you might expect of a former football star, only trimmer than someone his age had any right to be. He was eleven years older than the sheriff. It was part of why they were less close than many brothers. He'd been English's hero while the sheriff was a boy, but he was out of the house and living on his own before the sheriff entered the third grade. When Mad Dog underwent his sudden conversion from jock to hippie, from shit kicker to pacifist, it had been hard for English to accept, especially since Mad Dog, who never had much time for his little brother, suddenly had even less.

"I already told you." Mad Dog strained for patience.

"Yeah, you did, but why that particular spot. I always thought a man was supposed to climb a sacred mountain or something when he was seeking a vision, not sit in the grass at the edge of a public park."

"Makes me feel kind of guilty," Mad Dog admitted. "I spent a lot of time trying to figure out just where I should do this. By the way, seeking a vision wasn't exactly what I was attempting. It's kind of hard to explain." He looked down at his feet and sucked on his lower lip for a moment while he decided how to put it.

"You don't have to tell me that part if you don't want to, at least not right now."

"But it's all linked, you see." Mad Dog leaned forward and ran his fingers through nonexistent hair in exasperation. "I drove over to Wichita last week. That's where I got the body paint and the Speedos and all. But what I went for was to hit some bookstores and spend some time in the Wichita State University library. You know I've gotten pretty serious about our heritage. Anyway, I found some really interesting articles on *Tsistsistas* Shamanism.

"I spent the day plowing through a bunch of journals and a couple of books, made pages of notes. And I had an epiphany. The bottom line, Englishman, is that the Cheyenne world view is superior to western civilization's world view because ours allows recognition of theirs while the reverse isn't true. Rationalism, civilization's version, ethnocentrically rejects what it can't explain. The Cheyenne understood power and its spiritual potencies, spirits and the soul, both of which have unrestricted access to that cosmological power. They aren't limited by time or space. They're normally invisible but they can take on physical form, manifest themselves to us, control physical phenomena. We, the Cheyenne, used to be able to participate in the interplay between the spiritual and the physical. We could step outside of space and time or manipulate that power to suit our needs. That's what I was trying to do. Bring my *hematasooma*, my soul, into contact with others, or call up a *maiyun*, a spirit. I know this sounds weird, but I was trying to take a first step toward making the world right again."

"Do you understand what you're talking about?"

"Hell, I don't know. It all makes a kind of crazy wonderful sense to me. Understand it, no, not really, but I'm trying. Trying to know and learn and make it work the way it used to."

"What, and bring back the buffalo?" The sheriff was starting to lose it. "Get rid of the White Man?"

Mad Dog was so impractical. Sometimes that infuriated the sheriff. His older brother had inherited a full section of prime bottom land, the old Maddox farm, and mismanaged it to near bankruptcy. Then, all of a sudden, he was sitting on the only oil strike in the county, half a dozen producing wells and a nice steady progression of royalty checks that made it unnecessary for Mad Dog to work for a living. It didn't seem fair, but what really galled the sheriff was the way his brother squandered all the freedom that income gave him on half-baked notions and screwball schemes.

"Yeah," Mad Dog's voice was heavy with sarcasm. "Trading buffalo for White Men, that would do for starters."

"OK, Mad Dog, whatever you say. Just don't try to sell me any ghost shirts."

"My little brother, it would seem, remains a rationalist."

The sheriff put his face in his hands for a minute, rubbing his temples with his fingers and massaging the bridge of his nose. He was tired. He should have gotten more sleep last night. He put his hands back on his knees and drummed the fingers of his right hand. "OK. Believe whatever you want to. Exercise your freedom of religion however you see fit, just so you aren't doing human sacrifices or smoking something illegal. All I want from you right now is what put you in the park across the street from the church before dawn this morning. And, since you were probably there about the time the Reverend Simms got himself scalped and butchered, what or who you might have seen that could give me some clue where to start looking for somebody, besides you, to put on death row for this."

Mad Dog looked sheepish. "Well, since universal power is everywhere, and since spirits can be too, I decided the place didn't matter. And, hell, you know how I liked to tweak Simms' pompous evangelical ass. The costume, the special effects, it was all to cause Simms a conniption and get a few more people wondering what I'm doing. I figure once enough folks realize how the world really works, maybe we can hold a *Massaum*, the sacred earth renewal ceremony, get right with *Maheo*, the All Father, and start taking care of acid rain and ozone depletion and the greenhouse effect."

"Great. Now what did you see out there? What did you hear? Where do I start?"

"I only saw one person, Englishman. You. I heard some dogs howling. I saw some headlights a few blocks north, but that's it. No chilling screams, no hacking sounds, no blood-soaked folks out for a morning stroll."

Mad Dog's recital was interrupted by the sound of the jail door swinging open. Mrs. Kraus stood in the passage. A telephone was ringing in the distance behind her.

"I found Wynn," she said. "Not that I spoke to him by phone or radio, you understand. Just folks living over in Reverend Simms' neighborhood have started calling, complaining that Wynn's gone nutso. Apparently he's driving the patrol car across people's yards and taking pot shots at kids' toys. The consensus seems to be that you should go out there and stop him before a mob forms and takes after him with shotguns and pitchforks. I thought you might want to know. Now I got to go answer another complaint. I'll tell you if somebody saves you the trouble and kills him for you. I know you're a busy man."

The jail door swung closed behind her and the sheriff felt a sudden wave of doubt. Maybe he didn't want to get re-elected after all. "Shit," he said to no one in particular.

"He's your deputy, Charlie Brown," Mad Dog offered, helpfully.

"And you're my brother," the sheriff smiled wryly. "What more can a man ask?"

◇◇◇

The sheriff tried his radio again as he walked out of the courthouse and headed for his truck. No luck, of course. He climbed behind the wheel, fumbled with the shoulder belt and the ignition switch. He was normally faster, but, being in a hurry and dealing with what were still unfamiliar mechanisms....

The fuel injected 350 roared to life, revving a little higher than he liked. He found reverse, nearly killed it because he'd forgotten to disengage the emergency brake, then backed away from the building so he'd have room to make the turn into the driveway and avoid Mrs. Kraus' Toyota. He was going a little faster than he should have, but he was still yards from the rose bushes when the truck stopped dead, snapping his head back almost far enough to put it through the sliding rear glass. The sheriff searched all three rearview mirrors for evidence of what he'd hit. Nothing. He did the same with his memory and knew there shouldn't be anything but empty lot back there.

He threw open the door, ripped off the seat belt, and ran to the rear. A metal pipe, painted a bright silver and yellow and filled with drying concrete had been buried six feet in front of the nearest rosebush. Mr. York appeared to have made a stealthy advance on the rose front while the sheriff was in the courthouse. This new salient was undamaged by the sheriff's unintended counter attack, except for a slight scrape where its fresh paint had contacted the truck's chrome rear step bumper. The bumper had looked solid and massive. Now it looked a little bent and some of it's chrome plating was threatening to peel off. Chrome step bumpers were evidently not designed to survive five-mile-an-hour collisions.

The sheriff caressed the butt of his .38 police special and wondered whether any jury, on seeing the bumper, would convict him if he went over and turned Lanny York into fodder for his roses. Instead, he walked calmly back to the cab, buckled up, put the truck in low, pushed the throttle down to about four grand, and popped the clutch. The truck jerked, but not really forward, more down and sideways as the engine's torque transferred itself to the rear wheels and they started digging at the dry soil behind the courthouse. Twin streams of rocks and dirt exploded from beneath tire treads, doing no good to his undercoat and those patches of body work that curved under the fenders, but shredding every rosebush within thirty feet with his shrapnel. By the time he hit the street, the sheriff was proceeding with normal caution. Only the cloud of dust that hung behind the courthouse in the abnormally still air, and the rippled bumper on his new Chevy, remained as evidence of the latest battle fought there. There was a small smile on his face. He was remembering the dynamite Wynn had confiscated from some kids planning an over-zealous Fourth of July and imagining what it could do to York's post and the rest of the roses.

The alley between Peach and Plum streets doubled as a kind of slough. When it rained, water flowed down it into Kastleman's field where it bordered the edge of Buffalo Springs. About a hundred yards of brush extended into the field because it had been wet when Kastleman plowed his frost-damaged wheat under. As the sheriff's Chevy became a casualty of the War of the Roses, the black man took advantage of the cover to gain a head start across the tilled field.

Wynn almost missed him altogether because one of the property owners from the neighborhood had come out to inquire what the hell Wynn thought he was doing and who was going to replant his flower bed or smooth out the ruts across his front yard. Wynn had felt inclined to stay and argue until he noticed other doors opening and more irate citizens headed his way. The sight prompted him to recall that his first duty lay in finding the murderer, not soothing the public temper, and so he went careening back down the street in the way he happened to be pointed.

Between glances at the rearview mirror to keep track of the people pouring into the street, the deputy happened to look up in time to see a small, dark figure. It was at least two hundred yards beyond the end of the slough and hightailing it toward the distant row of trees and brush that bordered on Calf Creek. The man already had a considerable lead, and the crowd in the street behind looked capable of gaining on Wynn if he chose to pursue on foot. Without a second thought he floored the accelerator, leaped the shallow ditch that separated the intersection of Peach and Madison from Kastleman's field, tore through the rusty fence that served more as a boundary marker than a deterrent to passage, and left the remains of the patrol car's defective exhaust system behind. He bounced across the furrows, skewing this way and that as the wheels encountered clods too large to give way even to the irresistible force of the cruiser's unmuffled 454 cubic inches.

The black man never looked back. His progress, though less dramatic, was not much slower than Wynn's. The deputy considered aiming a warning shot out the window but he needed both hands to control the ferocious efforts of the steering wheel to carry him somewhere other than where he wanted to go. Besides, his .357 had bounced off the seat and was down on the floorboards, hopping about like some barefoot swimmer forced to hot foot it across blazing sands en route from water to bath towel. Wynn hoped he hadn't left the gun cocked.

The black man was in good shape for his age, but he'd had to push himself a lot harder than he was used to. He still had a hundred yards on the police car when he hit the screen of weeds, saplings, and underbrush at the edge of Calf Creek. Kastleman wasn't a farmer who willingly let land go to waste. He'd plowed as close to the stream bed as he could get, a lot closer than the black man expected. He hit the brush and the bank at the same time and went plunging face first down the slope into a few inches of muddy water. He sprawled there, what clothes hadn't been soaked by perspiration, now soaked by the creek. The trickle of hot water felt good against the abused muscles in his legs. He would have loved to lie there and soak and catch his breath, but the howl of the police car's exhaust was getting close. He glanced frantically around, scrambled to his feet, and began slogging upstream. No particular reason for his choice of direction except to get away. Somewhere, deep in his subconscious, Deputy Wynn had been transformed into a full-fledged man hunt complete with bloodhounds that would have more trouble tracking him if he disguised his trail by sticking to the stream.

Wynn watched the man disappear into the green curtain along the creek. The steering was getting harder, probably because of what he and the plowed field had done to the tie rods. Wynn kept his hands locked to the wheel and his foot to the floor as he closed the last few yards. At the final moment, he jammed the brakes on and threw the wheel to the side, a combination of moves designed to bring the cruiser to a dramatic broadside stop at the edge of the vegetation, leaving him ready to scoop up his .357 magnum and plunge into the underbrush in hot pursuit. There was a brief moment for Wynn to recognize that the wheel should turn further and the brake pedal was not supposed to go clear to the floor. The pedal should have stopped about half way down, and the car should have stopped as well. Hydraulic brake lines at every wheel having been torn out by contact with rock-hard clods of earth, neither pedal nor brakes functioned as expected. Long before Wynn could consider applying the parking brake instead, he was through the wall of vegetation and buried up to the nose of the police cruiser in sand and mud and water. The radiator jammed back into the fan and the engine stalled. The seat belts and shoulder harness the sheriff insisted his deputies use on penalty of extra night duty kept Wynn from cracking a few ribs against the steering wheel. He sat there for a moment, watching steam rise from the buckled hood of the only Benteen County patrol car and began to imagine what the sheriff was going to say when he saw it. Wynn realized he'd better come in with the murderer, or seriously consider not coming in at all. Failure and an alternative career track suddenly seemed synonymous.

When the door wouldn't open, he crawled out the window and dropped into the stream. There was no indication which way the murderer might have run. Wynn crawled up the opposite bank and examined the pasture beyond. Nothing moved out there except a flock of recently shorn sheep.

Calf Creek flowed, except in especially dry seasons, gently toward the North Fork of the Kansaw. If you went downstream you'd soon reach the highway, about a half-mile before the creek swept past the edge of Buffalo Springs. In the opposite direction were only farms and occasional back roads. Upstream seemed the only logical way to run, but a man could make up a lot of distance by cutting across the pasture with the sheep, thereby avoiding a gentle curve the creek made before slithering behind an abandoned farm house about a quarter of a mile away. Wynn slipped through the thick grass and weeds, avoided contact with the electric fence, and began trotting toward his distant goal.

It took the sheriff a little time to disperse the mob, especially because he hadn't the slightest idea what Wynn thought he was doing. Fortunately, they knew there'd been a murder in their midst and, even as angry as several of them were, they felt inclined to forgive and forget—for the time being—though a couple suggested Wynn as a likely suspect considering the way he was acting.

The sheriff pulled into the Reverend Simms' driveway, though there was no longer any reason to protect the truck from its first scratch. The weathered frame structure was in need of a visit from *This Old House*, as well as a new occupant. The curbside mail box still proclaimed that Peter Simms lived there, but it was probably the only resident of the street, and maybe even of Buffalo Springs, that didn't know better.

A sagging front porch held an old swing that looked incapable of supporting itself, let alone Simms' portly form. The front door was locked and the blinds were drawn. The sheriff walked around back, conscious of the curious eyes that followed his every move from behind neighboring curtains.

The back porch was screened, its mesh so fine and rusty that he could only make out vague, malevolent forms within. Its door was unlatched, however, and there proved to be nothing more threatening inside than a couple of ratty chairs and an old, round-topped refrigerator beside a dusty row of shelves filled with antique garden tools. The sheriff gave it a cursory look, then tried the back door. It opened without protest on an unlit hall leading into a gloomy interior.

It probably wasn't any hotter in the house than outside, but, as the sheriff traversed the hall he realized he was sweating. The feel of the cool metal and the cross-hatched plastic grip of his .38 Smith & Wesson Police Special helped a little, but not enough.

There shouldn't be anyone in Simms' house. It wasn't logical that a murderer would wait around in his victim's home until the law happened by, but what had been done to the Reverend indicated the killer might not share a view of what was logical with the rest of the world. The sheriff, who normally kept his .38 locked in a drawer in what he considered a commendable effort to avoid acts of blatant machismo, was glad for the deadly phallic symbol's company as he advanced into the dim interior.

Reverend Simms hadn't gathered many worldly goods, but someone had thoroughly searched those he had in no apparent hurry. Every drawer, every shelf, every closet, had been emptied. There were piles in all the rooms where the contents had been dumped when they didn't yield what the searcher was looking for. And, the sheriff guessed, since every room had received the same careful attention, it was possible that what was being sought had not been found.

The sheriff went back out to his truck and retrieved a fingerprint kit. He wasn't surprised when he found only smudges on the surfaces the intruder would have touched. The effort had a professional feel to it, and a professional would have worn gloves.

The sheriff tipped a bedroom chair upright after he finished his circuit of the house, then collapsed into it. His arms and legs ached, like he'd just run a hard 10 k after spending an hour with his free weights. The tension of following so closely in the footsteps of a killer wasn't what he was used to. He stared vacantly at the piles of clothing and empty drawers at the foot of the bed. It had been stripped of its sheets. Mattress and box springs leaned against a nearby wall.

What might a faintly pompous little preacher like Simms have that someone would be willing to kill for? And not just kill, but torture and then butcher. Had someone wanted answers? Was the killer sending a message? It didn't add up. The thoroughness with which Simms' house had been searched made what had seemed psychotic only moments before suddenly look cold-bloodedly rational and malicious. The sheriff knew that killers sometimes used gratuitous violence as a warning, but Simms seemed an unlikely candidate for involvement with the mob or international terrorists or the drug trade. So what was it? Something small enough to hide yet valuable enough to cancel a human life? The sheriff shook his head. No sense, it made absolutely no sense.

The sheriff wiped the sweat from his eyes. There was a small fan lying on the floor. It had probably been pointed at the bed before being tossed aside by the intruder. The sheriff righted it, made sure it was plugged in, and turned it on. Nothing happened. He thought it might have been damaged in the fall it must have taken. He tried the evaporative cooler in the window and got the same result. The light switch didn't work either. Strange, the overhead light had been on in the kitchen.

The sheriff returned to the back porch looking for the circuit breakers. They weren't there, but the power poles were in the alley and the feeder line ran to the southeast corner of the house. The sheriff followed it. He found a rusty metal box under the eaves near the corner with a pair of thirty amp circuits—the old fashioned kind with screw-in fuses. One of them was unscrewed, not just loose, barely hanging from its socket. When the sheriff tightened it, the cooler began blowing muggy air into the adjacent bedroom.

The dusty soil beneath the electrical box contained the scuffed prints of a pair of short flat slippered feet, the sheriff's boots, and the intricate waffled design of a pair of modern athletic shoes. The trails of boots and slippers paralleled each other from the house. The running shoes led behind some shrubbery near the back fence. There were several clear prints, just below average size feet but hardly average shoes. He'd given Wynn the department's camera, after documenting the mess inside the Veteran's Memorial Park restroom, and asked him to drop the film off at the Dillon's for developing and to pick up a fresh roll on his way here. Presumably, the camera was still in the black and white with his deputy, off chasing who knew what or where.

The sheriff tried the radio and, not surprisingly, got no response from Wynn. He'd seen the tire tracks leading off into Kastleman's field as he drove up Madison and made a right onto Peach. There hadn't been a Benteen County Sheriff's car out in that field then. The sheriff didn't feel like he had the time to go chasing after his deputy while a murderer was still on the loose. Wynn would turn up sooner or later.

The sheriff jotted a reminder to himself in his notebook. These prints were sufficiently clear that he should be able to identify the brand from the sole pattern, as well as the size of the wearer. Who that might be, or what their presence meant, were still mysteries. Did they belong to the killer? If so, why not slice and dice Simms in his house or his yard? Why trail him to the park and deposit his remains in an abandoned restroom? And why hadn't Simms felt threatened when he realized someone was fooling with his fuse box—or had the Reverend realized that at all? If he'd known, he should have called the deputy who was on duty last night and gotten someone to come check it out. That hadn't happened, maybe because Simms was involved in something he didn't want known. But even if the sheriff could convince himself to accept that absurd sounding proposition, why had Simms obligingly wandered out into the night to his fatal encounter in the park?

A slight movement in the far corner of the back yard caught the sheriff's attention. There was an open-topped fifty-five-gallon drum standing back there with just a hint of smoke rising into the improbably motionless Kansas air. Buffalo Springs didn't offer garbage removal. People either hauled their trash to the dump or burned it in containers like this in their back yards, then trusted the nearly constant wind to carry their pollutants a state or two away. It didn't seem likely that Peter Simms would have been burning trash before he walked off to the park to get murdered.

The Reverend Simms hadn't been good about watering his yard. There were plenty of weeds and some clumps of grass, but there were also dusty patches of bare soil that showed a trail of those waffled footprints going to and from the trash barrel. The sheriff avoided stepping on them as he examined the contents of the drum. The contents were, not surprisingly, ashes. It appeared that stacks of paper had been recently burned, or, perhaps not papers, but something smaller and regular, say three-by-five cards, or maybe not cards, maybe photos. The sheriff bent and peered intently into the container. Just the hint of an image seemed to stare back at him from the top of the pile. It looked like a figure, someone small, perhaps a child. He couldn't quite make it out. It was covered with a dusting of more ash. He bent and blew on it softly. It dissolved into fine soot that rose on a wisp of smoke and danced, unrecognizable and unrecoverable, in the steamy air. What had it been? Were they pictures? Had the searcher found and burned them, and if so why? Was this what someone had been looking for, what Peter Simms died for?

Too many questions, too few answers. The sheriff found himself wishing he was better qualified for his job. Some real police experience from somewhere would be awfully nice to fall back on about now. A decade as Benteen County Sheriff didn't qualify. No one in county history had been murdered before. What he knew about homicide investigation came from movies, TV, and novels. His qualifications for the job consisted of a brief military career that sent him home from Vietnam with a bronze star and a purple heart, just enough popularity with the voters, and the revelation that the preceding sheriff had been collecting cash payoffs instead of issuing traffic tickets at a speed trap on the highway over near Cottonwood Corners.

The sheriff decided to take one last look at the house, letting himself consider Simms as someone cunning and desperate, not just zealously intolerant. He went back through each room, looking for a perfect hiding place and finding nothing that hadn't received previous attention.

He stopped in the kitchen on the way out, picking up the phone to check in with Mrs. Kraus. There was a notebook and a pencil hanging from a string beside it. The sheriff thumbed through to be sure all the pages were present and there were names and numbers inside—people who would need to be informed.

The phone was one of the models that chirped at you instead of ringing the way a lot of Benteen County phones still did. Among its neat row of push buttons was one bearing the label REDIAL. Why not, the sheriff thought. He punched it and heard a staccato of tones flash into an electronic abyss. There was a long moment of stillness and then a phone, somewhere, began to ring.

"Hello," a familiar voice said. At first he thought he must be wrong, but he knew her voice. It was his ex-wife.

"Judy," the sheriff demanded, "where are you?"

◇◇◇

The two Heathers were currying a pair of big mares, one a chestnut Morgan and one a dappled roan and white Saddlebred. In the shadow of the barn the girls looked astonishingly alike, a fact their mothers were remarking on when the phone began to ring.

Judy was leaning her athletic frame against a wall, a contrast in her auburn ponytail, cotton shirt, denims, and boots to the tall, dark, intense and equally athletic woman beside her whose idea of casual dress—color coordinated exercise-wear by an athletic shoe manufacturer—seemed inappropriately formal in a place where the scents of straw and manure and urine blended to smell like all horse stables. The aroma was either aromatic or noxious, depending on your fondness for horses.

"We get it after the fourth ring," Judy explained. "If there's somebody up in the main house they'll pick it up before that. If not, we take a message."

The dark woman nodded. Judy wasn't the first person to explain the phone rules to her. She looked around nervously, as if searching for something to write on. Judy exchanged wide, calm-eyed stares with the sorrel in the stall across from the phone, then picked up after the fourth ring, surprise knitting her smooth brow as her "hello" was answered by her ex-husband.

Judy was no fan of the Reverend Simms' brand of Christianity. She normally took Heather over to Crawford on Sunday mornings where an Episcopalian service could be found. It was a long drive, but everything in Benteen County was a long drive. It was more or less on the way to Sam and Minnie Stark's Sourdough Ranch, the location of some of the best horseflesh in Kansas, where she'd made arrangements for her Heather to learn a skill that most girls, at some time in their lives, fantasize about more than sex.

The horses were a handsome pair, made more so by the girls' attentions. They stood patiently, knowing their day's work was done and the girls would soon lead them to their stalls for a reward of oats.

"How'd you get your name?" Heather Lane asked Heather English.

The latter blushed. She'd always thought the combination a bit much. "I don't know about the Heather. I think Mom must have read it somewhere and wanted to name me something unusual. Unfortunately, as I'm sure you've noticed, about the same time lots of mothers seem to have come up with the same idea. And English, I'm not real sure about either. My Grandma Sadie had lots of husbands during her life, only a couple she actually bothered to marry. My grandfather is supposed to have been a British soldier who was briefly assigned to a weather research station just over the county line. Nobody is real clear on whether that was his name or Grandma just didn't know, and when it came time to write something down on Dad's birth certificate, chose his nationality. Whatever, or whoever, by then he was long gone."

"Wow! She sounds neat."

"She died before I was born but Dad says she was something else. Before her time. She should have been a hippie, he says, cause she would have made a good one."

"Gee! She was pre-hippie. I thought they had hippies like forever."

"What the hell do you mean, where am I?" Judy countered.

"You called me, remember?"

"There's been a..." the sheriff paused, considered, and decided, for the time being, to minimize, "...crime. I'm at the scene. It's possible the last place called from here could be significant. The phone's got one of those automatic redialers and I punched the button. I don't know where I've called. Are you home?"

"A crime?" Judy watched Mrs. Lane's eyes widen at the words.

"Please, Judy, just tell me where you are."

"Where do you think I am? Where are your daughter and I virtually every Sunday at this time?"

"That's what I'm hoping you'll tell me."

"OK, OK," Judy sighed, her boundless patience once again pushed to extremes by her clueless former mate. "Sourdough Ranch."

"Aren't the Stark's basically atheists?"

"What's that got to do with anything? Is it a crime to be an atheist in Benteen County now? Actually, Minnie told me they were Druids. At solstices and equinoxes they perform bizarre rituals involving kinky sex out in the back pasture."

"Yesterday was the solstice."

"Oh Jesus, Englishman, lighten up. I was kidding. You know, a joke."

Judy always called him "Englishman" too. The nickname had originated with his mother, who loved the works of Noel Coward. Once she had a Mad Dog she had to have an Englishman as well. He still put up with it from Mad Dog and from Judy. Other folks had been persuaded just to call him Sheriff.

He looked around the ruins of the kitchen. "Whoever did this wasn't joking," the sheriff observed. "Why would Peter Simms call the Starks?"

"How should I know. Sam thinks he's what they call light in the loafers and Minnie just thinks he's a flake. I can't imagine them having anything to say to him, or vice versa, but you'll have to ask them and they don't seem to be around right now. And what's that got to do with your crime, anyhow?"

"I'm coming right out, Judy. Stay there. You see Sam and Minnie, keep them there till I come."

"Englishman. Go suck an egg!" Judy put the phone back on the wall. Mrs. Lane was looking at her with wide, curious eyes. "Obscene phone call," Judy explained, just as it started ringing again.

"How interesting," Mrs. Lane said with obvious curiosity. The phone kept chiming but Judy didn't pick it up even when it passed the fourth ring. Neither did Mrs. Lane. The two stood and watched each other and the phone until it stopped at the count of twenty-two.

◇◇◇

With mares chewing oats and mothers chewing fat, the two Heathers dug out the rags and the Neat's Foot Oil and began cleaning their tack.

"How do you like it here?" Heather English asked. The Starks had a couple of guest houses on the place where they put up buyers or rented space to horsey types with enough money to indulge an urge to improve their riding skills. Sam Stark could ride anything with four legs and make it like it and Minnie was an accomplished instructor of almost every equestrian form. Scores of medals and cups decorated her trophy room, including one Olympic gold.

"It's OK." Heather Lane caught the look of surprise her namesake showed at her lack of enthusiasm. "I mean, the horses and the riding are great. Minnie's terrific. It's just...well, you can only ride so many hours a day. Then...this is a nice place, a great pool and they've got a dish so you can watch all the TV you want, but what's the fun of doing all that with nobody but your mom?"

"Right." Judy's daughter could understand that. "There's just the two of you then? No brothers or sisters? Your dad didn't come?"

"I don't have a dad!" Heather Lane exclaimed with surprising passion. Then, more calmly. "My folks are divorced and I was an only child."

"Me too, on both counts."

"Oh, I thought...well, the way you talked about your dad...."

"He and Mom have been divorced for eternities. But he only lives a couple of miles away on what used to be Grandma Sadie's farm. I still see him all the time."

"What's he like?"

The question was asked with a kind of wistful intensity that made Heather English stop and consider how to answer it. He was just Dad. She'd never tried to define him before.

"He's OK. I mean, he's not a dweeb or anything, but sometimes he seems real surprised I'm not still a baby. He tries to listen, though, but you know how adults are. They never quite get it."

"He sounds...normal, you know. I wish my dad was like that.

"What is he like?"

"He's a monster. Mom's been protecting me from him as long as I can remember."

"A monster?"

"Yeah, a child molester. I was the child. Mom had him put in jail for it but he got out recently. He appealed and they overturned the original sentence. Now he's trying to fight Mom for custody. Can you imagine?"

Heather English could not, and the thunderstruck expression on her face was an eloquent answer. "You mean he...." She couldn't bring herself to even euphemize the word she'd tested her father with before dawn that morning.

Moments before, Heather Lane had seemed the younger of the two. Suddenly she was much older.

"I don't remember it. I mean, it was ages ago, back when I was an infant. I wasn't even two when she divorced him and the trial was just after that.

"I can't actually remember him doing it. In fact, I don't really remember him at all. I guess I was too little. But the doctors Mom took me to said he did it and Mom says she caught him at it and I'm not a virgin and haven't been since forever."

"God! I'm so sorry."

"Yeah. That's OK. I'm used to it." Heather Lane's face softened again. "But it must be neat to have a dad who's normal."

"Listen, Mom's promised to drive me into Hutchinson this afternoon so we can hit the mall, go to a movie, and get some supper. If you'd like to come...well, I can persuade my mom if you can persuade yours."

"Oh God, I haven't been in a mall since like the dark ages," Heather Lane said, her face flushing with genuine excitement.

Neither mother proved hard to convince. By the time they left, Judy had completely forgotten the sheriff's orders, a fact that would have surprised no one who knew either of them.

The blade sliced through flesh with so little resistance it was like opening the wound with a zipper—easier even. Of course, this flesh was far beyond the ability to resist and Doc Jones kept his scalpels honed razor sharp.

Eighty-six separate wounds. Doc had counted them carefully, after washing off what had recently been Peter Simms, and marked them on his autopsy chart. Eighty-six, and not one of them a puncture wound. All of them incisions, slashes. From the lack of tearing and abrasions and the similarity to the surgical Y-shaped cut with which Doc began his autopsy, it appeared they had been made with an instrument as carefully honed as his scalpel. Probably a razor blade, he thought, though modern blades were thin and fragile and might be easily broken in a fight. An old fashioned straight edge razor was more likely to have held up to the heavy use required of this weapon, though it could just as easily have been a pocket knife or even a scalpel.

That was what had always fascinated Doc about forensics. It was about half science and half art, from what he could tell. The dead didn't give up their secrets easily. There was a similarity between the autopsy process and an ancient oracle cutting open a goat or a chicken and reading the future (or, in this case, the past) by examining its entrails. Determining cause and time of death was as much a matter of interpreting what he found as what he didn't.

Peter Simms didn't smoke and didn't drink excessively. That left him with healthy pink lungs and a smooth and unremarkable liver. He ate too well and didn't exercise so Doc wasn't surprised to discover, beneath a thick layer of subcutaneous fat, that the Reverend had been a good candidate for angioplasty or a bypass not many years down the road.

The Reverend hadn't eaten that morning, but there were some internal surprises. Doc found the amputated genitalia stuffed deep into Peter Simms' throat. It had caused a blockage of the trachea and some damage to the larynx, but Doc was pretty certain Peter Simms hadn't lived long enough to feel that particular indignity. There was some blood in the lungs though, and a bit of bloody froth in the bronchial tubes.

The autopsy revealed little else beyond the sustained savagery that Peter Simms encountered in Veteran's Memorial Park sometime before dawn. Aside from the location of the genitals and the possibility that the Reverend might have suffocated on his own blood, Doc noted only two other unusual features on his report. Doc wasn't sure which of them surprised him most.

He had assumed the murderer took Simms' scalp as a trophy. That was why scalps were taken in the old days, or for the bounty sometimes paid by those who considered Indians to be vermin, fit only for extermination. Doc had felt confident that souvenir would prove to be valuable evidence, something Peter Simms' killer would have kept and hidden. When the sheriff found it, the scalp would be the final confirmation to put someone behind bars. He'd been wrong about that. He found the square flap of scalp inserted firmly inside the Reverend's rectum, though this indignity, too, was apparently post-mortem.

The other surprise was that the conservative, evangelical, self-righteous Peter Simms had a tattoo on his derriere. Quite near to where his scalp had been left, there was a small, colorful, intricately rendered cartoon figure. Doc was sure Walt Disney wouldn't have approved of this anatomically correct, though exaggerated, version of his favorite mouse.

◇ ◇ ◇

Wynn was in a lot worse shape than the black man. After about a hundred yards, he'd slowed to a brisk walk, reasoning that he could keep a better eye on the creek bank at that pace and that he should approach the abandoned farm with at least a little caution. He was almost there, watching both, when he discovered that one of the crew-cut sheep wasn't a ewe. He heard the hooves and started to turn just in time to get butted— literally—and somersault through the dry buffalo grass. Wynn found himself on hands and knees, only a few feet from where a big ram with a punk hairstyle was getting ready to show off for his harem again. Wynn took advantage of his stance, converting it into a sprinter's start. He hurdled the electric fence with a burst of speed and agility that might have earned him a starting spot on the Buffalo Springs High track team if he'd exhibited it a decade earlier. Sheep aren't bright creatures, but electric fences have a way of imprinting themselves on even the dimmest reasoning. The ram stopped a few feet behind the wire and began trotting back and forth, as if inviting Wynn to a rematch. Far behind him, among the thin patches of grass, a pair of items reflected the hot sun. Wynn checked his belt. His radio was missing. His hands were empty too. Before encountering the sheep, one of them had held his .357 magnum. The big ram eyed him and stalked the edge of the pasture staying between Wynn and the tools of his trade. Wynn began to realize this was taking on all the earmarks of another "lose some."

This had never been a particularly prosperous farm. The drought of the late eighties had driven it from ailing to terminal, along with the finances of the family who eventually lost it to the bank, and themselves to another chance somewhere in the sunbelt where it didn't matter if wheat here yielded less than twenty bushels an acre at under $3.50 a bushel. The place had been abandoned as a home for only a few years, but spare dollars had been required for payments or repairing machinery—nothing left for a weather- beaten house and outbuildings—and the place looked as though it had been without human companionship for decades.

There were a few osage orange trees in the yard, survivors despite the drought because they were a hardy plant and their root systems were close enough to benefit from the groundwater generated by the creek. Wynn used them as camouflage as he zigzagged his way toward the first of the outbuildings. He didn't really expect to find the murderer here, but with his .357 sunning itself in the pasture, he wouldn't take any chances. The first building had probably been a chicken coop. Wynn ducked inside, looking for a loose two-by-four he could take with him to revisit the ram. The place looked dilapidated enough, but Wynn was unable to budge any of the boards he tried to wrench free. The only weapon he found was an empty beer bottle beside a comfortable looking pile of straw and a used condom. Wynn resolved to check the place again some night. He wasn't prompted by a deep sense of outraged morality. He just thought it would be fun to scare a couple of kids and maybe cop a peek at a naked prom queen.

Unable to find anything better, he took the bottle. Not much of a weapon, not even enough to get him back into the pasture, but having something in his hand made him feel a bit more confident. It was just as well since the black man was trotting across the farm yard toward him as he exited the hen house. Wynn grabbed the bottle in both hands and extended it, sighting over its label and squaring his body in a perfect shooter's stance.

"Freeze!" he shouted.

"What did Englishman want?" Mad Dog asked, leaning against the door frame of the Sheriff's Office.

"Where Wynn is. Where French is. If Doc had anything for him yet."

"And?"

Mrs. Kraus couldn't decide whether Mad Dog looked more or less grotesque with the paint washed off. He'd spent the last twenty minutes in the restroom across the hall. From the way his skin glowed, as if it had been lightly abraded rather than gently scrubbed, she suspected he'd discovered the hard way, just as she once had, that the body paint didn't come off as easily as advertised. Mad Dog stood there in his black Speedos, his near nakedness emphasized by his shaved head. He was an uncommonly powerful figure for a man his age.

"I didn't kill him," Mad Dog said in response to her silent stare.

She leaned back in her chair, pulling the top drawer of her desk open as she did so, exposing the handle of the Glock to her view if not his. "Never thought you did," she said, reassuringly. She smiled, showing off her teeth. A few were still of organic origin.

"And?" he tried again.

"And nothing," she said. "'Wynn some' is lost, drove himself off into Kastleman's field west of town and ain't been seen since. French ain't home yet and nobody can find him. No other deputies in the county just now. Me and your brother's the only law enforcement anybody can reach. And Doc hasn't called."

"Englishman find somebody to tell Old Man Simms about his boy yet?"

"My guess would be that's one reason he's looking for a spare deputy. He's following up some lead he picked up over at the Reverend's or he'd probably go himself. I'd call, but the old man's pretty frail and that seems a heartless way to learn a relative's gone, even if neither had much use for the other." Besides, the sheriff had told her not to call when she'd suggested it. If the shock of the call didn't kill him, Old Man Simms was the kind to sue over a near miss.

"You know," Mad Dog mused. "I feel responsible." Mrs. Kraus let her fingers slide into the drawer. "Maybe I'll go out and tell him. That way, if a deputy does show up, Englishman can use him for something more important. Englishman calls again, let him know where I've gone."

"I'll do that," Mrs. Kraus agreed. She kept her hand near the butt of the gun until she heard Mad Dog's aging Saab start up. When his car was no longer audible she took the phone off the hook and went to visit the restroom herself.

She was out of the office when the short, swarthy man with the gymnast's build came in, knocked at the open door and called out "Hello," and "Is anybody home?" The only reply he got was the angry pulse of the phone demanding to be put back on its cradle and the sheriff's muffled voice interrupted by occasional bursts of static as he tried to raise Mrs. Kraus on the radio that occupied the center of her desk.

"I don't know if you can hear me," the sheriff finally told the stranger after repeating "Five-oh-one to five hundred" several times. "I tried to call but the line was busy. I'm in my truck and headed out of town. Simms' last phone call was to Sourdough Ranch and that's where I'm going. I'll phone from there, but if something comes up and you can't reach me on the radio, call ahead and leave a message or maybe get one of the neighbors to take it over and meet me there."

"Thank you," the man with the Mediterranean features replied in the direction of the radio. "All that time going through the house gets me nothing. I come in here and I don't even have to ask. Yes, thank you very much indeed."

"Did you copy that?" the sheriff's voice inquired. There was no longer anyone in his office to hear.

"**A**ssume the position," Wynn commanded.

"What position?" The black man seemed genuinely confused. At least he'd frozen when the deputy ordered him to do so and had yet to notice, or if he had, to mention, that what was aimed at him was an empty beer bottle.

"Uh...lean up against that tree and spread your arms and legs," Wynn instructed.

"This tree?" the black man pointed. It wasn't the one Wynn had in mind but it didn't matter. He wanted the man's back to him so he wouldn't realize Wynn was unarmed. And he wanted the man in a position from which it would be difficult to launch an attack.

"Fine," Wynn said.

The black man walked over to the tree and leaned against it. "I can't really spread my hands," he apologized. "The trunk's not big enough. Will this do?"

"That's OK," Wynn replied, beginning to feel in control again. "Just do the best you can." Wynn stepped up between the man's legs, stuck the mouth of the beer bottle in the small of his back, and patted him down. Wynn found nothing more lethal than a wallet and a cell phone. He removed them from the suspect and tossed them behind him. Wynn glanced longingly at the hand cuffs clipped to his belt, but his two-year-old had lost the key a month ago and the manufacturer hadn't sent replacements yet.

"Stand up real slow, but keep those feet spread," Wynn ordered, "and take your belt off."

The man did as asked. Wynn fashioned a reasonable substitute for the cuffs out of the belt and lashed the man's hands behind his back.

"Who are you?" the deputy asked.

"Neil Bowen."

"What you doing out here, Neil Bowen?"

"I don't know exactly," Bowen replied. "Trying to keep from getting lynched, I suppose."

"Now that I believe." Wynn bent and picked up the wallet and thumbed through a collection of plastic credit cards and photo IDs, all of which confirmed that the individual in custody was one Neil Raymond Bowen, Ph.D., Associate Professor of History at Fort Hays State University. That was surprising. It was one thing to expect a transient black man to kill Reverend Simms. Quite another to find that transient probably earned at least four times Wynn's annual salary. Folks like that seldom wandered around the country bumping off people according to some randomly psychotic pattern. Still, a black professor of history was an unlikely figure to find on foot in Simms neighborhood so shortly after the murder. That left him as a reasonable suspect in Wynn's mind.

"Well, Neil," Wynn asked, "care to tell me why you killed him?" Wynn wanted to see the black man's face when he answered, watch for clues that he was lying, so Wynn stepped around in front of his prisoner.

What he saw was surprise. "That's a beer bottle you've been pointing at me," Neil Bowen said, accusingly.

Wynn flushed a little but told the black man to just answer the question.

"I haven't killed anyone," Bowen finally said.

"Then why'd you run."

"Because you drove at me like you intended to run me down." Wynn recalled, that since he'd been sure the stranger must be the murderer, that had been pretty much his intention. He decided not to pursue the point any further.

"If you didn't kill him, who did?"

"Not knowing who was killed puts me at something of a disadvantage in making a guess, officer, especially since I don't know a soul among your local population."

"So then, what were you doing there?"

"I was looking for help. My car quit on a dirt road a couple of miles north of here. I couldn't raise anyone with my cellular. I could see that there must be some sort of community here because of the grain elevator and a couple of other buildings, including the spire of what looks like a courthouse, so I hiked across some fields and then started knocking on doors. I hadn't found anybody home yet when you started chasing me."

"A likely story," Wynn muttered around the uncomfortable suspicion that it just might be true. College professors didn't make good random serial killers, especially ones who carried the kind of identification that could be checked. A professor would surely be smart enough to avoid being found in front of his victim's home. Wynn clung desperately to the hope that a professor might be so clever that he would do something apparently stupid just to confuse investigators like himself.

"Well, Dr. Bowen, I got one dead body and one stranger on the street where he lived, so I hope you'll pardon me if I keep your hands secured till we get you back to the jail and I can check up on you. Either way, we're going to take a little walk, down the drive and across the road where I can borrow a phone to report in."

"You can use my cell phone if you'd like."

"Not much point," Wynn said, though he proceeded to do exactly that. The phone told him it had an adequate charge, but no cell was available. "These things almost never work here. Benteen County's supposed to be overlapped by two cells, but the sheriff thinks maybe we're underlapped instead. Not enough folks out here for the phone companies to worry over.

"Now turn around and follow the drive. We got that walk to take." Wynn hoped somebody would be home at the next farm. Otherwise they were going to have to walk down to the highway and over the bridge and all the way back to Buffalo Springs.

Old Man Simms' place was only about six miles south of town. It didn't take Mad Dog long to get there. He guided his Saab

Turbo through the gap in the evergreens. With the turn, he slipped from a landscape that resembled a solar anvil into a shaded forest of maturing hardwoods that almost hid the two-story frame house in their midst. Not so many years back, this yard would have been immaculately manicured, watered to a lush green on which you could practice putting. Green it still was, lush too, but grasses were being replaced by weeds and though someone had seen that the lawn got enough water to support the trees, no one had bothered to mow for about a month. That, Mad Dog recalled, was when Simms fired his last hired hand.

The Simms' place had never fit into the Kansas landscape, but now, untended, it had exchanged an elegant feel for an eerie one. In the sudden half-light of the yard, Mad Dog almost expected to hear a Rod Serling voice-over explaining that he had just stepped into the Twilight Zone.

The drive circled the house and Mad Dog parked his wolf in Swede's clothing under a massive maple that must have been planted when the house was built. A tire swing hung from one of its branches. The youngest Simms would have stopped using it about three decades ago.

The yard was unnaturally still. Normally by this time of day a steady south wind would have moaned through the leafy canopy. Not today, and no birds either. Probably too hot for them, he thought, wiping the sweat from his brow with the back of his hand, then drying it on his Levis. He still had the Speedos on underneath, but he'd donned a shirt and pants and boots before leaving Buffalo Springs. Bad enough to tell a man his son had been butchered without making a mockery of the scene by doing it bald and next to nude.

Mad Dog decided even the bald might be a bit much. He reached into the car for his weathered green and yellow John Deere cap, set it at a jaunty angle—he couldn't set a cap any other way—and climbed the porch to the front door.

He knocked and the door swung slightly open. Mad Dog found it surprising that the door wasn't latched, but not that it was unlocked. Most people in Benteen County still didn't lock their homes. Violence intruded into their lives through their TV screens, not their front doors.

"Anybody home?" Mad Dog called. The last time he'd been through this door was more than thirty-five years ago in hot pursuit of Janie Jorgenson, easily the pick of the Buffalo Springs High School cheerleaders. It was only hours after they'd won the state championship and he'd carried the ball for over 170 yards and intercepted a pass in the closing seconds to preserve the victory. Old Man Simms hadn't been old then. Simms and his wife had been among the team's most ardent boosters because their oldest boy, the Reverend's brother, Tommy, had been a big and mean-for-his-age sophomore lineman. This magnificent yard and home had been a natural place for a celebration. It had been a memorable night for Mad Dog. Janie had intercepted the first of his passes as he drove her home afterward, but then she'd let him fumble under her blouse and skirt and they'd soon achieved an even grander prize.

It wasn't Janie's trim little bottom, beckoning from within bright panties under a short skirt—scarlet under gold—he followed through the door this time, just a memory. Mad Dog wondered briefly what had become of Janie, and if she ever thought of him and their season of trial and Eros.

It was cooler in the house than outside, but not by much. And quiet, though you couldn't have heard a pin drop because of the plush pearl-grey carpet that lined the foyer.

"Mr. Simms?"

Still no answer. Mad Dog knew he should leave, go back to the Maddox farm his mother had made sure he inherited and call Mrs. Kraus or Englishman to report his failure from there, but something drew him.

There was a living room to the right of the foyer and a dining room to the left. At the rear there was a closet, a hall, and a stairway to the second floor. Old Man Simms was sprawled near the top of the stairs, his eyes watching Mad Dog's progress. Actually, his line of sight was slightly lower, almost straight down the steps, as if he were wondering how he could descend from up there. He certainly wasn't going to do it himself, not with his neck at that unnatural angle and the life gone out of him. He'd been dead for a while. Mad Dog could tell because the spot where the patch of scalp had been removed was dried and crusted. But for that you might have thought he'd simply slipped and fallen. Mad Dog's second corpse of the day had been more gently handled than the first. It didn't matter much, though. Mad Dog felt himself go wobbly in the knees and found himself sitting on the carpet, not quite knowing how he got there. A phone stood on a table nearby. Mad Dog reached out, picked it up, and punched in his brother's number at the Sheriff's Office.

Sunday was usually Bertha's biggest day. Under normal circumstances she outdrew the Buffalo Springs Non-Denominational Church. On a day when the only competition were the Methodists down on Jackson and the Lutherans out on Poplar, or the Buffalo Burger Drive Inn over where the highways intersected across from the Texaco, she had been swamped. By mid-afternoon, virtually every rumor had poured through Bertha's doors, been swapped across her formica tables, passed along the sweep of her counter, and washed up against the booths by the back wall. Most of the tale tellers had long ago given up and gone home when the stranger walked in and ordered a glass of iced tea. Bertha swiped the counter in front of him with a rag that smelled strongly of disinfectant but left a suspicious grey film behind. She was aggressive with it, challenging almost, as if she were waving a weapon under his nose.

It was impossible to tell if the glass she served his tea in was clean because it was sweating almost as much as he was after his walk from the courthouse. He took a chance and sipped it and smiled at her when it tasted like tea and not the stuff on the rag.

Bertha and her four remaining customers kept wary eyes on him while he drank, eyes that shifted innocently away whenever he looked in their direction, then flashed back at the first opportunity. Everyone was keenly aware that no arrest had been made yet. Peter Simms' murderer still roamed free. Strangers, who might normally be greeted with enthusiasm at least equal to the money they might be willing to spend in the county were, today, treated as if they might momentarily don a hockey mask and begin pulling the starter rope on a bloody chain saw.

The compact man with the international face finished his tea and Bertha came cautiously back down the counter. "More?" she inquired.

"No thanks," he answered. "But there is something you might be able to help me with."

Bertha raised her eyebrows and kept her hand near the bin with the steak knives.

"Can you tell me how to find the Sourdough Ranch?"

"Lookin' to buy a horse?" a farmer at a table by the front window asked.

"No, trying to find someone."

Eyebrows raised again. Bertha's, not having fully returned to a normal position after the first query, threatened to merge with her hairline.

The stranger reached into his pocket, pulled out a photocopy, and unfolded it. "Have you seen this girl?" it asked above a surprisingly good reproduction of a school photo. There was a reward mentioned, along with a series of addresses and phone numbers to contact with information. He passed it to the man by the window, a wise choice since Bertha might have hurled her rag in his face and gone for a steak knife if he'd reached in her direction.

"Why, this looks like..." the farmer said, then paused a moment, "...a right pretty young lady," he finished. "See you've got some numbers to contact on here. You mind if I keep this, let my family have a look?"

"No problem," the stranger said. "But about that ranch?"

The farmer considered a moment before deciding. "Get back on the highway and head east," he said. "Twenty-six miles. There's dirt roads every mile, one way or the other or both. There's a sign on that one directing you south toward Sourdough. It's easy to find, the turn's just a mile past a little old abandoned cemetery. After you leave the highway, Sourdough's another eight and a quarter miles. First driveway after you cross the bridge over Sweetwater Creek. Big sign over the drive. Can't miss it."

The dark man nodded. He dropped a fifty on the counter. "I've got this man's bill," he said, "and whatever change is left from that and the tea, just keep it." Before anyone could protest he was through the door and walking back into the sunlight.

As soon as he was out of view the farmer held up the picture of the girl. "Will you look at this," he demanded of Bertha and the others. "Where'd this fellow get a picture of Heather English?"

"You sure that's Heather?" Bertha asked. "Sure looks like her but the hair's different." Indeed, the girl in the picture was wearing her hair down over her shoulders, longer than Heather English had ever grown hers. This girl was a couple of years younger than Heather would be now and none of them were quite sure Heather hadn't looked exactly like that two years ago. They were sure, however, that the sheriff should know about it.

Bertha rang the Sheriff's Office and got a busy signal. Mrs. Kraus was back from the restroom and deluged with calls.

"Four AM," Doc said. "Give or take a day. Actually, I'm pretty confident he died within two hours of that. The weapon may have been a razor blade, maybe an antique one, or something with a finely honed cutting edge. Even with all the wounds that were inflicted, there's no indication the blade was getting dull. I'd say the victim probably lived a good five minutes after the cutting started. Cause of death is going to go on the autopsy as heart failure, after that heart ran out of anything to pump, but there's a chance one of those cuts across his throat was deep enough to cause bleeding directly into the trachea and he may have actually drowned on his own blood. On the bright side, if there is one, Simms was unconscious for the worst of it and the mutilations were all post-mortem." Doc cleared his throat.

"I'll have a written report for the sheriff by the time he gets back to town. You tell him to call me as soon as he checks in. There's a couple of things he and I need to discuss that you'd probably rather not know about, Mrs. Kraus."

Mrs. Kraus' imagination was equal to the hint. She scribbled her personal shorthand version on a note pad. "Soon as I hear from him I'll tell him to call," she rasped.

"And, Mrs. Kraus."

"Doc?"

"You aren't smoking again are you?"

"No sir," she said, honestly from her point of view. She was down to half a pack a day now and, as far as she was concerned, that wasn't smoking.

"Then your voice ought to be improving some. Come see me next Thursday. I smell tobacco on you and I'll stop renewing your birth control pills." Doc cackled into the phone before he hung up. Mrs. Kraus, who was delighting in the hot flashes and mood swings of menopause, failed to appreciate his sense of humor.

She put the phone back in its cradle and it rang again immediately, causing her to jump a little before she grabbed it.

"This is Wynn," the instrument told her.

"Where the hell you at? The sheriff's gonna have your badge and maybe your privates if you don't get yourself back in here and start helping on this investigation."

"Calm down, Mrs. Kraus. I got me a suspect here. Found him right in front of the Reverend's house and chased him half way across the county. I need you to send me some transport so I can bring him in."

"Transport? You're the one's got the patrol car."

"It's not mobile just now. Had some brake problems. Can't you send somebody out here? I'm at David Meisenheimer's and I need somebody to give me and my prisoner a ride back."

"Sure," Mrs. Kraus agreed. "I'll just lock up the office and drive right out in my Toyota. When the sheriff calls in for autopsy details and to direct the investigation of his deputies, well, I'll let you explain why nobody's here."

"Uh, maybe I can get one of the Meisenheimers to give us a lift," Wynn offered.

"I'd do that," Mrs. Kraus replied. "I'd do that right quick if I was you. Oh, and Deputy Wynn..."

"Yes?"

"Don't get lost on the way."

She put the phone down and reached for the radio to try to raise the sheriff again but the phone continued to demand her attention. It was Mrs. Curtis, with Mrs. Lake on the extension, complaining that the line had been busy and wondering what the latest news was. The ladies agreed that the County ought to spring for the cost of an extra line, or at least call waiting, especially to the Sheriff's Office. Mrs. Kraus told them how busy she was and reminded them that it wasn't right to tie up that line during the county's first ever homicide investigation. She complained that it seemed unlikely she'd get a chance for a belated lunch break. The ladies took the hint. They'd rush right over with a pitcher of lemonade, a sandwich and a fresh piece of pie. It was a gesture of kindness and civic responsibility, only slightly inspired by the chance to listen in on things as they developed and lend Mrs. Kraus a sympathetic ear should she feel inclined to vent her frustrations along with details about the murder.

The phone rang yet again as Mrs. Kraus was putting it back in its cradle. She thought she might as well stop bothering, just hit the disconnect button and then answer whoever was bound to be next.

"Benteen County Sheriff's Office," she wheezed, wishing for one of those cigarettes Doc had warned her about.

The phone was silent for a moment, conveying only the sound of heavy breathing and she almost decided the county's mysterious and occasional obscene caller was back on duty before Mad Dog spoke.

"Mrs. Kraus," he said. "I've got another one."

Mrs. Kraus had the sinking feeling she knew exactly what he meant.

Sweetwater Creek was visible from miles away thanks to the muddy trickle that snaked its lazy way across the prairie looking about as sweet as the coffee dregs it resembled. Irrigation agriculture had dropped the water table and bared the top soil to erosion, turning the flow of clear, sweet, spring water for which the creek was named, into something more like an open sewer. In any case, it wasn't the water that was noticeable, it was the luxurious vegetation that scrambled skyward from its moist banks. You couldn't see the stream itself, not until you were right on it, and these days, after a dry spell, sometimes not even then. But the line of proud cottonwoods it inspired proclaimed the presence of water and the absence of cultivation for a good six to eight miles.

Sourdough Ranch wasn't visible for nearly as far as the cottonwoods that flanked the creek running through its heart, but, occupying a full section of pasture, much of which had never been tilled, it stood out from the neighboring farms like some neatly geometric oasis in a desert of ripening wheat. There just wasn't much pasture in Benteen County anymore, and what there was raised mutton or beef, not Arabians, Morgans, and Saddlebreds.

The sheriff slowed and let his truck rumble across the ancient wooden bridge. He'd never noticed quite how rickety it seemed until viewed from the interior of a vehicle on which he still owed fifty-nine monthly payments.

There were lots of majestic shade trees around the house and outbuildings, beginning just after you passed under the arching sign that proclaimed Sourdough Ranch as the home of equine nobility, a list of names that would seem to require you to bow or curtsey if you were lucky enough to be introduced. Thick clumps of lilac and forsythia lined the drive and broke the wind as well as the monotony of a yard that grew almost nothing but shade trees and grass. Half a dozen flapper-style sprinklers ticked their way in great circles, advancing like aquatic second hands trailing a rainbowed mist of moments already past, encouraging grass whose hint of blue seemed more appropriate to lush Kentucky instead of semi-arid Kansas.

It was a big, sprawling house, late-fifties ranch-style red-brick with lots of space for his and hers offices, a trophy room, and rooms for all the little Starks that had somehow never come along. The drive circled the south side of the house, passing between it and the first of the stables and barns and outbuildings that surrounded the parking area. The garage door at the back of the house was open and Minnie Stark's Red BMW roadster stared impudently out from its comfortable lair. It was the ideal option for an early middle-aged woman with enough money to have her pick of a new Lincoln four-wheel-drive or her husband's no-nonsense Hummer whenever the weather wasn't conducive to top-down excursions. Today was a bit warm for this Teutonic triumph of engineering, but dry enough to leave the Hummer in the slot on the other side of the empty place where the Lincoln usually roosted. The Lincoln, with its blend of rugged luxury and air-conditioned creature comforts, had apparently been the day's choice for one or both Starks.

The sheriff parked near the wall surrounding the pool, less a barrier to prying eyes, with the nearest neighbors a couple of miles away, than to Kansas' incessant wind. He climbed out gravel-eyed and about twice as tired as he'd thought he was. Judy's car wasn't there. Since the Stark's sports-utility vehicle was missing too, that probably meant the Starks weren't back yet, and that Judy had simply ignored him and driven off after he'd implored her to wait.

He should have expected that, but he hadn't. He sagged against the side of the pickup and wondered what to do next.

There was only one unfamiliar vehicle in the yard, a Volvo with styling that seemed far too dull for what it must have cost. The New Mexico plates indicated it might have brought a buyer or a rider. It was parked in front of one of the larger guest houses the Starks provided their paying guests, but there wasn't any indication anyone was home there either. The air conditioning was off and the sheriff knew from experience that the place would become uncomfortable under a sun like this in less than an hour. He tried knocking anyway. He knocked on the doors of the other guest units as well, and the two old aluminum skin trailers used by hired hands, and he tried the main house too. All yielded the same absence of response.

The sheriff was pissed. Had he wasted an hour's drive? Could he afford to wait until someone returned? He needed to be back in Buffalo Springs, but he needed to know why a call had been made from the Reverend's house to Sourdough Ranch—an unlikely connection and doubly mysterious when it was the last call made, just before or after Simms was murdered.

The sheriff tried the radio. If one of his deputies had showed up, if there weren't any further complications, if Doc Jones had any results for him...well, maybe he could wait here awhile, push one of the Stark's lawn chairs into a shady spot and catnap long enough to clear his brain of its aching dullness, just long enough to help him survive the rest of this dreadful day.

The radio got him nothing. Occasionally he could get through from this far out of town, but not usually, and not today when he needed to desperately. Despite their unreliability in Benteen County, the sheriff wished he'd bitten the bullet and bought one of the cell phones he'd been asking the commissioners to supply for his department. After child support and on top of new truck payments, though, it had been easy to put off the expense.

There were phones in the house and trailers, but all the doors were locked and the sheriff wasn't inclined to break and enter just so he wouldn't have to drive a few miles and try some other farm house to borrow a phone. Besides, he suddenly remembered, there was another phone right here. He'd been at the ranch to watch Heather ride once. He'd been standing next to a phone that began to ring and no one else was around and he'd answered it and been offered a marvelous deal on aluminum siding. Where was that? One of the outbuildings, a stable...but which one?

He massaged both eyes with the heels of his hands and tried looking around again. House, garage, pool, guest houses, trailers, full size barn, an even bigger indoor-all-weather riding arena, and a pair of long, low buildings with a series of dutch doors, from the open half of which several pairs of equine eyes watched curiously. It was comforting to realize he, as Sheriff of Benteen County, brought such incredible skills of observation to the task at hand. And a memory like a steel sieve. He thought maybe it was the south stable. At least it was worth a try.

The main doors opened at both ends of the stable, flooding it with light and making it easy for the sheriff to spot the phone on the wall near where he recalled the tack room occupied a couple of converted stalls. He was almost to the phone when he heard the noises. A thud—something solid striking something unyielding. A second thud—this time accompanied by a splintering harmonic. Curious sounds, not those he expected, and, given what he'd found in the restroom of the Buffalo Springs Veteran's Memorial Park that morning, something to be investigated.

They were coming from the other side of the building, somewhere out back, opposite where he'd entered. A horse whinnied, another nickered, snorted, and made blowing sounds. The thuds were probably just a horse, he thought, trying to break out of the stable, though he wasn't convinced by his own explanation even as he tried it out on himself. Especially when he heard the whimper. Not a loud whimper, but nothing like he'd ever heard from a horse. The Smith and Wesson was in his hand and he couldn't have told you how it got there. His pulse was up, his adrenaline flowing. He crept forward, no longer aware of all those hours of missed sleep.

The back door opened on an avenue between pens with fences that were more functional and less pretty than the white pickets along the driveway—amputated phone poles on which two-by-six rails had been bolted to contain beasts regularly weighing in around a thousand pounds.

The source of the thuds was obvious. The last pen contained a mare, likely in season, and its rails separated her from a massive white stallion with a saddle of red hair and three stockings to match. The stallion wanted in. If his erection was any indication, the sheriff knew why. The top rail bulged, jagged splinters of wood gave proof of the stallion's determination. The mare chewed at the rail, tearing bits of it away and indicating her interest was probably similar to his. Her efforts were less productive but the stallion reared up and punched at the fence with his forelegs. The top rail split and collapsed against the one below it. The stallion was bleeding. He'd cut himself on the broken beam, but the injury seemed more evidence of determined lust than serious damage. The big white wheeled, threw himself in a quick circle, and launched himself over the fence. He cleared, but not by much and the sheriff felt himself involuntarily draw in every muscle of his groin as he thought, for an excruciating moment, the beast would catch that most delicate portion of his anatomy on the sharp splinters of the shattered rail.

The horses greeted each other, whickering and nuzzling and then the stallion moved behind her, nibbling at her rump before he mounted. The sheriff felt a renewed appreciation for the expression "hung like a horse," and some of the wistful envy that probably prompted it.

As the Saddlebred and the Arabian began mixing a pair of pedigrees in a way the Starks would not approve, the sheriff heard the whimper again, louder this time, and close. It was more like a moan now. It sounded human. It sounded like someone in pain.

A vivid picture of the butchered remains of the Reverend Simms flashed across the sheriff's mind. He had the awful feeling he might be about to discover a similar product of someone's awesome anger, one that had, so far, failed to find release in death. He experienced a momentary desire to tear his badge off, hurl it at the nearest manure pile, and abandon the job and this search to someone with the stomach for it. Then he remembered, Judy and Heather had been here. They might be victims. All doubts disappeared. The sheriff had to find the source of those sounds.

He couldn't tell where they'd come from. The stallion was snorting and the mare interjecting breathless little whinnies. Cicadas hummed, inordinately loud in the absence of the constant Kansas wind. There were only a couple of piles of used straw mucked out from the stables along with a few bales of hay and a portable sledge-like feeding trough standing between him and the line of heavily fenced corrals where an act of renewal was doing its best to offset what the sheriff feared he might find for a second time today.

He moved forward in an unconscious half-crouch, .38 cocked and extended before him. He rounded a stack of hay bales and thought he saw a furtive movement off to his right behind the trough. He was right. It was part of a gunny sack that a hint of breeze had found and toyed with and the sheriff almost put a couple of rounds into it before he was able to convert it back into a harmless bit of cloth instead of the savage killer his mind was expecting to find.

With his eyes occupied, however, his feet found and tangled with something else. He felt himself falling. He frantically looked down and saw, to his horror, human flesh. Naked human flesh streaked with parallel lines of fresh blood. He knew this was the source of the sound but he couldn't decipher the confused blur of images that confronted him as he lost his balance. Was this another victim, or were there two figures, victim and perpetrator, the act of butchery still underway, the fiend surprised while still at his mutilations? The sheriff fought for balance, fought for comprehension, and found neither.

He went down hard. He'd tried to catch himself with his right hand as he fell and got it partly under him, just enough to knock the .38 loose and send it skittering out of reach. He was part of a confused jumble of thrashing arms and legs. Fingernails slashed at his eyes and just missed. A fist slammed into his temple and flooded one eye with blood and made him turn his head away from the source of the attack, but also away from seeing what he was up against. Something hit him hard in the ribs but it was a glancing blow, more painful than damaging. He reached out blindly, encountered flesh, grabbed hold with all his might, locking one set of the arms and legs that pummeled him. Another set disengaged themselves and bare feet pounded away.

The sheriff shook the blood out of his eyes in time to watch a blond man run bare assed and buck naked around the end of the stables. The youth's long gold hair suggested it was probably Cody Mathews, one of the Starks' hired hands. There were bloody scratches on his back and buttocks.

The sheriff turned his attention to the source of those scratches, finally realizing exactly what he'd stumbled on and heard, and gotten hold of. She was tall and muscular and dark, much older than Cody, but with a body still suitable for stapling into a centerfold. She wasn't hurt, or hadn't been before the sheriff fell over her. She was apparently one of those women who had a thing about horses and, in Cody's company, had been caught up by the stallion's excitement. She and the boy had been in the midst of a private ride, their plans interrupted by the sheriff's arrival. They'd been down behind the hay bales—her spandex outfit and shorts lay atop Cody's jeans and cotton shirt—when the sheriff literally stumbled onto them. She still lay half under him, eyes wide, breathing hard, still writhing to get free.

There's something erotic about terror. Some ancient instinctive reaction takes over when we've been frightened, reminded of our mortality. It tells our bodies nature designed us to procreate before we die. That's probably why horror movies are so popular. The sheriff had been living his own personal horror movie all day. As he realized what was in his arms, he also discovered his body wanted her. If the painful bulge in his Levis was any indication, he wanted her pretty badly. It made him feel hot and embarrassed and ashamed. Letting go was one of the hardest things he'd ever had to do.

The sheriff lay in the dirt by the hay while the stallion finished and a dark exotic stranger sprawled under him, no longer fighting him now that he'd released her. Her eyes were deep brown, the irises such a rich chocolate color that they nearly blended with her pupils and made them seem even wider than they were—and they were wide. Those eyes seemed to look right past him, and the sheriff wondered if she'd even noticed that she was with a different partner than the one with whom she'd begun. He was about to offer some sort of apology, look for a graceful exit from this bizarre situation for both of them. He'd just opened his mouth in hope of finding something moderately appropriate to say when a voice spoke from the spot where her wide-eyed stare was focused.

"You slut!" it said. It didn't sound happy. The sheriff wondered how he was going to explain, or if he'd get the chance.

◇◇◇

Doc Jones' Buick station wagon was a nondescript beige that blended well with the layers of Benteen County dust it collected, lying thick enough in places to have begun developing their own stratigraphy. The Buick's patina was nearly indistinguishable from the twin columns of dust that rolled up off its back wheels to hang suspended in the heavy afternoon air.

Just past the third crossroad from the highway, and after navigating around a washed out bridge over Calf Creek, Doc began to slow down and watch for mailboxes. There was a time when he'd been a regular visitor at the Simms' place, but that was years ago. He hadn't been to the house since Old Man Simms decided Doc Jones was personally responsible for medical science's inability to cure Mrs. Simms' fatal breast cancer.

As it turned out, he didn't need to read mail boxes after all. He recognized the place at once. It still sported a lush stand of hardwoods behind an evergreen windbreak that separated it from the road.

The Buick swung into the driveway and slid through a verdant tunnel that allowed entry to Doc and the car while filtering out the dust he'd brought along. The big two-story wooden frame house sat in an enchanted glade dappled with shadow and sunlight. Doc had almost navigated the entirety of the drive before he realized Mad Dog's Saab was parked under a maple behind the house and that Mad Dog, himself, was sitting on the steps of the front porch. It gave Doc a momentary pause. Until today he might have questioned Mad Dog's sanity about any number of things and never considered him dangerous, but until today he'd never conducted an autopsy on someone who'd been tortured to death and scalped and otherwise treated in very much the way the ancestors Mad Dog claimed might have welcomed another White pilgrim to this stretch of prairie in a previous century.

The sheriff should be here to deal with this, Doc told himself with a brief flash of hostility that evaporated almost as soon as it surfaced. The sheriff probably should be lots of places this afternoon. Wherever he was, Doc knew, he was doing his best. This was just one of the places the sheriff would get to as soon as he had the time. Until then, and until this thing was over and solved, Doc would just have to pitch in and help shoulder the load. He remembered the day the sheriff had spent almost fifteen minutes giving CPR to the Hoffman girl after the family's pickup avoided a Hereford bull and rolled into an adjoining field tossing Hoffmans, and pieces of Hoffmans, every which way while Doc had been too busy performing a Caesarian in an unsuccessful effort to save the girl's mother and baby brother to come tell the sheriff that even those heroic efforts couldn't have saved her. In other words, the sheriff would do what he could for others, so Doc would do what he could for the sheriff. Still, Doc wished he'd stopped by Bertha's to see if someone would come along for the ride, or that he had a pistol hidden in his medical gear, or that Mad Dog hadn't felt the need to wait for him. Hell, he wished he was young again, and rich....

He pulled up near the front door and crawled out from behind the steering wheel and into a steam bath this riotously green patch of vegetation and shadow had fooled him into forgetting. It was still summer in Benteen County.

"Mad Dog." Doc Jones said, bobbing his head as he extracted his leather satchel from the car and proceeded toward the porch.

"Hi Doc," Mad Dog said, coming slowly to his feet and extending a hand that was still streaked with a little body paint.

Doc wasn't about to refuse it on that account. They shook. "Mrs. Kraus tells me you found another one," Doc said. Maybe Mrs. Kraus had somehow got it wrong and Mad Dog would tell him so and he could turn around and go home and try not to think about what someone had done to Peter Simms, try not to let his thoughts drift back to what he'd left in a body bag and a series of containers in the refrigerated back room of Klausen's mortuary. He could see from the unhappy look on Mad Dog's face that this was one more wish that wouldn't come true.

"Old Man Simms," Mad Dog said, nodding and turning to open and hold the door. "He's right in here, on the stairs."

Doc didn't go in yet. He stood there and let his free hand rub the bridge of his nose. Just at that moment, he couldn't bring himself to turn his back on Mad Dog.

"How'd you come by this one?" Doc asked.

Mad Dog stood there, holding the door and shrugged his shoulders. They were broad shoulders, strong enough to have stuffed the Reverend Simms, or what remained of him, head first down the toilet in Veteran's Memorial Park, adding the insult of a post-mortem swirly to the injuries of ante-mortem butchery.

"I felt pretty guilty about Peter Simms," Mad Dog said. "When I heard he'd been identified, and when neither Englishman nor any of his deputies were available to come break the news to his old man…well, I thought it was the least I could do."

There it was, the part about guilt. That was what bothered Doc. Why should Mad Dog feel guilty? Doc decide he'd rather ask straight out, face to face, than feel the razor's touch from behind as he went through the door.

"Guilty?" he asked. "You trying to tell me you killed the Reverend?"

"I'm not real certain," Mad Dog replied. Hardly the reassurance Doc had been seeking.

"I don't understand," Doc observed.

"Me either," Mad Dog said. "That's the problem."

Doc found his hand at the bridge of his nose again. It was the sort of gesture a man might use whose glasses didn't fit right. Doc didn't wear glasses, he wore contacts. He decided it was also the sort of gesture a nervous man might make to waste time in the hope that something might come up to let him avoid doing what frightened him. The realization made Doc mad.

"Well, fuck this!" Doc exclaimed. "If you're the murderer and you're going to kill me too, get it over with. Otherwise, show me the body."

Mad Dog didn't say anything, he just stood there looking sad and holding the door and Doc used the burst of anger and adrenaline to get past him. He made it safely, and once inside, the sight of Simms' lying on the staircase captured his full attention.

"He hasn't been butchered," Doc observed, surprised and relieved he wasn't going to have to scoop parts of another human being into plastic baggies to take back to Klausen's.

"No," Mad Dog agreed, "but look at his scalp."

A small square patch was missing, Doc could see that from the foot of the stairs. "Just like his son," Doc whispered.

"I thought so," Mad Dog whispered back. It would probably have bothered Doc but he was on his way up the stairs by then, eyes noting details and processing them as he climbed to the corpse's side

"Did you touch him?" Doc asked, reaching out and doing so himself.

"No," Mad Dog said, finally providing a simple answer, now that he wasn't dealing with a question he considered metaphysical.

The body was about the same temperature as the house. Rigor had set in and there was marked lividity in the portions of the corpse that were lower on the stairs.

"He's been dead for some time," Doc said, as much to himself as to Mad Dog. "Probably at least ten or twelve hours." He took a cotton swab out of his bag and dabbed it at the missing square of scalp. The swab came away dry. "This wound didn't bleed and it isn't fresh. Whoever took his scalp did it after he was dead, maybe even quite awhile after."

Mad Dog couldn't think of anything to say so he just stood at the foot of the stairs and nodded his head. None of what Doc was telling him made much difference, metaphysically speaking.

"Go get me the stretcher out of the Buick," Doc commanded, his mind now too occupied to be concerned with the possibility he might be talking to a killer. "I want to take him right down to Klausen's. I've got a feeling whoever scalped him didn't kill him. He maybe even died of natural causes, but I'll need to open him up to find out. And I need to check for his scalp."

Mad Dog went for the stretcher, but he wasn't particularly interested in, nor relieved by, Doc's conjecture. He was pretty sure that Old Man Simms' murderer, as well as the killer of the Reverend Simms, was capable of acts that could be mistaken for natural causes. So, even though Mad Dog was positive he knew the murderer's identity, he had no idea what to do about it.

The Sheriff slowly turned to face the voice. It was one of those things he didn't really want to do, but for which there was no alternative. He tried to let his face relax into a friendly, non-threatening smile and merely succeeded in looking guilty and foolish.

The speaker wasn't a big man, but he was very solid. The muscles in his arms rippled under a pelt of dark hair and olive skin as he clenched his fists. His slacks and shirt fit well enough so that the sheriff knew there was no excess flesh on the man. He had an athlete's body and a face that looked Turkish or Greek, or maybe Spanish. He didn't have any accent. The sheriff noticed that as the man spoke again.

"I've often thought about how it would be when I found you. This isn't what I expected, but it's appropriate. It's all you were ever good for."

Angry husband, the sheriff had thought. He still might be just that, though the remarks didn't quite fit—not that this was a good time to analyze them. He was just glad the man didn't seem to be paying him any attention as he tried to wiggle free of the naked woman who was the target of this abuse. The man didn't seem to be armed either, though his shirt hung over his belt, not tucked into it. Almost anything that wasn't too bulky could be hidden under there, say a knife or a razor, given what had happened to the Reverend Simms. The sheriff's gun was only a few feet away near a pile of pungently fresh road apples. If the woman would just hold the man's attention while he got his boot out from under her butt and crawled over there, the situation might revert to his control.

"I'm going to kill you," the woman said as the sheriff extricated himself. He was still watching the short dark dangerous-looking man and hoped she hadn't suddenly chosen to address him instead of the intruder. At least he knew she wasn't armed. She didn't have any place to hide anything.

He rolled off her in the direction of the pistol but she chose that moment to lunge at the newcomer, nails extended, going for his eyes. The sheriff knew how dangerous those nails could be. He'd seen Cody's backside and he was pretty sure the wounds on his own cheek had been caused by them. There was nothing half-hearted about her attempt. She might have made it if she hadn't tripped over the sheriff's freshly freed boot. She fell short and incidentally knocked the sheriff's hand away from the pistol just as his fingers were on the verge of retrieving it. It also might have saved her serious injury. The dark little man with the muscles chopped a foot into the place her face would have been if she'd been free to get there. He'd expected to make contact with the martial arts kick and he lost his balance too and then all three of them were there in the dirt and the hay and the manure and two of the three seemed bent on maiming each other and not especially concerned if the sheriff happened to get in the way.

Somebody hit him in the ribs as someone else tried to tear his left ear off, or maybe it was the same someone in both cases. The sheriff got to his hands and knees and seemed about to disengage himself when someone kicked him solidly in the butt. The kick sent him sprawling. He ended up with his face in the dirt, spitting gravel through bruised lips, but his nose was only inches from the .38. He latched onto it with the fervor of a tent meeting convert to instant salvation. He rolled and saw a whirl of clothed muscular masculinity and naked muscular femininity in search of each other's jugulars.

"Freeze, God damn it!" he shouted, and when they didn't, added, "Sheriff" and pumped a pair of rounds into the thick lumber of the portable feeding trough.

It worked. Two pair of taloned hands ceased searching for eyes to gouge out and a pair of bloodied faces turned toward his voice.

"What the hell's going on here?" the sheriff demanded in an outraged tone that might have been more appropriate if asked of him by either of them at separate times a few moments earlier.

"Who are you people?" The sheriff had had a tough morning. He was tired of surprises. He wanted answers for a change.

Nobody gave him any though. They just stared at him until the man finally asked a question of his own.

"Sheriff?"

The Benteen County Sheriff's star was attached to the pocket of his shirt. He waved a hand at it. "What do you think this is," he said, "a merit badge for mud wrestling?"

"I see," the dark man replied, then moved a little faster than the sheriff would have thought possible. One of his hands dipped to the vicinity of his belt and came back with something thin and sharp and shiny. The other hand grabbed the woman by her hair and the first hand put the blade at her throat as the man looked calmly at the sheriff and said, "Drop the gun, asshole. Drop the gun or I rip her throat out and maybe get blood all over your badge. I won't do her much good either."

That wasn't how this was supposed to work. If you were the good guy, you got the drop on the opposition and then he just gave up or you plugged him. He didn't grab a handy hostage to thrust between himself and your weapon and tell you to drop it and call you an asshole. What, the sheriff wondered, would Clint Eastwood do in a situation like this?

"I said drop it," the dark little man repeated. His voice sounded just a little shriller this time. "Don't think I won't kill her."

The sheriff had no reason not to believe him. He didn't know who either of these people were, but he couldn't see how putting his gun down would help the woman. Dirty Harry wouldn't put the gun down. Of course, Dirty Harry wouldn't have given the man a chance to make the demand. He'd have put a couple of fist sized holes from his magnum in the guy and dropped him in the dirt and manure. It would have made Harry's day. The sheriff was just about angry enough to do something similar. He'd killed before, back when he was just a kid, up close and personal in those final days when Vietnam was already a lost cause but American servicemen were still going out to meet little dark skinned men who didn't offer any choices but kill or be killed. The sheriff had had enough of it to last a lifetime. He didn't shoot game animals anymore, or even targets. Maybe he wasn't capable of enough anger to just blow this guy away, but he was mad enough not to obey.

"No," the sheriff said. The little man looked surprised. "I'm keeping the gun. You cut her and I pop you. I drop the gun and you can cut her and maybe get to me or away before I can pick it up again. No, I'm gonna keep the gun and if you cut her, you're gonna be dead before she is."

"He won't kill me," the woman said, her voice a harsh whisper through a larynx constricted by the dark man's corded arm. "At least not now. I've got something he wants and doesn't know where to find. He won't kill me now."

The man with the muscles and the blade didn't deny it. His eyes had suddenly begun to flash from side to side as if looking for an exit.

What was going on here, the sheriff wondered. This was starting to sound like something from a Bogart movie. When would the fat man and his gunsel put in an appearance? These two would do for Brigid and Cairo. Maybe he should ask them about the black bird?

"Maybe you should let her go," the sheriff suggested.

"Shit," the man said. "You're both idiots if you think I'm going back to jail."

Jail? What was this about going back to jail? And what did the little man want worse than killing this beautiful woman, something he'd given every indication he was seriously interested in doing?

The man began backing away. "Stay put," he ordered the sheriff, who immediately disobeyed.

She didn't exactly fight him, but she didn't cooperate either. It made his retreat awkward and slow. Too slow to bear. About ten feet before the sheriff had decided he'd do exactly that, the man suddenly lifted and shoved the woman back at him and whirled and dove for the entrance to the stables. The sheriff wasn't quite ready for it. He managed to avoid being knocked down but he couldn't have gotten off a clean shot even if he wanted, and he wasn't ready to risk killing someone over something he clearly didn't understand.

"Halt! Halt or I'll shoot!" the sheriff shouted, hurdling the naked woman and flailing his arms to help keep his feet under him. The angry little man didn't halt and the sheriff didn't shoot and by the time the sheriff got through the stable and into the parking lot a motorcycle had been kicked to life and was showering everything in the vicinity with rocks and gravel.

The Chevy made its own dust cloud and the sheriff did some creative steering to keep it from spinning out and going ass first into the ditch across from Sourdough's entrance. He went airborne as he crossed the bridge at Sweetwater creek, the 350 howling in frustration at losing contact with the earth and the traction it needed to continue to accelerate. The sheriff was doing better than seventy at the first intersection and close to a hundred by the second but the motorcycle was getting away. The Chevy could go faster still, but not on this washboard and sand country road. The sheriff was just beginning to recall the RPM limits and moderate speeds he was supposed to keep his new truck under during its break-in period when the back end started going squirrelly on him and he knew he'd blown a tire as well as maybe voiding a warranty. By the time he got it stopped between two empty wheat fields, he couldn't even hear the scream of the motorcycle's exhaust anymore. Nothing but dust remained as the bike carried yet another mystery out of his control and back into Benteen County where it could do all manner of harm to his chances of being elected to another term, to say nothing of its possible impact on the life expectancy of the local population.

OK. So where was the jack? The sheriff knew his spare was hanging under the bed just in front of the recently remodeled chrome step bumper. He leaned over and opened the glove box and grabbed his owner's manual. A plastic baggy containing a package of M&Ms and a note fell into his lap.

> "If you find this it will probably mean your new truck isn't as trouble free as it should be. In that case, we'd like you to remind you that Heather favored the 'way cool' Dodge and I thought a Ford would be more reliable. We told you so, but your problems will best be faced knowing you are loved and have chocolate. Thus, this care package and our affection. XOXO!"

It was Judy's handwriting. The sheriff shook his head and tore open a corner of the package and poured some M&Ms into his hand. Having spent the day baking inside the cab of his pickup, they defied their slogan and melted in his hand as well as his mouth.

He'd been so angry that she hadn't waited at the ranch he'd thought he might never speak to her again. And now.... He munched another handful of the nearly liquid candy and began thumbing through the manual's index. He found what he needed to know about the jack, but for the more confusing topic of Judy, there was no entry.

"You should have killed him," she told the sheriff as she emerged from the doorway to the stable. She was back in her spandex outfit and shorts. It did more to confine things than hide them. There wasn't much point in not staring at what was already familiar, so when the sheriff looked up, he didn't bother just focusing on her eyes.

The little man who'd gotten away on a motorcycle had been wearing an expensive pair of athletic shoes with interesting waffled soles. Since returning to the Sourdough, the sheriff had been fruitlessly examining the gravel parking lot for a good impression to compare with his memory of the prints he'd found in Peter Simms' backyard. While he was eyeing her, he checked. She was wearing sandals.

"Why?" he asked. "Why should I have killed him?" The sheriff was in the mood to kill someone about now. He was willing to listen to nominations. The jack the truck came with wasn't really designed for changing flats on country roads. He'd spent more time than he could afford figuring out how it was supposed to work. Wrestling the spare—at least there really was a spare and not one of those mini-tires more appropriate for dunking in coffee—out from under the bed, and then making the swap while the truck swayed and threatened to topple on some important part of his anatomy had caused his patience to run out. He'd be ready to resubscribe after he solved a murder and the mystery of this woman and the motorcyclist.

She shrugged. The spandex emphasized nipples that stood erect from emotion or exertion. She looked as good in her clothes as out. With most women it was one way or the other, not both. She looked dangerous, but she looked good.

"If somebody doesn't kill him, he'll kill me, not that that particularly matters. What matters is that he'll also get to my daughter again."

The sheriff looked down at his hands and tried rubbing a smudge of grease off. The smudge stayed. He couldn't wipe it away any easier than he could wipe away his confusion. He dabbed at the blood that was still oozing from the cut above his eyebrow, then used a thumb and forefinger to massage his jaw. It was a gesture that would have plainly told anyone who knew him of his stress and frustration, and his growing intolerance of whoever continued to contribute to either.

"I think maybe it's time someone told me what this is all about," the sheriff said through teeth he somehow managed not to clench.

"What do you want to know?" the woman asked.

"Everything," he replied. "Just start at the beginning and if you're not sure whether to tell me something, do it. Let me decide what's important."

"I'm not sure what the beginning is."

"God damn it! Tell me what the hell is going on and tell me now!" the sheriff shouted, his composure finally gone.

"He's after Heather, you idiot," she screamed right back. "He wants to get his hands on her, and probably his prick in her again too, and I'm going to kill him before I let that happen."

The sheriff felt his jaw drop. Who is the dark man and why is he after my daughter, he wondered? If the woman was right, the sheriff might have found a reason to kill again, but he was still thoroughly confused. He was pretty sure the dark man hadn't sexually assaulted his daughter as of the early hours of this morning when he'd seen her last, or since, up to the time he'd spoken to Judy when he was at Simms' and she was here. Like everything so far, it just made no sense.

"Who are you?" the sheriff asked. "What have you got to do with Heather?"

"I'm Heather's mother."

The sheriff thought he had reason to know Heather's mother. The woman's reply just further confounded him. The two of them stood and stared at each other, waiting for the other to say something that made sense or related to the moment of sex and violence they'd just shared...or for the Mad Hatter to invite them to tea.

. A stallion whinnied and the sprinklers ticked off a few more moments of eternity in a landscape that seemed to reach from alpha to omega and maybe back again. A man and a woman failed utterly in their mutual attempts to communicate, and in this way, as in most things, the universe went on as normal.

Judy English stared at the pretty girl in the revealing camisole and felt properly shocked. Not because everything bordered on being indecently exposed, but because she looked so good just this side of naked. For Judy, the shocking part was that the pretty girl was her own reflection in a dressing room mirror, beneath lights so harsh they seemed designed to help a woman find her flaws and remind her not to commit sins of the flesh or purchase erotic offerings improbably discovered in a boutique in the Hutchinson Mall.

Judy was power shopping, and about out of time. The movie she'd dropped the girls off to see would soon be over. She knew she should get back before it let out to make certain they didn't start trolling the mall for boys or scarfing up junk in the food court. Judy had taken a sandwich to the ranch for Heather but skipped her own lunch. Now she was hungry. She had her heart set on eating at the Red Lobster across the parking lot before heading home to Buffalo Springs. The closest you could get to seafood in Benteen County was the tuna salad at Bertha's. Judy had promised herself a reward if her scale read under 110 pounds that morning. Thanks to Englishman, she'd burned a lot of calories last night. Enough, if the scale's reading of 108, and her reflection in this mirror, were to be believed.

She slowly pivoted and glanced over her shoulder for a rear view. It wasn't bad, especially not for a small-town schoolmarm pushing forty. But what on earth did she want with a camisole? She couldn't remember the last time she'd actually had a date. Not that there weren't offers. The shop teacher and the basketball coach had made it clear they were willing to provide for her physical needs. So had several farmers, some of them already married, and even one kid who wasn't much more than Heather's age. Most of them were cute enough, a couple were even hunks, but…. Well, when you got right down to it, the "but" was that they weren't Englishman. She hated him down to his bones, sometimes, except when she still loved him so much she couldn't wait to jump them.

She tried a side view and consciously stopped sucking in her tummy. Not horrible.

Judy had wanted something that Benteen County didn't offer for as long as she could remember. She wasn't sure what that was, and she hadn't been able to explain it to Englishman when she tried to persuade him to move away, maybe even outside of Kansas. He'd seen the world, or at least the collection of army bases at which he'd been stationed on his way to and from Vietnam. Benteen County was home. It was familiar, comfortable. He didn't want to leave. Well, in comparison to where he'd been, she supposed, that was understandable. But what about Paris, or even Kansas City, Missouri? There was more to be experienced out there and she wanted to discover it strongly enough to fight for it. Their fights had gotten to be about all kinds of things, mostly, she supposed, that neither of them were who each other had expected. After the divorce when she was free to leave, she hadn't. She didn't think it would be fair to deprive Heather of her father and a familiar home. Not while their daughter was young. Not, apparently, until she was old enough for college. And then, well there were still things Judy wanted to see but she was afraid the men in Paris, or Kansas City, still wouldn't be Englishman.

She looked at the price tag again. Absurd! The money should go into that travel fund she'd been promising herself she'd start sometime soon. Her reflection smiled wickedly out of the mirror. Englishman would like this view even more than she did. Paris would wait a little longer.

"Hey Lois, here's your double-bacon burger combo." Heather English plopped an immense stack of food down on their table. She and Heather Lane were spending the last of the funds Judy had left for them to entertain themselves with while she went on her shopping spree. They were in the north end of the Hutchinson Mall in the fast food cluster by the cineplex and the video game arcade. Nearby, a silver haired matron sat at a piano and made elevator music of REM's "Losing My Religion." Even if the girls had recognized this sanitized version, they wouldn't have thought anything of it. REM already belonged to an ancient generation from their view point.

"Lois?" the other Heather paled. "Why did you call me Lois?"

Heather English began unwrapping her chili-cheese burger. "Cause your name is Lane. You know, like Lois Lane from Superman."

"Oh, yeah." Heather Lane's reply was subdued enough to get her companion's attention.

"Gee! Did I say something wrong? I didn't mean anything by it." Heather English was concerned enough to delay her attention to the mound of food that awaited.

"No, it's OK," the visiting Heather sighed. "It's just funny, you know. It's like, you just guessed my alias."

"Wow! You have an alias?"

Heather Lane was recovered enough to pop a straw into her cherry coke and the wrapping from her burger. "You told me about your name. I guess it's only fair for me to tell you about mine. Lane's not really it. Heather is, but even though I trust you like eternally, Mom would kill me if I told you our real last name.

Lane's the one she picked for us to use while we're hiding out from my dad. And it's funny you called me Lois, because that's where it came from, Superman's Lois Lane. See, I've got these aunts. One of them is Linda Lois...well, I guess I shouldn't tell you her last name either. Anyway, a long time ago she got in this tough spot and needed to pretend she was someone else and that's what she came up with. Lois Lane. I thought it was so cool, you know, cause she picked it so she could be the heroine of her own story, the girl the superhero will always come rescue."

She filled her mouth with bacon burger and Heather English shook her head in admiration. "That is so awesome. It's like something from a movie."

"Speaking of movies," Heather Lane said as she dunked a seasoned french fry into a pyramid of catsup and mayonnaise, "I never thought your Mom would let us see *Scream*. Mine won't let me see Wes Craven's films."

"Actually," Heather English confessed around a mouthful of chili-cheese burger "I think Mom may have the impression we went to that Robin Williams, Billy Crystal movie. I'd kind of take it as a personal favor if you wouldn't say anything."

"Sure," the pseudonymous Lane girl agreed. "My Mom'll be a lot happier if she thinks the same."

"I thought you didn't enjoy it," the rural Heather observed. "You never screamed once."

"Just inside," the urban Heather replied. "Mom taught me not to scream, not unless it'll do me some good. She says if you scream around a guy, you just make it worse. She says it was that way with Dad. She taught me to clam up and wait for my chance, so I sat on the edge of my seat in the movie and did the white knuckle bit.

"Anyway," Heather Lane continued, "this is just one more thing it's better Mom doesn't know."

"Mothers are so...." Heather English couldn't find an adjective that was sufficiently inclusive of overly protective, warden-like, up-tight, not-with-it, and lacking-in-understanding.

"Too true," her look alike agreed around a sip of cola. "I've been stuck in convents and girls' schools and stuff all my life. It's like Mom does everything to keep me from ever getting close to a boy. Like at the ranch. You know that Cody who works there?"

The sheriff's daughter did. In fact, he was the source of the offer of assistance in losing her virginity she'd told her father about. Well, maybe not a direct offer, but he'd made reference to showing her how to sit a different kind of saddle. She'd known what he meant. Cody was several years older than she was, but the Buffalo Springs school system was small enough that she was aware of his reputation as a letch. He'd bragged about bagging most of the homecoming queens in his age group. The homecoming queens denied his claims. Basically, Heather English thought Cody was a dork who probably hadn't scored as often as he maintained, though maybe often enough to deserve his reputation. He was a cute dork, though.

"Sure, I know him."

"Well, like I think he's got the hots for me. He's been hanging around all the time and giving me the eye, only Mom won't give me a chance to be alone with him. She's always there, always part of the conversation. But I'm hoping, you know. Just yesterday he whispered to me that he had a plan to win Mom over."

The Heather of Buffalo Springs could believe that. Cody had a way of hanging around anything female. She even caught him trying to hit on her mom once, which had made Heather English feel more than a little weird. She thought Heather Lane really ought to know about Cody, but she didn't want to hurt her feelings.

"He's got the cutest little butt and all that sweet blond hair. I'm thinking maybe I might like to re-lose my virginity to him."

"Re-lose your virginity?"

"Sure. I mean, it's not like I can remember what my father did to me. I may not have a cherry to pluck anymore, but that doesn't mean I know what I'm doing. Oh, I've read lots of books and had some sex-ed classes. I know what goes where and I even bought some rubbers out of a machine in a service station restroom for just in case, but I'm still, like, terrified of doing it. I mean, what if I don't like it or what if he can tell I'm not pure and then he expects me to know what to do and I like blow it."

Heather English couldn't help the giggle that escaped her. "From what I hear, blowing it is exactly what he'll be hoping for."

Heather Lane chortled Cherry Coke through her nose and Heather English snorted some partially masticated fries across the table. When Judy English, carrying enough merchandise to supply an expedition to darkest Arkansas, returned, she had to drag a pair of hysterical Heathers from the food area to the parking lot. In spite of all the food they hadn't managed to swallow, it was obvious neither of the girls would have an appetite for supper in Hutch. Judy endured her own hunger and disappointment, along with an endless harmony of girlish giggles, as they abandoned metropolitan Hutchinson for the long drive back to Benteen County.

If he hadn't brought in a prisoner, Wynn knew he'd have been catching holy hell from Mrs. Kraus about the missing police cruiser, revolver, radio, and the fact that he'd been out of contact for most of the day. He did have a prisoner though, so all he got was a lot of angry muttering when he asked her to arrange for somebody to tow the cruiser out of Calf Creek. As he escorted his prisoner back into the jail he could hear her making snide comments about him to the pair of old biddies who'd brought in her lunch and their prying curiosities. Neil Bowen was more respectful of him than anyone else he'd encountered today, maybe because the man was still a little concerned about getting lynched or shot for resisting arrest, especially since Wynn had borrowed a spare pistol out of the armory closet and let the black man see him load it.

Wynn didn't take Bowen straight back to the cages. He didn't want the man to see what a sorry state of repair most of them were in, not until he was prepared to lock him up and go tell the sheriff he had the murderer (or at least a suspect).

"Take a seat," Wynn invited, gesturing to one of the old wooden chairs that had been stacked in the corridor for as long as the deputy could remember.

"Thank you," Neil Bowen said, and took the best one. Wynn had to do some sorting to find another that looked solid enough to offer reasonable support. This was not quite the way he'd pictured the interrogation starting, but then none of the day had born much resemblance to his expectations. He pulled his selection around to put it between a west facing window and the spot Bowen had selected. That put the light behind him and in Bowen's eyes, except that the sun wasn't low enough to make it a problem. Still,

Wynn didn't have a collection of lamps to stick in Bowen's face. This would have to do.

"OK," Wynn began, "why'd you kill him?"

"Who?"

"The man you killed," Wynn thought that was a clever rejoinder that might just trip up the professor and start a confession.

"I haven't killed anyone, Deputy. Therefore I'm afraid I can't tell you why."

"What were you doing in front of Reverend Simms' house."

"I've explained that. I got lost and had car trouble. I'm not very mechanical. Maybe I just ran out of gas. My cell phone wouldn't work. I was looking for help so I hiked across a field to that neighborhood and started knocking on doors. I hadn't tried more than a couple when you started chasing me."

"What's your connection with the Reverend?"

The black man shook his head. "I'm afraid I have no connection with the Reverend Simms whatsoever."

"Ah ha!" Wynn pounced. "How'd you know his name then?"

"You just told me," Bowen replied.

"I did?"

"You did," Mad Dog agreed. Wynn hadn't noticed him back there in the cells. "Aren't you supposed to read him his rights first, Wynn, before you start questioning him?"

"What are you doing back there?" Wynn asked, in the hope Mad Dog and the black man might forget that stuff about rights.

"I'm waiting for Englishman, Wynn. What are you doing with this guy. What makes you think he's got anything to do with the murders?"

"Aw, Mad Dog, mind your own bees wax, will ya. I maybe got me the killer here."

"Excuse me, Deputy Wynn," Bowen said. "I believe you are supposed to inform me of my rights, and one of those rights is the presence of an attorney. Since you seem to think I've killed someone, I rather think I'd like to speak with my lawyer if you don't mind."

"Jeez, Mad Dog! See what you've gone and done."

Mad Dog stood up from the bunk he'd been lying on, pushed open the cell door, and walked around to the corridor. He offered his hand to the black man and said, "Hi. I'm Harvey Mad Dog. I'm Cheyenne."

"Really," Bowen said, accepting it. "I didn't think there were any around here anymore."

"Not many," Mad Dog agreed. "Just me and my brother."

"Neil Bowen, Mr. Mad Dog. I'm an historian. I hold the Benjamin Singleton endowed chair at Fort Hays State, and I'm very pleased to meet you."

Wynn got to his feet. "Now hold it just a minute. This is an interrogation here, not a social gathering."

"Oh, come on, Wynn. What would an historian from Fort Hays be doing murdering one of our local preachers. Give me a break. What'd you do, go after the first stranger you saw just because he's black?"

That was an uncomfortably accurate assessment. "Course not," Wynn protested. "I found him prowling around near Simms' house."

"And you've heard him tell you why. Have you checked to see if it might be true, or where he was when the Reverend was murdered?"

Wynn just stared down at his boots and didn't say anything.

"He didn't did he," Mad Dog asked Bowen who shook his head to acknowledge Wynn's failure. "Well then, sir, where'd you spend the night last night?"

"Why, at home in Hays. I drove down here this morning."

"And can you prove that?" Mad Dog continued.

"Well, my wife and children know I was there, and we have company staying with us, my wife's mother and sister. I stopped for breakfast in La Crosse on my way down. That would have been about eight. I paid with a credit card. Deputy Wynn, I believe you'll find the receipt in my billfold if you'd care to look."

"Wynn," Mad Dog said. "From what Doc tells me, Peter Simms was killed between two and six this morning. Sound's like Professor Bowen can prove he was a considerable distance from here in that time frame, and like he's maybe got a good reason to consider suing Benteen County for false arrest. I'm not too sure the county commissioners would look favorably on retaining the deputy who drove the county into bankruptcy by violating an esteemed academician's civil rights, even if your old man is chairman. Might be a good time for an apology, and maybe a little assistance in helping the professor find his car and getting it towed in and running so we don't waste any more of his day."

"That would be very kind of you," Dr. Bowen agreed.

"Yeah, well," Wynn muttered. "I may have made a mistake here, but you just set tight a few minutes while I make a couple of calls and check out your story. Then, if everything's like you say, you can go."

"After you find and fix his car," Mad Dog supplied.

"Yeah, after that," 'Lose Some' agreed.

The gossips of Buffalo Springs had enough material to last a month. Not that they'd managed to pry much from Mrs. Kraus. She was too busy, but they had overheard some interesting phone calls and witnessed more than a little first hand drama. The phone had kept Mrs. Kraus almost constantly occupied. Then some folks who'd been at Bertha's came in with a picture of Heather English and a wild tale about a stranger who was looking for her. Just after that, the frightening and newly bald Mad Dog arrived and asked for his brother. When he heard the sheriff was still out of touch, he'd solemnly let himself back into the jail. As the phone started ringing again, Mrs. Kraus whispered that the always peculiar half-brother of the sheriff was acting even more oddly today and had—perhaps coincidentally—discovered the bodies of both Reverend Simms and his father. Then along came Wynn, riding up to the front of the courthouse in the back of the Meisenheimer's pickup without his patrol car, his gun, or his radio. He did have a colored prisoner, though, a dangerous looking stranger who came in with his hands lashed behind his back. It was a thrill to watch Deputy Wynn dig out a pistol and load it, unbind the Negro, and lead him back into the jail for an interrogation that would not begin to match their imaginations.

That was when Deputy French finally called in. He was about half-way across the county at his sister's place. He'd just gotten word and was ready to come back on duty wherever the sheriff needed him. Mrs. Kraus filled him in, adding a few details for the gossips, and then French asked her what she thought he ought to do. Should he come into the courthouse? Should he try and find the sheriff—drive around the county using the radio every few miles until he got within range and could raise him? Should he drive over to Crawford and see if maybe the last of the Simms men happened to be home and/or inform the man of his tragic family losses—maybe make sure there wasn't another Simms in danger, or establish that the survivor wasn't the perpetrator? Should he try to find Judy and Heather English and let them know some stranger was looking for them?

What French and Mrs. Kraus had was an abundance of options and an uncertainty of priorities. French finally made his own choice. "I'm only maybe twenty minutes from Crawford. I'll start there. I'll turn my radio on and start hailing the sheriff as I go and keep an ear open for anything new from you. After I check on Tommy Simms, I'll circle around to the south so my radio should reach that end of the county and keep trying the sheriff as I head back to Buffalo Springs. Hopefully, by then, we'll have found him and somebody'll have orders for me. If not, we'll see where things stand and go from there."

Before Mrs. Kraus hung up, Wynn was back in the office pestering her for the phone to make some important calls, but the minute she disconnected French, Doc Jones was back on the line with preliminary results about Old Man Simms.

"Natural causes. Massive heart attack. Must have broken his neck when he collapsed on the stairs. Maybe, whoever cut him scared him to death. Or maybe they found him that way, then decided to leave us a message connecting him to his son, though the scalp was just stuffed in one of the old man's pockets. The sheriff might want to send somebody to check the place out for signs of who did it. Don't think Mad Dog and I disturbed much and whoever scalped him is probably the one who carved up his boy."

Mrs. Kraus thought about sending Wynn, but the way his day was going he was the last person the sheriff would want to give the opportunity to contaminate a crime scene. Simms Senior's residence would have to wait.

So would Wynn's demand for a phone, since the moment Doc hung up the Sheriff's line rang again. This time it was a concerned citizen reporting the sound of gun shots from Sourdough ranch, followed by a high speed exit from the same location by a man on a motorcycle hotly pursued by someone in a new Chevy pickup.

Mrs. Kraus put her hand over the receiver for a moment and glared at Wynn. "Can't you see I'm tied up with official business right now. You need a phone, go down the hall and borrow your daddy's."

It was a good idea, though Wynn was surprised to find it ringing when he let himself into the abandoned office. Who would be foolish enough to call the commissioners on a Sunday? Wynn picked it up and announced, "You got the wrong number."

He just managed to stop from breaking the connection when he heard the sheriff shout, "Don't you hang up on me Wynn or I swear I'll kill you with my bare hands."

"No sir," Wynn said.

The sheriff thought that eliminating Wynn's County Commissioner father would be preferable to doing in "Wynn some" himself. After all, it was Wynn Senior who was behind the preferential hiring policy that had forced the sheriff to trade a deputy's position for Wynn Junior in exchange for a vote to maintain his department's marginal operating budget. If something were to happen to the commissioner, the sheriff thought he could deal with "Wynn some, lose some." At least Junior meant well, even if he was generally incompetent, and it wasn't like the sheriff had been able to keep all his low paying positions filled. Besides, the county usually didn't need much in the way of law enforcement. If Wynn could be controlled, made to fear the possibility of, say, losing his job, the sheriff thought he could turn him into an acceptable law officer. At a moment like this, for instance, when Wynn seemed to believe the sheriff was angry enough to inflict bodily harm, he became the soul of efficiency. He hadn't even tried to explain everything that had happened in the sheriff's absence, not his questionable arrest, nor the damage he'd caused to county property. He just did as the sheriff asked and ran down the hall and got Mrs. Kraus to come provide the synopsis in her precise if opinionated fashion.

It was a lot to take in. Then the sheriff reciprocated. He gave a description of the motorcycle operator. She didn't match it to the odd guy the folks from Bertha's had told her about. The flyer with the picture had ended up face down on Mrs. Kraus' desk, its back covered with hastily scribbled notes to herself. It wouldn't resurface for days. What with all the insanity she and the sheriff were encountering, they both missed the crucial link.

"The man's to be detained as a material witness," the sheriff told her, "so far, nothing more. Make sure the deputies know and circulate the word around town as best you can so folks can tell us if they see him." The word was already circulating, and given the velocity of the galloping gossips, it would spread beyond the county line before dusk. "I've got a few more questions for Mrs. Lane, then I'll be headed back. I'll call and leave a message on the answering machine for Judy if she's not home—Mrs. Lane tells me she probably won't be before nine or ten—and I'll maybe swing by the house just to be sure before I come back to the office. Get French to examine both the Reverend's and Old Man Simms' homes for evidence and have him take pictures of the shoe prints under Peter Simms' fuse box. Have Wynn check out this Professor. Unless his story's a house of cards, Wynn should apologize, get his car brought in and repaired, and otherwise offer the county's hospitality.

"I'm here at Sourdough for a while if you need me, then I'll be on my radio and should be in range within ten minutes of when I leave. If anything breaks, let me know."

"You got it," Mrs. Kraus rasped. "You want I should accidentally shoot Wynn in case he decides on his own to do any more investigating?"

"Placating his professor ought to keep him busy for a while, Mrs. Kraus, but use your best judgement—and maybe your hollow points."

Mrs. Kraus' cackle easily carried across the stable to where Ellen Lane sat on a bale of hay and listened curiously. Her attitude seemed a little shy now. It was hard for the sheriff to reconcile this meek figure with the naked hell cat he clearly recalled being a willing participant in savage acts of sex and violence.

"OK." the sheriff turned to her. "Let me run through this one more time to be sure I've got it straight. You're Ellen Lane. *You've* got a daughter named Heather who just happens to have gone off to Hutchinson for the afternoon with *my* daughter Heather and *my* ex-wife."

"Right."

"You're here because you're hiding from your ex-husband whose conviction for sexually molesting his daughter was recently overturned by an appeals court and you're afraid he means you and your daughter harm."

"I'm sure of it. You saw him."

True enough. The muscular little man with the dark complexion might not be the murderer, but he'd threatened to kill, and had obviously been willing and able to hurt this woman. That didn't prove he was as deadly as she claimed, but it didn't hurt her case any.

"Tell me about him again." Clearly, he could parrot what she'd already said the rest of the afternoon, but it wasn't getting him any fresh information.

"OK," she sighed. "His real name is Benjamin de la Jolla. Lane's a name I took to try to keep him from finding us when he got free. Obviously, it didn't work. He was an aeronautical engineering student at Wichita State working for Bauman Aircraft on the side when I met him. Ben was handsome and charming and good in bed and I married him. He also had this thing about children, a kind of fascination with them that I didn't think anything about until I found some children's underwear in his den not long after Heather was born. I still didn't understand. I didn't pursue my suspicions until I caught him having sex with our baby daughter. I tried to kill him right then and he damn near killed me before the cops came and I had him arrested. I took her to a specialist and got the proof and had him charged and held with too much bail for him to make. Ben was tried and convicted, but I knew he'd come after me if he ever got out. And I'm terrified of what he might do to Heather, especially after what he's already done."

"Where's he live?"

"I don't know. He was held in the old Reformatory at Hutchinson until the appeal. All I know is he started looking for us the minute he got out."

"Any idea how he managed to follow you here?"

"No. Sorry. I've just kept my head down and tried to stay out of touch since he was released."

"Does he have any ties around here? Can you think of where he might run?"

She shook her head. Bizarre. Someone who might be a madman on the loose in Benteen County at the same moment as the county's first murder. On the surface, it looked like the two events were unrelated, unless the man's shoes matched the footprints at Simms'.

"Do you have any reason to think he might know a Reverend Peter Simms in Buffalo Springs, or Elmer Simms, the Reverend's father, of a rural route of the same town?"

Something flickered in her eyes, but she just shook her head again. "No, I think I've heard the Starks mention the Reverend, but I can't imagine that Ben would know either of them. Even Heather and I don't know anybody around here but the Starks, your wife and daughter, and the Starks' hired hands."

"That reminds me," the sheriff said. "I should have a word with Cody."

"I don't think you'll find him. He's lusty enough, but none too brave, as I expect you've noticed. He tends to disappear whenever there's trouble. I think he's got a hiding place along Sweetwater Creek where he goes to give things time to settle down."

The sheriff didn't have time for a search. In fact, he didn't have time for more questioning of Ellen Lane, though he didn't like the idea of leaving her there alone either.

"Why don't you ride into Buffalo Springs with me, Mrs. Lane, just in case your former husband decides to come back?"

"I have a 9 mm in our cabin, Sheriff, and I know how to use it. I can't take a chance that Heather might come home with no one here to look out for her. As soon as Judy gets back with the girls I'll drive to Buffalo Springs and come by your office. Besides, the Starks are just off looking at some land a neighbor wants to sell them. They should be back soon, and I've seen both of them shoot. We'll be as safe here as with you."

The sheriff reluctantly agreed. There was more to this situation than he'd uncovered, but he had a murder investigation that needed his attention and a nut case riding around on a motorcycle looking to kidnap the daughter he might have molested as an infant. The sheriff would have to find time to decipher the puzzle that was Ellen Lane after Benteen County was back under control.

"Tell the Starks I need to talk to them as soon as they get home," he said, climbing into his Chevy's cab, "and tell them it's important." He still needed to know about that last call from Peter Simms' phone.

"I'll do that," she agreed, "and if I see my ex-husband, I'll be in touch."

Yes, the sheriff thought. That would be nice. He fired up the Chevy and aimed it for the county seat.

Since they'd left Hutch at least two hours earlier than she'd originally planned, Judy English decided to go home to Buffalo Springs before taking Heather number two back to the ranch. That would give her a chance to fix herself and the girls sandwiches, and quell her raging appetite before she did something stupid like going by the Buffalo Burger Drive Inn for a triple cheese burger and a banana split, the kind of meal that might go directly from her mouth to her thighs and spoil the look of her new camisole. Besides, it would give Ellen and Heather Lane a little extra time away from each other. Judy was experienced enough, both as a mom and a teacher, to know when parents and children had been spending too much time together. The two Heathers had obviously hit it off. Her plan would benefit them as well.

Judy decided not to pull into the yard. That way she wouldn't have to deal with the gate and worry about keeping the dog from getting out. Or make him move. Boris, the German Shepherd Englishman insisted she keep as a combination guardian and playmate for Heather, was sprawled in the driveway sleeping the sleep of a dog who works the night shift.

She pulled up at the curb and reached down to pop the trunk as the two Heathers bailed out like a pair of skydivers intent on the intricate aerial ballet they had to perform before getting back to Earth. Around giggles and whispers, and with a complex system of gestures that would have profoundly shocked Judy, Heather English had persuaded Heather Lane to show her one of the rubbers she now carried "just in case." They headed for the privacy of her bedroom where Judy couldn't witness her daughter's terror, delight, and amazement when she discovered how big the thing was. They were at the front door fumbling with the lock when they heard the voice and saw the shadowy figure who'd been hidden from the street by the trellis of morning glories that were Judy's pride and joy.

"Heather," the voice said.

Both girls turned toward the muscular little man with the dark complexion and the hypodermic needle in his right hand. He seemed surprised at seeing two of them, especially since their builds, features, eyes, and hair, even to the way it was cut—short as practical for a small-town tomboy and short as a disguise for a daughter in hiding—forged a resemblance identical enough for twins.

"Heather?" he said again, though this time it was obviously a question.

One Heather had been taught to fear strange men, taught to remain quiet when making a noise didn't offer immediate salvation. The other was home, in a town where she knew everybody and everybody knew her. Her father was sheriff and her dog, Boris, was only a few feet away.

"Yes," Heather English said.

"Whoa, Sheriff. We must be paying you too much if you can afford a truck like that."

The sheriff was coming out of the Texaco after settling for his gasoline and the repair of his flat. The tire had picked up a piece of rusty barbed wire but had taken a patch and the sheriff was feeling lucky that he didn't have to buy a new one. It made the 350's expensive thirst for fuel less painful than it might have been. The farmer who'd made the joking comment worked about three sections out the Stark's way. While he didn't live too high on the hog, most folks seemed to think he owned enough hogs, and other profitable investments, to pretty well live however he wanted.

"Yeah. Five years of payments and it's all mine, which means you've got to re-elect me to at least one more term."

"Don't worry, Sheriff. If the citizens fire you I can always use some extra help around harvest."

"Mighty kind of you," the sheriff observed. He'd been in contact with the office by radio for long enough to know he had time to stop to deal with the tire and top up his tank on the way in. No more disasters had struck the county since he'd spoken to Mrs. Kraus from the Starks'. The only new information he had was confirmation from French that Tommy Simms was not at home in Crawford and could probably be reached in care of his custom cutting crew of traveling harvesters, thought to be somewhere in central Oklahoma. That, and the fact that Wynn's professor checked out and Wynn was seeing to the retrieval of his car personally, and therefore staying out from underfoot.

The farmer started to pass the sheriff on his way to pay for his own purchase, then turned at the last minute with another question. "Oh, by the way, that nephew of yours find his way to Judy's?"

"Nephew?" the sheriff asked.

"Yeah, as I was heading to town I come across this young fellow sitting by the side of the road on his motorcycle studying a map. Stopped and asked could I help him find someplace and he showed me a picture of your daughter and asked me where she was staying. Took one look and I knew it was Heather. Figured she'd be at her mother's place, so that's where I directed him. Ain't that hard to find. I was surprised a relative of yours would get lost around here that easy."

"Nephew? He give you a name?" The sheriff was beginning to connect the dark man from Sourdough to the guy with the pictures at Bertha's. He suddenly knew who the man on the motorcycle was, but not where his Heather fit in. Ellen Lane hadn't mentioned that their daughters looked surprisingly alike.

"No. I took him to be from your side of the family though, given his complexion."

"Short, muscular guy, blue polo shirt and tan slacks?"

"Then you've seen him? He found the place all right? I was afraid he might have missed them since Judy was just turning off the highway toward her place as I was coming into town."

"Sweet Jesus!" The sheriff said. Judy was back early and a knife wielding maniac might have located her and both Heathers.

The flip side of the Chevy's thirst for fuel was how quickly it got him out of the Texaco and on his way to the sleepy neighborhood where he and Judy had disagreed over almost everything, except their daughter, who, for reasons that were completely beyond him, could be in extreme danger.

◇◇◇

The sun was noticeably lower. Its light streamed across the floor of the corridor in the jail and made Wynn's positioning of chairs to aid his earlier interrogation of Professor Bowen belatedly effective. Elsewhere in Benteen County, the day was moving to the frenzied pulse of the sheriff's muddled investigation or Mrs. Kraus' efforts to meet the incessant demands of telephone, radio, and gossips. Back in the jail, however, time flowed at a different pace, syrup-slow as shadows lengthened and the old clock on the wall across from the cells seemed to pause forever between swings of its brass pendulum.

It was hot and still back there, as it was across the county. The atmosphere was heavy, so thick with humidity that objects just across the room seemed less sharply outlined than normal. Neil Bowen longed to get out of there and, technically, there was no longer any reason he couldn't. Until the now apologetic deputy returned with his car, however, he didn't have anyplace else to go. Finding himself in the middle of a murder investigation, a stranger whose skin color had been enough to make him a prime suspect of local law enforcement, he was in no rush to explore the community and test the racial attitudes of any other citizens. One near lynching a day was enough.

He'd spent a few minutes out in the Sheriff's Office, but it was obvious he was just in the way. The two middle-aged women occupying the only available chairs that weren't behind desks had seemed to watch him with more than a hint of suspicion. He had hardly felt welcome and so he'd wandered back into the jail where the only man in the county to actually befriend him was spending a quiet afternoon contemplating the ceiling from a bunk in a rear corner cell. He didn't understand what the big fellow was doing back there but he obviously wasn't locked up and it was comforting to stay in the vicinity of a man who had come to his rescue once, and, if necessary, might again.

"Feels like tornado weather," Bowen ventured.

"I looked outside a little while ago," Mad Dog replied, "while you were up front. Not a cloud in the sky. It's unnatural."

"I've come to think that unnatural is the natural state of Kansas weather," the professor laughed. "I'm no longer surprised when it snows in May or bakes in January."

Mad Dog rolled over and sat on the side of the bunk, apparently willing to chat. "Yeah, but when the wind stops blowing...."

"Well, yes," Bowen agreed. "I'll have to admit, I can't remember the last time it was still like this all day. Not since I took the job here and moved from East Tennessee State."

"What brings you to Benteen County, Doc?" Mad Dog inquired.

"Well, I believe I mentioned that I hold the Benjamin Singleton endowed chair of history at Fort Hays State. Do you happen to know who Mr. Singleton was, Mr. Mad Dog?"

"Just Mad Dog, no mister to it. I assumed he was a benefactor of the college, but since I don't know any Singletons in this neck of the woods, I'd guess I'm wrong and you weren't dropping by to see about funding new scholarships."

"No. No indeed. Fortunately for me, fund raising is left to those who are not quite so uncomfortable at asking for handouts. No, Mr., or rather just, Mad Dog, Benjamin Singleton was a former slave who, after the Civil War, inspired the 'Negro Exodus,' what some call the 'Exoduster Movement.'"

"Don't believe I'm familiar with either him or the movement, Doc."

"He was something of a black Moses, leading his people to the promised land, bringing former slaves to establish black colonies here in Kansas. You've heard of Nicodemus, Kansas, no doubt."

"Of course," Mad Dog agreed.

"Well, that's an example of what Singleton intended. Sadly, the result was usually less successful. After the first few colonies were established in an orderly fashion the word got out and hundreds of poverty stricken and disorganized former slaves followed on their heels. They didn't have anything but their strong backs and their will to survive to build on. Most of their efforts led to disasters of varying magnitude. Kansas weather, as we've just said, tends to extremes that offsets the benefits of its rich soil.

"One of those disasters occurred right here in Benteen County, Mad Dog. Fourteen families established a community along Coyote Creek a bit east of Buffalo Springs. Nearly seventy souls marched here with only one yoke of oxen and the supplies and implements that could be carried on a single wagon and a collection of push carts. They brought yellow fever with them, endured a fearsome blizzard, two summers of drought, and one plague of locusts. The few survivors turned back east after that. Their descendants are spread all the way from Wichita to the slave states from which they'd come. There's supposed to be a graveyard out there, almost fifty dead they left behind. I was here looking for that, Mad Dog. The Kansas State Historical Society has some interest in placing a marker and I've been researching this particular settlement. New Zion, they called it. That's what I was looking for."

Mad Dog came out and stood against the open door that led into the cell block while Neil Bowen spoke from where he'd leaned his chair against the wall to what had once been the jailer's office.

"I have heard of the lost colony, Doc. I just never knew they were black. I even think I know the place," Mad Dog told him. "It's almost straight east of here. There's a few old weathered markers and a broken stone cross in a grove of hardwoods that aren't natural to this part of Kansas. I'd always wondered who was out there and what became of them. I'd be happy to show you the place, Doc, only right now we got some bigger troubles around here and I think I need to maybe talk to my brother, see if I can find a way to explain to him about *Tsistsistas hematasooma* and *maiyun* and *havsevama'tasooma* and that's not gonna be easy."

"What do Cheyenne spirits have to do with the murder of Reverend Simms?" Professor Bowen asked.

Mad Dog's jaw dropped. "You know about that stuff? You understand Cheyenne Shamanism?"

"Well, a little," the professor admitted. "The Cheyenne were an important part of the history of this state as well."

"I'll be damned!" Mad Dog exclaimed. "Then maybe you can help me undo what I think I've done."

Judy was hysterical. After more than a dozen attempts to call the Sheriff's Office netted her only a succession of busy signals, she lost it. She beat the phone into a heap of plastic and wires, slamming the hand set against the desktop unit until little that was recognizable was left of either.

Heather Lane was catatonic, curled up in a ball on the front porch where she'd collapsed when her father snatched Heather English, injected her with something that dropped her like the price of wheat during a good harvest, and began brandishing a knife while hustling her toward where he'd left his motorcycle under a pear tree across the street.

Boris lay at the edge of the street. He was panting heavily and fighting to keep his eyes open against the powerful tranquilizer the stranger had tossed him in an irresistible meatball.

He knew Heather needed him but wasn't sure where she'd gone and couldn't make his legs work well enough to get to his feet, let alone give chase.

The sheriff did a kind of stunt car stop in front of the house, going broadside the last thirty feet or so and enveloping the shady street in a fog of dust that the wind would normally have immediately cleared from view. Instead, it just hung in the air and gave the scene a kind of sepia quality like something out of an old photograph.

A couple of neighbors stood on porches but nobody rushed to the sheriff's side as he tumbled out of the truck with his .38 drawn and sprinted toward the house. He stopped at Heather Lane long enough to determine that she had no obvious injuries and seemed in no immediate danger, and just barely long enough to realize this person looked like his daughter but was someone else. He found Judy on her hands and knees in front of the remains of the phone, trying to fit pieces back together that were far beyond salvage.

"Judy," he demanded, and, when she didn't even look his way, bent and pulled her to her feet and shook her until her eyes finally focused on him.

"Damn you, your line was busy," she said.

"Where's Heather?"

And then the tears came. "Oh God, Englishman, I don't know," she wailed. "This guy came out of nowhere. He must have been waiting on the porch. The first I knew was when Heather screamed. I dropped my packages and came running and Heather was fighting him and he did something to her and she went limp. I threw myself at him and he just pushed me aside like I was nothing. He had some kind of plastic things and he looped them around Heather's wrists and ankles and drew them together and then just kind of threw her over his shoulder as casually as I would a purse. I remembered the pepper spray I've got about then. I grabbed for it but he kicked it out of my hand and waved a knife at me and said something like 'she's mine and nobody's ever going to take her away from me again' and then he ran down off the porch and poor Boris tried to stop him but he couldn't even get up. Boris kind of fell a few steps closer to the street and made the most miserable sound, kind of like a howl, and I suppose I was screaming cause the next thing I remember I was standing in the middle of the road watching him do a block long wheelie on that motorcycle with our daughter swung over his shoulder before he put the bike practically over on its side and just barely kept Heather from scraping the dirt as he took the corner down there at Lincoln and then all I could hear was that thing screaming up through the gears. And then the damn phone was busy and busy and busy and...God damn you Englishman, where were you when I needed you?"

"**S**omeone has kidnapped Heather!" Mrs. Kraus cried as she burst through the iron door and into the jail. It was an effective conversation stopper. Mad Dog and Professor Bowen looked up with equally stupefied expressions.

"Heather? Englishman's daughter?" Mad Dog managed to stammer.

Mrs. Kraus was nodding her head wildly. "Kidnapped," she reaffirmed.

Mad Dog turned to Bowen. "My niece," he explained. "You see, this makes an awful kind of sense and fits right in. The evil magic often reflects back on the friends and family of the incompetent sorcerer."

"Harvey Mad Dog, will you shut up." Mrs. Kraus stomped her foot like an infuriated school teacher. If she'd had a ruler his knuckles would have been in danger. "You stop this foolishness right now. Your brother needs you. Your niece needs you. Heather was stolen off Judy's porch just minutes ago by a madman on a motorcycle and he's getting away. Wynn's not here and not competent. French's somewhere on the road between here and Crawford. You've got a car. You can help find him."

"Which way did he go?" Mad Dog asked, sounding like a bad line from a worse movie.

"Went down to Lincoln and turned left, the sheriff said. Lincoln only goes five blocks so he must have turned again, but the sheriff doesn't know where. Says he didn't see any motorcycles on his way in from Sourdough Ranch to the Texaco, nor from there direct to Judy's."

Mad Dog could still move fast for a big man. He managed to get around Mrs. Kraus at almost a full run without knocking her down just as Professor Bowen was saying, "Is there anything I can do to help?" Mad Dog crashed through the iron door, streaked through the foyer, and went over Mrs. Kraus' desk like a halfback breaking through the defensive line and hurdling a linebacker. The gossips broke and flew for the exit like a flushed covey of quail as Mad Dog tore open his brother's desk and ransacked drawers until he found the leather container he was looking for. And then he was out of the Sheriff's Office on the gossips' heels, almost faster than they could clear the way, carrying the leather case and the radio he'd grabbed from Mrs. Kraus' desk. He didn't head for the front doors, though. He cut back left just as Mrs. Kraus and Professor Bowen emerged from the jail in time to see him dash up the stairs toward the second floor of the courthouse.

"Mad Dog, you damn fool," Mrs. Kraus shouted after him. "The kidnapper's not gone up there, and just where do you think you're going with my radio?"

Mad Dog didn't answer. He pelted down the main hall between empty courtrooms and offices, most of them abandoned for want of much needed repairs. At the end of the hall there was a solid wooden door with an ancient brass handle. It bore a faded sign that Mad Dog knew had once read STAIR.

The attic rooms were mostly unfinished, empty but for boxes of ancient files that had been ruined by a roof that seeped in more than a few places and pigeons that had found entry through windows broken in some long ago hail storm. The center of the attic was occupied by a six-by-six foot cistern into which water had once been hand pumped so that the building's primitive facilities and its fire hose could be served with gravity powered running water. Yet another crude staircase, this one metal, circled the cistern and led to the tower. It was the highest spot in Buffalo Springs, or Benteen County, for that matter, until the co-op constructed its grain elevator beside the railroad tracks. When the courthouse was new, the tower had been quite an attraction to a populace to whom the idea of a flat earth still seemed rational based on their personal observations. As the building deteriorated, the tower had been officially closed to the public. Empty beer cans and a pair of discarded pantyhose indicated that it still got occasional use.

"Englishman, this is Mad Dog, you hear me?" he asked the radio as he began scanning a horizon that promoted thoughts of eternity because it seemed to reach that far. He popped open the leather container with his other hand and put the binoculars to his eyes, making clumsy adjustments while he spoke to the radio again.

"Englishman, can you hear me?"

"Mad Dog," a tinny voice replied. "Go ahead."

"I'm in the tower of the courthouse," Mad Dog said. "He can't have got far yet, and I can see more than ten miles from up here. You got any clue which way he went?"

"Turned right when he hit the highway. West. That's all I know so far."

"Hold on then," Mad Dog said and set the radio down and steadied himself against one of the tower rails. The highway stretched with Euclidian precision toward the purple mountains' majesty half a day's drive away.

"Nothing to the west," Mad Dog reported. "Just a semi coming in from Barnett's Corner and an orange pickup maybe a mile behind."

"He could have turned either way on the north-south blacktop," the sheriff observed, his voice and his personal involvement sounding equally remote, "or maybe on Adams if he knows his way around.

"Tow truck two miles north," Mad Dog said, not realizing he was reporting the location of Deputy Wynn, who might have contributed his own observations if he hadn't left his radio in the custody of sheep earlier in the day. "Then, something way off and going, but it's definitely a car, not a motorcycle."

Mad Dog changed positions. "South is clear as far as I can see. There are two cars and one truck coming and a pair of cars going East, but no motorcycles. There'd be dust if he took Adams out of town and I don't see any. He's either pulled off the highway somewhere outside of town or he's still here."

"You see any suspicious dust anywhere else?" the sheriff asked.

Mad Dog pulled the glasses down to scan the horizon. He wouldn't need binoculars to spot dust. Miraculously, there wasn't any. At that particular moment, and for the last quarter hour or so, it appeared that not a single citizen of Benteen County had driven along a dirt road within a ten mile radius of Buffalo Springs, except maybe to the southwest. That was the one direction in which Mad Dog's inspired observation post failed. Between the Benteen County Courthouse and that wedge of flat and endless horizon, stood an even loftier skyscraper.

"Nothing, Englishman," Mad Dog said. "There's not a bit of dust out there anywhere I can see. He's either still in town or he's gone southwest. I can't see through that damn grain elevator."

"Southwest," the sheriff echoed. "I'm on my way." Mad Dog heard the distant sound of tires squealing as they bit pavement and the roar of a V-8 being stressed. Through the trees that lined Main Street, Mad Dog saw his brother's new pickup flash by on its way around the only obstacle that might be between his daughter and rescue.

"Go get him," Mad Dog whispered, though not as hopefully as he could have and not into the radio. Just in case, he started at the east edge of the elevator and began to sweep the horizon again. His results were the same as what the sheriff discovered on the far side of the Buffalo Springs Co-op. No dust, no motorcycle, nothing.

"She should be in a hospital," Doc Jones complained as he helped the sheriff maneuver Heather Lane out of the back of his Buick on a stretcher that had seen too much use that day. At least this occupant didn't require a body bag. In fact, physically, there didn't appear to be anything wrong with her. Psychologically could be another matter. From the time Doc Jones got to her she'd been catatonic or unconscious. It hadn't been long, only a few minutes after Heather English was seized, thanks to a quick call from Mrs. Kraus and the fact that he'd only been a few blocks away, still in the back of Klausen's writing up his notes from Old Man Simms' autopsy.

"I need her here, Doc," the sheriff said. "She may be able to tell me something that will help. And, more important, I need her mother here. She'll come for her daughter even if she'd prefer to avoid seeing me about now. Besides, just at the moment I can't think of a safer place for her. We're too undermanned to send anyone along to guard her on the way to a hospital at Great Bend or Larned, and the maniac that has my daughter will come after her if he realizes he's grabbed the wrong Heather. We'll have a lot of people here until we find him. It's the best I can manage, Doc."

"I'm not arguing with you," Doc said. "It's not her physical health I'm concerned with. I don't think she was even touched. But I'm just an old country Doctor. I don't know a Freudian slip from a Jungian petticoat. This girl may need someone with skills I don't have."

"What did you give her, Doc?" the sheriff asked as they maneuvered the stretcher up the steep front steps and through the doors that an unfamiliar black man had stepped forward to hold open for them.

"Just a shot of Valium to calm her some, and not a strong one at that. Certainly not strong enough to account for her doing this sleeping beauty number on me. That worries me, Sheriff."

"Tell you what, Doc. She doesn't come around once her mother's here, we'll call for an ambulance and a highway patrol escort. But I need some time with Ellen Lane. There's got to be stuff she hasn't told me."

They wheeled Heather Lane into County Commission Chairman Wynn's office, since it was the only one with a full sized sofa, and made her as comfortable as possible. Doc Jones checked her pulse and blood pressure and reassured himself that her vital signs were still normal. The sheriff started across the foyer to his own office.

"Hold on a minute," Doc said. "There's something you need to know about."

The sheriff was clearly impatient to be elsewhere. Doc wondered how to put it, then decided quick and to the point was best.

"Sheriff, the Reverend had a peculiar tattoo on his tush."

"What?" The sheriff was as taken aback by the idea as Doc Jones had been.

"He's got a Mickey Mouse on his right cheek, but not just any Mickey. This one's got a penis that's almost as big as he is, and is clearly in the process of practicing the safest kind of sex available. We used to call it self-abuse."

"You're kidding."

"Nope. Now, like I said, I'm no expert on matters psychological, but that tattoo indicates to me that the Reverend probably was involved in what folks around here would call perversions. You ever hear of him dating any of the local women?"

"No, can't say that I have."

"I don't know of any men folk he hung around with that much either, but that particular tattoo tends to make me wonder about homosexuality or...."

"Or what Doc?"

"Or pedophilia. God help me, Sheriff, but I think that tattoo might have been aimed at interesting kids. I've never had much to do with Simms or his church, but all of a sudden I'm remembering families with kids who suddenly stopped going there, a couple who even just up and moved out of town."

"Jesus, Doc. If you're right it could sure expand my list of suspects, but how would Old Man Simms fit in, and what about this maniac who grabbed Heather?"

"I don't know, Sheriff, but I needed to tell you. You go on now, do what you have to. I'll keep an eye on this one."

The sheriff was hardly through the door to his office when Mrs. Kraus started filling him in. "The highway patrol has dispatched units to cover the east-west and north-south blacktops and they promise to send us some help as soon as they can free it up. French is only about five miles out on his way back from Crawford and should be here in minutes. Don't know where Wynn is but he's due back any time. I did like you said and called Sourdough and the Starks are home. They promised to stay around the phone in case you still need to talk to them. They said they'd get word to Mrs. Lane that her daughter is here and ask her if she can maybe come into town to pick her up. I told them Judy had car trouble and had dropped the girl off here and was sorry but just couldn't manage to deliver her back to the farm."

"Good," the sheriff said, forcing himself to concentrate on what she was saying and not what he wanted to be doing. It might all be important. Any of it could affect his daughter's life. "Have you heard from Judy."

He'd found the best way to relieve his ex-wife's panic was to put her to work. What the sheriff lacked most was manpower. Judy could be a legitimate help. He'd asked her to go question people along Main Street, find out if they'd seen the motorcycle and which way it had gone. She could talk to people at the Texaco or the Buffalo Burger Drive Inn, check if they'd maybe seen the bike and its passengers as it made its getaway.

The strange black man wandered in and plopped himself down in one of the chairs across from Mrs. Kraus' desk. Mrs. Kraus didn't pay him the least attention as she continued updating the sheriff.

"Yeah, she called. Said she talked to a couple of the baggers at the Dillon's store. They said the bike went past them quick as a bank foreclosing on a farm loan. They never got a look at it, but they heard it slow down and turn south somewhere, they thought before the highway, maybe about Jackson or Van Buren. Judy was gonna head over that way and see if she could find any more witnesses."

Mad Dog came clumping down the steps from the second floor. He'd abandoned his lookout post in the tower when he saw Doc Jones and the sheriff pull up in front of the building.

"Englishman!" Mad Dog burst into the Sheriff's Office. "I know you aren't going to want to hear this but I think you and I need to talk about evil spirits."

Mad Dog was right. "Jesus, Mad Dog," the sheriff said. "I've got two dead people, one murdered and both scalped, and the murderer might be the lunatic who kidnapped my daughter and carried her off in the last half hour. I got no time to listen to your drug-induced, expanded-consciousness, lamebrain theories. You want to help, get out of here and go find out where that motorcycle went, figure out who killed one Simms and mutilated the corpse of the other. Just leave me the hell alone."

Mad Dog stopped like he'd taken a punch. From the sick look on his face, a low one at that.

"Tell him, Professor," Mad Dog said, not much above a whisper. "Maybe you can make him see."

"Oh no," Professor Bowen said, waving his hands in denial. "I said I agree. You've raised a reasonable philosophical interpretation of events within the *Tsistsistas* world view. I do not, however, believe it is one whose understanding is likely to do your brother much good in solving his current dilemmas. What you argue is fascinating, Mad Dog, but I'm not sure even I, who am moderately well versed in that world view, would accept your interpretation. I'm sorry. I can hardly suggest that the sheriff take time from his investigations to familiarize himself with an ideology of which he is unlikely to be able to make use in order to solve these crimes."

Mad Dog looked crushed. The sheriff looked at the little black man and finally succumbed to his curiosity. "Who are you?" he asked.

"I'm an historian, an accidental guest in your office while Deputy Wynn helps retrieve my stalled automobile. I apologize for any inconvenience I may cause you and offer any aid that I might render. Best, I suppose, I can offer to stay out of your way."

"Good idea," the sheriff agreed before heading down the hall in search of an open phone line to call the Starks. Mad Dog turned and watched him go like a man who's lost his best friend, or his only brother.

The sheriff sat behind County Commissioner Bontrager's desk and watched Mrs. Kraus usher in Ellen Lane. She swept in with an air of cool formality in stark contrast to the way she'd looked when they first met. Despite the afternoon's oppressive heat, she looked crisp and comfortable, very much the antithesis of the way the sheriff felt. There were a couple of chairs on the other side of the desk, and some privacy here, luxuries to which the sheriff was unaccustomed without making use of the jail.

"Where's my daughter?" Ellen Lane asked. It wasn't quite a demand, but it was obvious her patience had been stretched a trifle thin. Whether she'd been upset by Mrs. Kraus' insistence that she'd have to see Sheriff English first or the hassle of driving all the way to Buffalo Springs he couldn't tell, but it was clear she expected a quick answer.

"She's here," the sheriff said. "She's with the doctor and she seems to be coming around fine, recovering from the shock. She's not been physically hurt in any way."

Ellen Lane suddenly looked scared and angry. "What's all this about? What happened? Why would she need a doctor? I want to see her now."

"No," the sheriff said. There was a no nonsense tone to his voice that commanded attention even from an angry parent who didn't know him. Ellen Lane controlled her wrath and sat forward, listening expectantly.

"You'll talk to me first. You can see her after. She's doing fine and she wasn't hurt, but she could have been. It was a very close thing. She was almost kidnapped by your former husband, Mrs. Lane, but she wasn't. Instead, he took my daughter, and that's who may or may not be all right and may or may not be in grave danger. That happened, at least in part, because you weren't entirely open with me when we talked before. Now, with my daughter's life at stake, I expect you to tell me everything I need to know. If you don't, I'll lock you up until this is over and then I'll charge you as an accessory to whatever happens to my Heather. Do you understand me, Mrs. Lane?"

Ellen Lane was good at controlling her emotions in the presence of an angry man. Considering the relationship she'd come from, that wasn't surprising. "You didn't know our daughters looked so much alike, did you?"

"No," the sheriff said. "I didn't know that."

"I'm sorry. I thought he would back off for a while. After coming face to face with a sheriff, I didn't think he'd try again. And I never thought he'd be able to tie her to your wife and daughter. That was stupid. I should have thought that he could be flashing pictures, and, if he was, people might point him toward your Heather."

"Good," the sheriff remarked. "That's a start, but I want more. I want it all."

"All being what, Sheriff? I don't know where he is."

"Are you sure, Mrs. Lane? Don't you even have a guess?"

"Look, Sheriff. When I heard his conviction had been overturned, that he was facing a new trial and would be out on bail, I grabbed Heather and we ran and hid."

"From where?"

"We live in Santa Fe. I own a gallery. It's been pretty successful. I left it in the hands of a manager and cashed out some investments and bought enough traveler's checks for us to live on for a while, long enough, I hoped, for him to do something stupid and violate his bond and get thrown back in jail so we could come out of hiding."

"Why here?"

"I don't know. Because Heather likes horses, I guess, and so do I. Because I thought central Kansas was the last place on Earth he'd think to look for us."

"And why would this be such an unlikely place for him to look? You met and lived in Wichita. You've spent time at the Stark's regularly over the years. If he might trace you to Santa Fe, why couldn't he trace you here."

"I gather you've talked to the Starks then, or someone who's seen us there."

The sheriff nodded. The Starks hadn't taken the call from the Reverend Simms and had no idea of why he might have called their ranch, but they'd been helpful in other ways. "Minnie Stark say's you've been spending a week here nearly every fall, usually by yourself, for the last six years."

"I'm disappointed in Minnie," Ellen Lane said. "I told her what our situation was and she assured me she'd be discreet."

"We're a little past the time for discreet here, Mrs. Lane. In 1905, a brother and sister named Ketchum walked across the road to their neighbors', the Campbells. When Mr. Campbell opened the door they blew him apart with a shotgun. Then they entered the house and proceeded to execute Mr. Campbell's wife and three children. It was never clear whether it was before or after they died, but the Ketchums took sexual liberties with them. The children ranged in age from eleven down to five. That happened about half a mile the other side of the Benteen County line, but, for some reason, the Ketchums chose to come to Buffalo Springs to turn themselves in. Three days later, the family, friends, and neighbors of the Campbells followed. They planned to take the Ketchums out of their cells and string them up on a telephone poll at the end of the block. When they broke into the jail in the back of the courthouse they found the pair had beaten them to it. They'd torn blankets into strips and hung themselves from the bars on the top of their cells. Until this morning, that's the closest we ever came to having a murder in this county.

"Today, the Reverend Peter Simms of the Buffalo Springs Non-Denominational Community Church was murdered across the street in Veteran's Memorial Park. A few hours later, his father's body was discovered in his home. Both corpses had been mutilated in a peculiar and identical way.

"If that wasn't enough to make this an unusual day for Benteen County, you were attacked by your former husband while he was searching for his daughter at the Sourdough Ranch.

"Then, in a bungled attempt to seize your daughter, he mistakenly kidnapped mine this afternoon. Those events put us well past Minnie Stark's discretion boundary, and far beyond my tolerance for evasions. Now, do you or your former husband or your daughter have any connection to the Simms family? It's time to talk, Mrs. Lane. If that crazed husband of yours harms my daughter because you don't tell me what I need to know to save her, the fact that I'm sworn to uphold the law won't protect you from me."

Ellen Lane sighed and sat back in her chair. "That sounded like a threat, Sheriff. But I guess I don't blame you. I feel pretty much the same way as you. What the law tells me I can do to protect my daughter has very little relationship to what I'm prepared to do."

"That reminds me. You said you had a 9 mm. Are you carrying it now?"

She nodded. "Yes. It's in my purse."

He reached out and picked up her purse from where she'd deposited it on the desk and pulled the pistol out. "You have a permit to carry a concealed weapon I assume?"

She didn't say anything.

"Then you won't mind if I hold on to it for the time being, until we get this settled. And maybe being without it will refresh your memory. All that stands between your ex-husband and you and your daughter in this county, Mrs. Lane, is me. Sooner or later he's going to discover he's made a mistake. Then he's going to come looking, unless I find him first. You can help me do that."

She paused and stared out the window at an afternoon that was darker than it should be at this hour. The sheriff wondered if a storm was building up in the west, and whether she was organizing her thoughts or composing fresh lies.

"I used to live here when I was little," she said. "Ben knows that."

"Ben's your ex-husband, right?" The sheriff was so focused on his daughter's plight that her revelation hardly registered.

"Yes."

"Tell me about him. What's he like? Where's he from? Do you know why he was sexually abusive to your daughter or what the extent of his deviance might be? Would it include pubescent females like my daughter, for instance? Does he have a history of violence? Give me the stuff I need to know, not his favorite color or his shoe size." Even as he said it, the sheriff realized that last one might be important too, but not now. After Heather was OK he could go back to being a law enforcement officer instead of a frightened father.

"I know surprisingly little about him, considering that we were married for almost four years. Most of what I thought I knew turned out to be lies. I thought he was Spanish. I thought that was why he had kind of an olive complexion and that dark, curly hair and brown eyes. He spoke it fluently, and he talked about going back to visit the old country, only after he was arrested, it turned out he was just a mix of Mexican and poor white trash.

"The main thing I can tell you about him is that he's false. He hides behind some kind of mask all the time, picks a role and plays it. I never had a clue until I came home unexpectedly one afternoon and caught him in the act. Up to then, I would have called him a great guy, attentive, sexy, a good provider. Then the mask came off and I found out none of it was real. I'd never seen him violent except when a drunk in a bar gave him a hard time once and he broke the guy's nose. But from the moment I became aware of what he was doing to our daughter, my life was in danger. He's tried to kill me before this afternoon.

"I don't really know if he's just a pedophile or whether it runs wider than that. We had a very active and, how shall I say this...creative sex life. He wasn't into sadomasochistic stuff, but he seemed to want to try pretty much anything else. He volunteered to coach the girls' softball team for our church. I wonder about that now, though even after everything hit the Wichita press, nobody came forward with any other complaints against him. I have suspicions, but there's such a stigma attached to the person who's been violated that people keep quiet. I can't say for sure. I'm sorry. I guess that's about all I know."

"You really aren't helping me," the sheriff said. "I've assumed from the beginning that my daughter may be in mortal danger, regardless of whether he finds out who she really is. Come on, I need something here. There's got to be a Benteen County connection somewhere."

Ellen Lane nodded. "Me. Like I said, I grew up here. But we moved away when I was twelve. As far as I know, Ben never did anything other than pass through Kansas until he came to Wichita to go to school. He spent most of his life in East Texas before enrolling at Wichita State and convincing me he was my own personal Romeo."

"You then, do you have any connection to the Simmses?"

"Yes. Does the name Todd mean anything to you Sheriff?"

"Todd? That rings a bell. There was some trouble, wasn't there? I think that was when I was attending a little one-room schoolhouse, before it closed and I started getting bussed into town. We didn't hear much about it out in our neck of the plains and Mama wasn't much of a gossip, she'd suffered too much from the gossip of others, but things like that get talked about for years in a place like Benteen County."

"Yes, there was some trouble, as you kindly put it. Todd was my father. He was accused of molesting Mr. Simms' daughter. It didn't happen, but the Simmses were important people here and my father was just a hired hand, the child of dirt poor farmers from out of state. Nobody believed him."

"I remember now. He committed suicide, didn't he?"

"He climbed the silo behind the barn at the Simms' place. It's a tall one, probably sixty feet. Then he jumped. He landed on a spring tooth that was propped against the wall. It tore him up pretty bad but it didn't keep his head from exploding on the concrete sidewalk alongside the barn. I was the one who found him."

"I'm sorry," Englishman said. "But that's a link. That's what I need, only I'm confused. If your former husband hated you, why would he have anything against the Simms family? You'd almost expect the opposite."

"I don't know. He was always fascinated by that story, even though I told him my father was innocent. He'd really get off on arguing Daddy's defense. The Simms girl was old enough to know what she was doing, he'd say. She was a kind of Lolita, some preadolescent sex kitten who lured a simple country boy on. It was absurd because he didn't pay any attention to the fact that Daddy just didn't do it. It used to make me angry. I thought he was saying all that because he thought my father was actually guilty. Now I think he was arguing his own defense, putting himself in my father's place and imagining how he'd try to get out of it."

"OK," the sheriff said. "That's a start. It's pretty twisted, but it gives me a motive to work with. But I've still got to find your husband and my daughter. I'm almost certain he's right here, in Buffalo Springs, or no more than a few miles out of town. But you tell me he's never been here before. That means he has to have chosen the place he's hiding from out of your memory. Think, ma'am. Where were your secret places as a child here, places you may have told him about? If you had done what he's done, where would you run to hide?"

"There was a place under the bridge on Calf Creek, about a quarter mile from the house. I used to go there to play all the time and..."

"No, too far. I'm sure he's closer in. Besides, that bridge washed out more than ten years ago. I think there's only a couple of posts and crossties left."

"God I don't know. We weren't in town much, unless...."

"Unless what?"

"Well, my family was pretty conservative. We didn't believe in dancing and movies and such, but I used to sneak off and ride my bike to town on Saturday mornings and go to the Strand Theatre for the cartoons and the children's matinee. I came off without enough money one time and I was so disappointed I couldn't afford a ticket that I hung around and started exploring. I found a door to an old freight entrance in the back that was sprung. They couldn't close it tight. After that, that's how I always got in. I remember I searched around back stage a couple of times. They must have had real plays there in the old days, because there was a dusty old room under the stage with lots of trapdoors and a couple of exits into what might have once been an orchestra pit. And there was an iron rung ladder up the back wall that led to a series of catwalks and all sorts of ropes and pulleys and weights where they maybe hung scenery or lights or curtains. There was a door out onto the roof, too, and I remember going up there sometimes because it was the highest place around except for the grain elevator and the dome here at the courthouse. It was my most special secret place, my safe place. I told Ben about it."

"Bingo," the sheriff said. He was almost out of the room when she grabbed his arm.

"Hey, what about my daughter?" she demanded.

The sheriff kept going and she stayed with him. As they passed the next office, he pushed the door open. Heather Lane and Doc were playing a complicated form of double solitaire on the floor.

"Hi Mom," Heather Lane said. "Come look at the neat game Dr. Jones is teaching me."

"Look," Dr. Bowen said, "it's not my place to trivialize anyone's religious beliefs and you've been very kind to me, offered me some important assistance at an awkward moment. Still, I have to say I don't think you understand Cheyenne religion that well."

Mad Dog reached up and turned on the Saab's air conditioning, adjusting the flow so that his guest would receive its maximum benefits. Those benefits would be limited. Mad Dog had a theory that the Swedes, however remarkable their engineering, did not understand efficient air conditioning because they were conditioned to Swedish air. When a hot summer day in Stockholm might just push ninety, you built your system accordingly. You were not prepared to produce the cooling needed in Saudi Arabia, the Sahara, Death Valley, or Benteen County, Kansas. On a day like today, all Mad Dog's Saab would do was blow air that was slightly cooler than what might come through an open window.

Mad Dog nodded and put the Saab in reverse, backing out of the parking spot he'd taken behind the courthouse and avoiding the new line of posts that guarded a row of bedraggled rose bushes. "You're probably right, Professor. I haven't been doing serious research very long. What I know is just what I got from a little reading. Tell me where I've gone wrong."

Wynn had finally returned a few minutes before. He'd had the professor's car towed over to the Texaco where it had been filled with gas and where it was currently on a battery charger. It should be ready to go by the time Professor Bowen called for it. Wynn would have given him a ride to pick it up, but he was without wheels himself. The tow truck had already departed on its second excursion of the day, retrieving the Benteen County patrol car. The sheriff was interviewing Mrs. Lane and Wynn thought he needed to stay where he'd be available for whatever his boss might require. Frankly, Neil Bowen was just not that comfortable in the presence of a deputy who, he felt, had been willing to kill him for being black and in the wrong neighborhood. He'd been pleased to accept Mad Dog's offer of a ride to his car.

"It's not that simple, Mad Dog. Surely you wouldn't expect me to explain all the intricacies of Christianity in the course of a short drive. I assure you, while Cheyenne culture was at a more primitive level technologically than that of Western Civilization when the two met, the religious philosophy of these plains nomads was no less sophisticated. And then, of course, there's the problem that I'm not an expert. As an historian whose interest focuses on matters that occurred in the same era and locale, I've given myself a basic grounding in the subject, of course, but I'd hardly feel competent to explain it in the sort of minutiae that your situation would seem to dictate."

"So you're saying I couldn't have summoned a *havsevama'-tasooma,* an evil spirit?"

Dr. Bowen was not accustomed to dealing in absolutes. History was filled with them, names, dates, places and the like, but he was not the sort of historian who limited himself to such concepts. For him, history was a grand and constantly evolving process that could only be described in the abstract. Mad Dog seemed to want his knowledge dispensed vending machine fashion. Put your money in and push the button and get what you want. Neil Bowen preferred the magic of ideas, conjuring up notions for his students like Legos that they could assemble as they saw fit. Mad Dog wanted the final product ready made.

"No, I'm not saying any such thing," Professor Bowen said. "Anything, of course, is possible, especially within the framework of the world view that you're discussing. Let me attempt to generalize, and perhaps offer a little advice, Mad Dog. But please don't accept what I tell you as gospel, especially not Cheyenne gospel. I am not part of that culture, nor am I even a worthy student of it." He paused.

"However, I can offer an informed opinion." Dr. Bowen cleared his throat and straightened his collar as he always did just before beginning a lecture. "First—and bear with me a moment because I'm sure I'll restate some of what you already know, and do it in a very simplistic way—let me outline the world view of which we speak. And excuse me, I'm going to use the English terminology, for instance Cheyenne rather than *Tsistsistas*, because I don't speak *Tsistsistas* and neither do you and while we may use the same *Tsistsistas* term, it may translate in a different way to each of us.

"The Cheyenne universe is divided into the visible world in which we live and the invisible world of spirits. The visible world is further divided into three parts, the world above, the world below, and the middle world—the place where people live and interact with plants and animals. There's a whole pantheon of gods, or spirits if you prefer, of varying power and influence on day to day life. I won't bother going through them because it serves no purpose as regards your particular question.

"What is important, is the nature of the individual soul. The Cheyenne basically believe that every living thing has a soul. Many non-living things too, such as certain mountains, the directions, the sun, the moon…but I'm getting off into that pantheon I was going to avoid. Essentially, that which lives has a form, a body—a shell in which it exists while it is alive—and a soul or spirit that is released when life ceases. Among the pantheon are spirits that oversee the souls of these life forms. They are a kind of supra-spirit, a great wolf spirit for wolves, a great buffalo spirit for buffalo, a great Cheyenne spirit for people, and so on. These oversee the spirit lives of the souls of creatures that are not currently living."

Bowen shut his eyes for a moment. "The first fallacy of your reasoning, Mad Dog, is yourself. To my understanding, the Cheyenne doubted that White People, whom they called spiders, had souls. Thus, while they would have conceded there was some sort of over-spirit to watch out for the souls of other Native Americans, even enemies, they thought the White Man had none to be guided. When Whites died, they simply ceased to exist."

Mad Dog pulled the Saab into the Texaco and found a parking space behind the building near where Bowen's car sat, still attached to a battery charger. He kept his engine running and the air conditioner straining as he turned in his seat to give the professor his full attention.

"Pardon me, I should correct a possible misconception there," Bowen continued. "I use the term White Man generically to include the forces of Western Civilization in general. Thus, Hispanics and Mexicans would be included, as would Orientals and people like me, African Americans—Buffalo Soldiers, for example were just Black White Men to the Cheyenne. That is, they were not people. They had no souls.

"Now, by your own admission, you are no more than one quarter Cheyenne and it is possible that, though you almost certainly are descended from the people, you could be less than that quarter. Since you were not raised into Cheyenne culture, I think that very probably makes you a non-person, a White Man, according to traditional Cheyenne standards, and therefore an individual without a soul and thus, by definition, incapable of contact with the souls of Cheyenne or spirits existing within the Cheyenne invisible universe. However...."

"Ah ha!" Mad Dog pounded the steering wheel in delight. "I knew there had to be a however coming up."

"Yes, well," Professor Bowen took a deep breath. "That was then and this is now. I understand that the Cheyenne world view has evolved and reconsidered that particular tenet. It's not that they have become, like so much of the modern world, more politically correct. That wasn't what led them to decide that non-people, that is the non-Native American population of the rest of the world, might have souls after all. Rather, Cheyenne religious leaders have begun to encounter representatives from that world with whom they feel a certain kinship, people in whom they recognized shared views and behaviors that give evidence of the great life force, that same soul, that makes a Cheyenne a human being."

Bowen rapped his knuckles against the Saab's dash and paused to give it an accusatory stare. He had the habit of gesturing flamboyantly when he addressed an audience and there just wasn't enough room in the front seat of a Saab.

"But not everyone. You have to give the Cheyenne credit there. Theirs is hardly an evangelical belief system. They look at that immense mass of humanity that threatens to overflow our globe and they do not reach out to embrace them. All men are not brothers, or even humans. There are simply too many people, and not enough souls to go around. It's like comparing buffalo with cattle and sheep. Buffalo have souls, cattle and sheep do not. They are domesticated animals, as are, Cheyenne theologists would argue, most of humanity, even including some modern Cheyennes. There are only so many souls available. The rest of us are just animals like those sheep and cattle. We're just meat. Given all that, still, I will have to admit, Mad Dog, that there is a chance that modern Cheyenne spiritual leaders would accept the possibility that you might have a spirit that is separate from your living form, and, therefore, a tool through which you might contact or manipulate spirits within the Cheyenne invisible realm. However, again...." The professor raised his hand as if to ward off interruption and further marshal his thoughts.

"First, while I would not rule out the possibility of the existence of that invisible realm, and, in fact, I rather admire the rationale for its authenticity, I remind you that there is no independent empirical evidence for its existence. Much like any religion, it must be accepted as a matter of faith.

"Second, it is a faith in which you do not have sufficient knowledge or training to expect, on your first try, to be able to make contact with some malevolent spirit within that world and allow it access into this, our physical world. Such a spirit, in other words, might well exist and have the power to affect us, but it would have no need or use for someone such as yourself, other, perhaps, than as part of some sort of cosmic joke.

"And third, even if you are right and I am wrong and, in an effort to outrage some local citizens and make fun of their own religious beliefs, you were somehow able to make that contact and inadvertently become an instrument of its evil actions, it is now operating within the visible world and it is within that visible world that you will most likely have to find the opportunity to confront and defeat it.

"Finally, if you are, despite all outside appearances, a natural born shaman who, quite casually has been able to release this evil into the world, then you are probably the only one who is also capable of finding a way to suppress and destroy it. In other words, there's no point in listening to me or trying to explain it to your brother or anyone else because they won't believe you and they won't be able to help you. You must simply decide for yourself what is right and what is not and then you must do what you must do."

"Wow!" Mad Dog said. "A natural born shaman. You know, that just might explain it."

Neil Bowen looked out the window and rolled his eyes, but he didn't say anything because it was true. It just might explain everything.

Heather English drifted on the edge of consciousness. She was aware of the voice and she was aware of the pigeons, but neither of them seemed connected to her. The pigeons were cooing madly among themselves and the voice seemed to be cooing to her as well, but she didn't understand what it or the pigeons wanted. She was still very sleepy. It was hard for her to concentrate and connect the words with each other and then connect the words with herself.

"I've got you now," the voice was saying in a kind of soft monotone, almost as much to itself as to her. "You're safe from her, at last. We're both safe from her. For now, anyway, and before this is over you'll be safe from her for good.

"My God, Heather, the things she's done to us. Do you have any idea what it's like to have your life swept out from under you, to be accused of atrocities too horrible to imagine, so horrible that everyone thinks there's no way she could have made them up, no way that she might have some terrible tangled purpose all her own, and so they believe her and they don't believe you and suddenly you're not a member of society anymore? She turned me into a pariah, an outcast. I was an exile, even from the company of outcasts and pariahs. I'm something worse than any of them. I'm so detestable that thieves and murderers and rapists feel disgust for me, for the things they believe I did. For years, I had to live with them, locked up among amoral beasts who loathed me, who felt they could somehow diminish their own guilt by abusing me, causing me harm. Can you imagine that, my darling? Can you wonder that I detest her so? That I'll do anything to save you, to save me, to save everyone from an evil only I can recognize?"

There was something in this that Heather, at some primal level, comprehended. Deep within her subconscious, part of her knew it was important to grasp this, to regain her senses, to resume some control over herself and her situation. By some massive force of pure will, she forced her eyes to flutter open. Shadows, and incomprehensible shafts of sunlight on which she could not clearly focus, greeted her, shapes as baffling as the sound of pigeons, or the voice. She seemed to be suspended high above a shadowy pit into which confused beams of light fell, failing to illuminate. There were ropes and cables down in that darkness, and great lengths of cloth that draped still further. She was lying on a slatted wooden platform, peering through the bottom rung of a railing, suspended between the shadows below and the light and the pigeons and the voice above. She had never seen a place like this. She didn't recognize the voice. She could only decipher an occasional word and puzzle out its meaning and by the time she had done that, the voice was several phrases further along and the next word she understood was unconnected to the last. She tried to fathom it and the light and shadows swirled in her mind and the cooing and the crooning mingled and the crooning became a shushing sound, an insistent demand for silence just as she heard the terrible creaking of a mighty door. It was as if God himself were telling her to be quiet as he reached out to close the crypt in which she lay and commend her to the darkness she found again behind eyelids too heavy to hold open and consciousness too tenuous to maintain.

The Strand Theatre, like most of downtown Buffalo Springs, had long since been abandoned. Unlike many remnants of the city's more prosperous past, it had not yet been torn down. The sheriff's Chevy slid into the alley between Jackson and Van Buren Streets and stopped behind the windowless brick cliff that was the Strand's backstage.

"Wynn some" came out of the passenger's door with a borrowed .44 Colt semi-automatic at the ready. It had been a hard choice, Wynn or French, but the madman who'd taken his daughter was clearly after Heather Lane. If the man realized his mistake and got by the sheriff, she needed competent protection. That was not

Wynn. Wynn, the sheriff finally decided, needed to be where he could keep an eye on him. French would escort Ellen and Heather Lane back to Sourdough Ranch and stay with them until relieved.

"Looks like they never got around to fixing that door," the sheriff said. Wynn nodded, the sheriff had filled him in on what he'd learned from Ellen Lane on their drive from the courthouse.

The door was padlocked, but a piece of heavy equipment had torn it away from one of the bottom hinges, leaving an opening a kid like Ellen Lane could have slipped through with ease. It was a struggle for the sheriff, but he was just trim enough to squeeze in, and found himself rewarded for his effort. A motorcycle was parked only a few yards inside the door that could evidently be swung quite a bit wider if necessary. Heat still radiated from the machine's manifold, not that the sheriff had any doubt that this was the means by which his Heather had been stolen away.

"I can't get through," Wynn complained. He was shorter and rounder than the sheriff, evidence of a slower metabolism and a weakness for desserts.

"Quiet!" the sheriff hissed, not that Wynn had spoken above a whisper. "Wait in the alley if you can't get in. I'm going to take a look."

It was dusky and silent inside the abandoned theater. Dimmer than it might have been, with Wynn stuck in the damaged door, blocking most of the sunlight. There were no windows to supplement the hot flash of brilliance that spilled around Wynn and across floorboards warped by heat and rain and snow and a Kansas wind that had sandblasted them nearly every day since the door was originally damaged.

The motorcycle sat among curtains that, at first glance, seemed plush and expensive. As the sheriff's eyes adjusted, they turned out to be just ancient and dusty.

There must be windows somewhere because the power to this building would have been shut off for years and yet there was enough light to reveal a confusion of boxes and spotlights and cables, even a few pieces of what must once have been scenery stacked against the rear wall. The source of that light seemed to be high overhead in the loft above the stage. Shadows hung up there amidst poles and ropes and pulleys, but through them an occasional shaft of light tentatively probed the gloom.

More curtains separated the stage from the theater's auditorium, but they were in no better condition than the ones hanging beside the motorcycle. Through occasional gaping tears the sheriff could see the empty trough that had once been an orchestra pit and rows of vacant seats sporting stained and tattered fabric. Abandoned, the theater had taken on the aspect of a set itself, the perfect place to search among phantoms of operas long past for a modern murderer, a frighteningly real villain given to torture and mutilation and the abduction of the sheriff's young daughter.

The dust was everywhere, and it was through the dust that the sheriff trailed his quarry. The footprints of a small man wearing athletic shoes whose outline looked familiar covered the stage. One set was different than the others, made broader because of the heavy burden it carried. They led across the boards, weaving their way through a forest of drapes and between a complex topography of boxes, all of it spotted with the droppings of a flock of pigeons whose cooing, far above, provided the only sound the sheriff could hear.

Otherwise, it was absolutely quiet in the theater. There was no wind, today, to provide a distant moaning backdrop. No traffic sounds on this sweltering Sunday afternoon, with most of the city's few remaining businesses shut down. Only on Main Street and Harrison, which were also highways, and thus nearly the only arteries through which the commerce of Buffalo Springs still trick-led, were any businesses open today, except for Bertha's. In here, it seemed as if there was no living thing for miles, except the pigeons gossiping quietly among themselves. Their presence was evidence that those shafts of light above did not necessarily enter the building through windows, or if they did, that some glass was missing.

Other than the pigeons, the only sounds the sheriff could make out were his own quiet breathing and Wynn's almost equally silent struggles with the back door. The sheriff debated going back to deal with Wynn, then found he couldn't. His daughter might be only a few feet away. Even the slightest delay might cost her life. He moved softly, in an almost slow-motion imitation of similar tense scenes that had been projected on the great screen that once hung between him and the amphitheater beyond. It was gone now, sold while its silver surface was still of a size to be used in more prosperous communities, before the advent of multiplexes rendered it as outmoded as a newsreel or the concept of the family farm.

The trail led past an ancient electrical board filled with graphed switches whose metal arms reached toward the sheriff as if desperately seeking his attention. Under other circumstances, the curious machine would have riveted him until he deciphered how it might have been used to give audiences the illusion of bright sun, soft moonlight, violent storms, and other magics. Not today. The footprints didn't pause there and neither did the sheriff.

The footprints led to the far wall. It was lined with ropes and pulleys and stacks of counterweights. It was a place as fascinating as the light board, but, the footprints had not paused here either. They only curved toward the back wall, circling around stacks of boxes and more falls of dusty curtains, toward the darkest corner of the stage. The sheriff followed, his .38 drawn and ready.

At first, the sheriff thought there must be a hidden door, for the burdened footprints only went to the wall and did not return. And then he saw the metal rungs set in brick and mortar, slowly let his eyes follow them up that vertical face through a web of shadows to what might be a catwalk. There were no safety devices associated with the rungs and they rose to a dizzying height that the sheriff would not have ascended under normal circumstances. This was not a normal circumstance. He reached out, grasped a rung and tested it. It seemed solid and so he reached for the next one and slowly, gun still in hand, began his cautious climb. If he was right, his daughter was just above, in the company of danger.

Wynn watched the sheriff fade into the darkness. It was an uncomfortable feeling. This wasn't a place where he wanted to be left alone, especially not half in and half out the alley door. He should be at the sheriff's side, but, try as he might, he couldn't squeeze through. Unable to follow, he decided to retreat and search for another entrance. He began backing out and discovered he was stuck.

He'd hooked some portion of his clothing on the door or the jamb and wedged himself, butt out to the world. It was the sort of predicament that had gained "Wynn some, lose some," his nickname.

This had already been the kind of day that would add to his reputation as a screw up. It took only a moment for Wynn to picture himself being discovered in this humiliating condition, then having to live it down for the rest of his years. Or worse, he could be caught by the killer here, his corpse savaged and left stuck in this final indignity. The idea gave Wynn strength he hadn't realize he possessed. With one giant heave, he pushed himself through, then listened to the echoes of complaining rusty hinges fill the auditorium and send a clear warning to any occupants that they were no longer alone. Company was here.

"I've been everywhere," Judy English complained, "and I can't find a trace of the motorcycle. It's like he turned off of Main and just disappeared."

"The sheriff got a lead from that Lane woman," Mrs. Kraus rasped. She'd been able to overhear the sheriff as he hurriedly briefed his deputies and shared the highlights of Ellen Lane's dissertation. So had Doc Jones who was sitting in one of the Sheriff's Office chairs, feet propped on an old coffee table that held a few outdated magazines even the original owners hadn't cared enough to read. It had been a long day, but Doc was sure it wasn't over. Staying in the Sheriff's Office seemed likely to give him a head start toward the next emergency.

"What? Where's he going? Has he found Heather?" Judy demanded.

"He got a lead," Mrs. Kraus said. "Mrs. Lane, she lived here when she was a kid. She told him about a secret place she had in Buffalo Springs. Her husband knew about it. The sheriff and Wynn have gone to check it out."

"Where?"

"Oh no, Judy," Doc interrupted. "You wait right here. The sheriff's got problems enough without having to worry about you too. Besides, you go barging in there, you just might make matters worse."

"How much worse can I make them?"

"Far as I know, Judy," Doc said, "your daughter's still alive. You show up in the wrong place at the wrong time, that could change."

Judy's shoulders slumped. "I'm sorry Doc. You're right. I'm just so damn scared. I promise I'll stay here, but please tell me where they've gone."

Doc nodded and Mrs. Kraus told Judy about the Strand, then filled her in on the rest of the story as best she'd been able to get it. It all seemed fantastic to Judy, unreal. Unreal was how she felt too. Her hands and feet and nose were numb and tingling. Her heart was racing and she had to stop and remember to breathe. It seemed like she couldn't get enough oxygen. She thought maybe she should ask Doc if his earlier offer of sedatives was still open, then rejected the idea. Her daughter needed her. While Heather was in danger, Judy wasn't going to hide behind any pills.

Doc had been sitting there, massaging his temples with the slow circular motions of a man who's very tired and has the kind of headache that cannot be ignored. He was listening to what Mrs. Kraus had to say because he didn't have anything better to do, but even with only half his attention it was making more sense to him than it was to Judy. Up to a point, anyway.

"Whoa, Mrs. Kraus," he interrupted. "Back up a minute there. Did I hear you right? Did Mrs. Lane claim she was the daughter of that Todd fellow who was a hired hand of the Simmses?"

"Yes sir, that's what the sheriff said."

"I must have missed that part, Mrs. Kraus. You sure? We talking about the Todd who killed himself after he was accused of molesting the little Simms girl, Lord, must be more than twenty years ago?"

"That's what I understood," Mrs. Kraus agreed.

Judy's patience was gone. "What the hell does it matter, Doc?" she asked.

"That Todd," Doc replied, "the way I heard the story, I don't remember him having a daughter. Mrs. Kraus, you were here then. Think on it. Is my memory really that bad?"

Mrs. Kraus thought, and as she did, you could see the light dawn behind her eyes. "Well," she said, "I ain't real sure Doc. I remember a child but it seems to me it was a boy."

"Boy, girl, what's the difference?" Judy asked.

"The difference between truth and lies," Doc said. "Judy, you got a key to the school?"

Judy was totally baffled now. "Sure," she said, "but why?"

"Yearbooks," Doc said. "You and me need to go look at some yearbooks."

The Buffalo Springs Elementary, Middle, and High Schools were located only a few blocks east of the courthouse and, like everything else in the village, within easy walking distance. They were in a hurry, though, so Judy piled into Doc Jones' Buick and learned that her husband wasn't the only local driver who'd become skilled at high speed maneuvering. Like the sheriff, Doc Jones had frequent cause to get places faster than the posted limit. He didn't bother with a parking place in the empty lot, pulling to a stop immediately in front of the door to the elementary school.

The three age divisions of the local educational facilities were distributed into the two buildings that had originally served as grade and high schools only. By the time junior highs, and then middle schools, became popular, the two original structures were serving fewer students than they once had. The addition of a single-story walk way containing a few administrative offices and linking the pair of two-story buildings had been sufficient to accommodate the third branch of academia.

Judy let them in the main entrance, a wide hall from which steps led both up and down and corridors branched into a maze of classrooms. There was something eerie about the silent, abandoned building. The place, when occupied, was never still. It constantly echoed with children's voices. Today, not even the wind called down the empty corridors. Rows of lockers stood mute and unslammed. Only the whisper of Doc's and Judy's shoes on worn tiles interrupted the building's well earned vacation.

"There should be a set in the library, but things in there tend to get torn up and misshelved, Doc. That's why there's another set kept in administration. I think that'll be quicker. They go all the way back to when the school was founded."

"I'm thinking Sixties is what we need," Doc said as he hurried to match her frenzied pace down the hall that led toward a principal's office, past teacher's lounges and faculty meeting rooms. "But we may need to get into students' records, too. Todd's not that uncommon a name."

The yearbooks were neatly stored in one of those old bookshelves with the glass doors that kept out dust without hiding contents. It occupied the back wall of the secretary's office, midway between a row of file cabinets and a bulletin board displaying children's art and out of date announcements. They started with the 1965 and 1966 copies of *The Bison*, with Doc traveling back in time and Judy aiming for the future.

"No Ellen Todd," Judy reported, after skimming through the books to 1970. I've got a Jimmy, a Karen, and a Lyle. No way the Karen could have been Ellen Lane, though. This one was a pale little blond."

"I think I've got something interesting," Doc observed. "Take a look."

He passed the 1962 *Bison* across for Judy's inspection. A swarthy, Mediterranean looking little boy whose eyes refused to meet the camera's gaze sat in the collection of first graders. The caption said he was Benjamin Todd. Doc flipped some pages and displayed a dark, intense young lady's face peering defiantly from a flock of fifth graders. It bore a definite resemblance to Ellen Lane's, but the name underneath was neither Ellen nor Todd. It was Sarah Ann Simms.

The sheriff paused as the sound of the door echoed through the building. He watched the outline of what he thought was a catwalk above for any sign of movement. And suddenly it was there. A dim face peered down from beside where the ladder's rungs disappeared into the gloom. The sheriff flattened himself against the wall and tried to make himself invisible, but he kept the pistol pointed in its general direction. That was probably the madman he saw up there, but it could be his daughter instead.

"Is that you, dear?" A voice he recognized from their encounter at Sourdough Ranch called softly from the loft.

The sheriff didn't answer. Having announced them, he hoped Wynn would now have the sense to come provide back up, to offer some sort of distraction that might let him finish this climb and pluck Heather from harm's way.

The face disappeared for a moment, then returned.

"Peak-a-boo, I see you," it said.

There was a scraping sound and something solid and dark came hurtling down toward him. It struck two rungs above and ricocheted out from the wall, brushing at the sheriff's back before careening down to the stage, and, from the sound of its impact, perhaps through it as well.

It took the sheriff a moment to understand that the man had dropped one of the long, brick-shaped counterweights at him. The sheriff hadn't stopped to examine them as he passed the array of ropes and pulleys and stacked weights below, but he'd noticed they were all metal and even the smallest must weigh ten pounds or more. The larger ones might weigh fifty. If any of them struck him on this uncertain perch, they would tear him from the wall and throw him to the stage, more than thirty feet below. That didn't matter. The fall wasn't going to kill him. The impact of one of those weights would do it first if the damage it had done to that steel rung so near the sheriff's head was any indication.

"Jesus, Sheriff, you all right?" Wynn's voice echoed from the vicinity of the motorcycle.

The sheriff didn't answer. He just held his pistol and watched for the face or his doom to appear above.

"Is that you, Sheriff?" the voice asked. "I didn't think she'd send someone else to do her dirty work for her. I thought she'd come herself."

The sheriff decided the time for silence was over. "Time to give it up, mister. You've climbed into a trap. There's no other way down from up there and I've got a sharpshooter on the stage with a night scope. You throw any more weights or do anything else threatening and I'm going to have him blow the top of your skull off."

"Sorry, Sheriff. I was only aiming for a near miss. Still, I wouldn't have dropped the first one if I'd known that was you. On the other hand, I can't just let you come up here either. In doing so, you understand, you'd put the girl's life at risk. We've nothing more to lose, she and I. We won't be taken. I won't go back to jail again."

"You won't hurt the girl," the sheriff said. He hoped it was true. He was pretty sure it was true if the man still thought he had his own daughter. If he knew he had the sheriff's instead, all bets were off. He might be willing to let her go, or he might be willing to kill her or turn her into a real hostage.

The voice was quiet for a minute. "No," it mused. "You're right, Sheriff. I won't hurt my daughter. Nor will I hurt you for that matter, though I still won't let you up here. It's my wife I want to see. When you speak to her, tell her there's something we need to discuss face to face. Tell her if she wants her daughter, she'll have to come find me and we'll have a nice long chat. Tell her, after that, Heather can go anywhere she wants, anytime, and I won't interfere. OK Sheriff?"

"Sure. I'll tell her, but let me come see that the girl's all right first."

"Sorry, Sheriff, I'm afraid you'll just have to trust to a father's love on that one. No point coming up anyway. I've seen enough of your operation here to feel pretty confident that whoever's with you is neither a sharpshooter nor equipped with any sophisticated night vision equipment. I also have my doubts that we're sur-rounded and trapped, though I suppose, if I waited around long enough, you could find the volunteers to do it. That's why I'm afraid we'll be leaving now. Please pass my message along to my darling wife. Tell her she'll know where to look, if she thinks about it. Heather and I'll be waiting, but she's got to come by herself next time so we can, one way or the other, finish this."

There was a loud crash above and the sheriff felt himself go cold inside as he saw the faint light that must be the entry to the catwalk darken. He was sure the man was about to drop another weight down the ladder and there was no place to go hide. Nothing more deadly than a sifting of dust fell out of the darkness. The crash was followed by some brief scuffling noises and a sound like a muffled thump. The sheriff was suddenly sure he was alone up here. The other Heather's father must have gone through the exit to the roof. But where did he expect to go from there? A vacant lot hugged the north side of the Strand. There was an alley in the rear. The front of the theater and a single story building next door offered adjoining roofs, but both were at least forty feet below the Strand's summit.

"Wynn," the sheriff shouted. "Get outside, check for a fire escape or some way down from the roof. Don't take a chance on him hurting Heather, but don't let him get out of your sight."

"Right," Wynn's voice echoed up from beneath him as the sheriff began to ascend the ladder again, more rapidly now that he was so close behind. Too rapidly, almost, he discovered, as his hand grabbed for the rung that was no longer where it should be because of its encounter with the weight. Somehow, the sheriff not only held on, he kept from dropping his pistol as well, then, more cautiously, continued into the darkness.

It was a catwalk, all right, and the ladder went through a narrow opening in its latticed surface. Or, rather, had gone through. The man had found a piece of plywood that nearly filled the space and, judging by the sheriff's inability to budge it, had piled counter weights on top.

The sheriff smothered a heartfelt curse, holstered his gun, gathered himself on the rungs immediately below the blocked opening, and applied his back to the obstruction. The angle was awkward and the plywood, heavily weighted, but the sheriff brought a father's desperation to the task. Gradually, the plywood began to slide, the weights to shift. The sheriff nearly fell again when it gave way, spilling two weights over the edge and into the darkness.

But for more stacks of weights and another row of ropes and brakes and pulleys, the catwalk was empty. At the far end, additional rungs led to a skylight, most of its panels missing. Gun back in hand, the sheriff sprinted for it.

At the top of this ladder, the sheriff briefly considered the impossibility of raising his head for a look in all directions at once, and the danger of encountering a bullet, a two-by-four, or even a solid kick. Still, he had to go on.

When he did, he found the roof was empty. The sheriff hurried to the nearest edge. The distant top of the theater's auditorium was also unoccupied. He checked the wall facing the vacant lot next, thinking it was the most likely to have a fire escape. He clearly remembered the alley wall was nothing but bricks and a weathered suggestion that he chew Redman, the irony of which he might have enjoyed at another time. No one there. No one in the alley either. That only left one wall and one adjoining roof. The sheriff reached it just in time to see a tiny figure coil a rope and sling it over one shoulder as he bent to lift a curled human figure over the other.

The man looked up. "It's called rappelling." His voice was faint but distinct. "You should try it, but I'm afraid I haven't left you a rope."

The figure touched a hand to his head in mock salute, then turned and trotted to where a stairwell opened into the adjacent building. He was gone from view before the sheriff could scream for the deputy he feared was having as much trouble getting out of the Strand as he'd had getting in.

"Wynn!" Only the pigeons wheeling in tight formation above the theater appeared to hear him.

Shadows in the Benteen County Veteran's Memorial Park had lengthened, giving the place a deceptively cool and gentle look. Mad Dog left his Saab parked across from the Buffalo Springs Non-Denominational Church and wandered slowly across the parched grass to the spot where he'd begun his day. His talk with Professor Bowen had done wonders for his confidence. He realized Bowen, though he'd been kind enough to answer and answer honestly, probably thought that he, Mad Dog, was as nutty as his years of outrageous behavior had made him in the eyes of the community. It didn't bother Mad Dog. He marched to the beat of his own drummer. Always had, always would, experiencing only an occasional passing pang over what others thought of him.

Mad Dog found the spot where he'd begun his vision quest. His cow skull was still right where he'd left it, along with the blanket he'd spread to sit on and a bundle of odds and ends he'd brought in case he needed them. It probably should have been a medicine bundle, he reflected, though, in a way it was. There was a bottle of Aspirin in there, along with some insect repellent, salt tablets, a bottle of water, and assorted tubes of body paint. He gathered everything and folded the blanket around them, slinging it over his shoulder.

This is where it started, he thought, glancing across at the restroom, swaddled now in yellow crime scene tape. At least it had been hosed out and the flies were gone. This was where he'd sat when he'd somehow contacted evil, provided a channel for it to reach out and touch his world.

The Reverend Simms' butchered body was probably already stuffed in that toilet when he arrived and began to set things up here. The thought hit him like a semi encountering a jack rabbit whose concentration had been on the curious properties of asphalt instead of approaching headlights.

If Simms was dead before Mad Dog began his attempt to contact the spirit world, then how could he be responsible for raising the evil that acted here. Uncertainty paralyzed him, but only for a moment. The timing didn't matter, he realized. While in spirit form, the thing he'd loosed upon the world wasn't confined to time and space as he knew it. Once unleashed, it could go where and when it wanted to begin its terrible crusade. Slipping back in time a few minutes to plant a corpse was nothing.

Mad Dog sighed and his confidence flooded back. Uncertainty, that was the danger to him in this conflict. He mustn't allow himself to doubt.

Who was his adversary, he wondered, or what? Was this the soul of some long departed evil shaman, killed by his tribe and exiled to eternity until Mad Dog happened along with his immense but previously unrecognized powers? Or might these be the tortured shades of the Ketchums, who'd taken a shotgun and their perversions to their neighbors almost a century ago. Weren't the Ketchums supposed to have been half-breeds, part Indians? Wasn't that why, in retrospect, nobody was surprised at the unspeakable things they'd done to the man's wife and children before slaughtering them, too? Mad Dog thought he remembered hearing that all the Campbells had been scalped, though those had been among the least of their injuries. There was something about the Ketchums— murderers, brutalizers, and suicides—that felt right to Mad Dog, but it probably didn't matter. The Ketchums could have simply been another manifestation of an evil that originated long before.

What did matter was where his opponent was now, and where and how he should seek it out and meet it in order to send it back into the invisible world until it mended its ways and learned to exist in harmony with the universe. Mad Dog looked around the park, searching for a sign, an answer. He wasn't particularly surprised when he found one.

The eagle sat near the top of one of the elm trees. There was a lot more wildlife in Kansas than there had been when Mad Dog was a boy. In those days, you could hunt for quail and pheasant and rabbit with some success. You might even bag the occasional duck, and if you had the patience for it, there were deer to be found along a few rivers and creeks and in the desolate sand hills near the county's northern border. With economic collapse and a continually declining human population, however, Benteen County's wildlife was returning. Oh, you still wouldn't find herds of buffalo to darken the horizon, but deer were common now, and turkeys were back, and bobcats, and now here, right in the heart of downtown Buffalo Springs, a Golden Eagle.

Mad Dog began to walk toward the elm. There was no doubt in his mind that this raptor was a messenger to him. The question still remained, though, could he decipher the message? Would he understand?

The eagle ignored him. It let Mad Dog come almost directly beneath its perch. The bird casually groomed himself, and as Mad Dog stopped, dropped a single golden feather that Mad Dog was able to reach out and pluck from the air.

The bird screamed. It was not a cry of fear or defiance, just the voicing of its pleasure in being here and now, of accepting its place in the visible world. It spread its wings and soared, rising steadily until it was out of sight.

Mad Dog bowed his head and looked at the feather he'd captured. It was perfect and holy. He was about to offer up a prayer of thanks when he noticed that something gleamed at his feet. He bent and found a broken razor blade, its shiny metal surface partially obscured by a crust of dried blood. Only a few yards away, not far from one of the paths that crossed the park, the grass was bent and trampled, and worse, spattered with a prodigious amount of dried gore, too dry for flies, though every ant in the park seemed to have discovered it and come to reap the unusual harvest. The eagle, he decided, had given him more than a message and a token. It had given him a reminder. Dr. Bowen was right. The spirit he fought had taken on physical form. If he was to meet and defeat it, he would have to do so on both physical and spiritual levels.

The rest of the message also seemed clear. The spirit he'd released would have spent its imprisonment in the underworld, away from the joys of physical being, far from the great blue vault of the upper world. If Mad Dog wished to seek it out, he should remember that it would shun the underworld as it sought its pleasures or its vengeance. Mad Dog wasn't certain, but he thought he knew what that meant. He turned and started back across the park toward his Saab.

As he emerged from the trees he became aware, for the first time, of the distant black line that stretched across the southwestern horizon, flickering as it teased the earth with tongues of lightning. Another sign, Mad Dog decided. They would not fight this fight alone. The spirits of his ancestors, of the three levels, and of worlds visible and invisible, would join with him. The spirits of Cheyenne Contraries would ride the thunderheads into battle. The evil one would call on its own friends, random violence and fear and rage. Like the eagle, Mad Dog let out a scream at the joy of being what and where he was, of knowing the challenge he faced and the certainty that he would do his best to answer it.

The dinner crowd at Bertha's looked through her windows and across the park. They spotted a tall man emerging from the trees, bald head thrown back, howling at the sky.

"Whatdaya think, Bertha?" one asked. "Mad Dog our murderer, returnin' to the scene of his crime?"

Student records were private. They weren't meant to be available, even to teachers. That was why current ones were kept in locked files next door to the principal's office. Of course, everyone knew where the keys were kept and faculty and staff took unauthorized peeks when they felt the need.

Old records were harder to access, not because there was even the semblance of security surrounding them anymore, but because they'd been shoved into boxes and transported to the basement where they were stacked in a haphazard fashion. Doc and Judy got lucky. The boxes they wanted were near the surface of a pile in the back corner.

"Look at this, Doc," Judy said, apparently meaning only to get his attention since she didn't offer him the document in question. She was calmer now that she felt like she was accomplishing something useful. It was a third grade report from Sarah Ann Simms' teacher to the principal. "Even then she was acting out sexually. There are all kinds of indicators of abuse here. Someone should have followed up on this."

"It was a more innocent time," Doc mused, "or maybe we just didn't want to believe what our friends and neighbors were capable of."

"Nobody locked their doors then, but the Simmses sure should have locked up access to their daughter. God, Doc! I can't believe her parents wouldn't have been aware that something was going on. They must have had suspicions."

"Maybe, but nobody did anything about it until she was just starting the sixth grade. That's when Todd took his dive."

"You find that there?"

"No, not specifically, but her attendance stopped in mid-September that year and there's a letter here from her parents explaining that, 'due to a serious illness, Sarah Ann has been hospitalized and will not return for the current term.'"

"Wow! They shipped her off to the loony bin, huh?"

"Looks that way," Doc agreed, as he burrowed deeper into the file. "Here's a letter from the Psychiatric Hospital in Larned asking for her transcripts."

"Oh, that's so sad. She never came back home. How long was she there, do you suppose, and what were the circumstances of her release? Gee, Doc, our Ellen Lane might be a pretty scary character."

"Well, she certainly had problems, but it appears she was released no more than a year later. Here's a letter from a Miss Mary Ellen Chandler of Wichita requesting those same transcripts. It appears she'd become the child's legal guardian in the interim."

"Who's this Chandler person? How does she come into the picture? Do you suppose the Simmses just didn't want their daughter back?"

"I don't know," Doc said. "The name Chandler rings a bell with me, though. I'm pretty sure that was Mrs. Simms' maiden name. Perhaps Miss Chandler was the child's aunt. The fact that she became legal guardian is unusual. At the very least, it indicates the problems that hospitalized Sarah Ann Simms went beyond molestation by a hired man. There must have been issues involving her parents or her family.

"We need more details, Judy. Considering the autopsies I've performed today and what I've just seen in these records, our Ellen Lane may just make a pretty good suspect, regardless of whether we've got some nut who's kidnapped your daughter. Is the phone system still working here?"

"Yes," Judy English said. "They don't shut it off for the summer, but we'll have to go back up to the administrative offices. The phones in here are all internal lines. To get an outside line, someone's got to switch you through and there's no one to do that but you and me, Doc."

"I want to try the number on this letter, see if it still gets us a Chandler or, if not, if I can manage to get someone at the state hospital to break some confidences. We need to check and see if there's any word from the sheriff too, and have Mrs. Kraus tell Billy French to keep an eye on the lady whose body he's guarding."

"God yes!" Judy led the way toward the stairs. "Maybe there's word from Englishman. Let's get to those phones."

It was lonely in the courthouse with all the action elsewhere and nobody calling in anymore. Mrs. Kraus kept checking her radio to be sure it was not only on, but on the right channel as well. She desperately wanted to go on the air and ask the sheriff what he and Wynn had found over at the Strand or to be sure Billy French's escort duty was going all right. She couldn't do that though. Everybody had strict orders from the sheriff to stay off the radio until he called in and cleared them for use again. All he needed was to be sneaking up on the bad guy when one of them read off their call numbers.

Mrs. Kraus wanted a cigarette too. She'd brought a pack along with her when she reported in to help out over the emergency that morning, but even though she couldn't recall lighting up more than a half-dozen or so, the pack was long gone. The emergency pack she kept in her bottom drawer was now empty too. She would have picked through her butts for a recycle or two, but when Doc Jones put in an appearance she'd had to pitch them and make heavy use of the aerosol deodorant.

Most of the day she'd been too busy to think about a cigarette, even though she'd apparently been going through them regularly enough. Now, she was alone in a quiet office with nothing to do but wait and worry.

The sheriff had made her promise to keep the phone line open in case he, or anyone, needed to communicate with the office without using a radio. That was reasonable, but how long would it take for her to call over to Bertha's and get somebody to walk a pack across the park, or, considering what had happened out there today, more likely around the park?

She strolled over to the window and peered across the square. Bertha's was drawing a good supper crowd. Surely one of them would be willing to....

The thought stopped half formed. There was a tall figure out there, almost hidden in the underbrush back beneath the elms. She leaned forward and squinted, as if subtracting a couple of inches and contorting her face would make him any more recognizable. As she watched, he turned and came back out into the sunlight where he stopped again and seemed to look back her way. It was Mad Dog, and he had something long and slender and blade-shaped in one hand. Lordy Pete, she thought. Is that a knife? With the thought, her doubts about the sheriff's oddball brother came flooding back. He had been out there in that park before dawn, about the time the Reverend Simms was being sliced off this mortal coil. Mad Dog had been known to experiment with mushrooms and cactus buttons. Lord knew what kind of psychotic flashbacks he might be having from his hippie days.

Mad Dog seemed to be staring straight at her. She thought about backing away from the window a little, but decided cowering from Mad Dog was the last thing she wanted to do. Then he opened his mouth and screamed and she found herself stumbling back across to her desk and digging for her Glock. She stood there, breathing heavily for a minute wondering if she should try to hide or just march down to the front steps and pop Mad Dog as he came across the street to murder her. Finally, she compromised by peeking out the front window. Mad Dog was climbing in his Saab and backing out into the street, paying not the least attention to her or the courthouse, or the expensive new Volvo with the out-of-state plates that should have had the right of way and nearly had to lock up its brakes to keep from rear ending him.

Mad Dog headed down the block toward Bertha's. The woman driving the Volvo turned a familiar face toward the courthouse and studied it with dark, intense eyes, then continued along the street in Mad Dog's wake.

Now what the hell was Mrs. Ellen Lane doing back in Buffalo Springs without her daughter or, more important, her bodyguard, Billy French? Mrs. Kraus didn't get time to give it much consideration. That was the moment when the phone began to ring and the radio, using a poor imitation of the sheriff's voice, insistently crackled her call number. Glock in hand, Mrs. Kraus hurried to answer both.

"Go ahead, get the phone," the sheriff told Mrs. Kraus. "It might be important."

He stood on the Corner of Poplar and Jackson, just south of the Strand. There was no one in sight and no indication which way the maniac might have gone with his daughter. Wynn was waiting with the truck, or better be. His future as a Benteen County Deputy was in doubt, first, for warning the kidnapper that the sheriff was in the theater by forcing the door when he'd been told to stay put and stay quiet, and second, for getting stuck in the door again and failing to cover the outside of the building when the sheriff asked him. It wasn't likely Wynn could have stopped the man, but he might at least have seen him descend and followed him.

The sheriff didn't feel like playing the numbers game they normally used to code their calls. Heather's kidnapper wasn't listening and if others were, maybe they'd seen something that could help.

"Billy," he asked the radio, "you receiving me?"

Something staticky and incomprehensible crackled in his ear. It was probably Billy French. Englishman fiddled with his squelch control, boosted his volume, and repeated his question, suggesting Billy try some adjustments too. All he got was more interference.

"This is Sheriff English," he told the radio. "Anybody else on this channel?" He was hoping some of his deputies had come back into the county and gotten the word they were needed, or just turned on their radios out of curiosity about what was happening on an otherwise dull Sunday night.

Nothing but static. The sheriff turned and retreated toward the alley. He wanted to be sure Wynn was still there and not getting into further trouble, and he wanted to start driving streets, looking for hints or witnesses, anything to point him toward his daughter and her captor.

"Five hundred to five-oh-one," Mrs. Kraus' voice croaked through increasing static.

"Go ahead, Mrs. Kraus."

"That was the KBI," Mrs. Kraus said, sounding more worked up over talking to the illustrious Kansas Bureau of Investigation than the sheriff would have expected. "They called, wanting us to do a notification of next of kin. They.... Oh, damn, there's the telephone again."

"I don't care about the KBI just now," Englishman said. "Check the phone and see if it's something important. If it isn't, get rid of them. I need you to call the Sourdough for me."

"But the next of kin was for Tommy Simms, Peter's brother, the old man's first born son. They just identified him. He was all cut up and scalped and.... Aw, hell, hang on a minute and let me get the phone."

"He was what?" the sheriff demanded, but there was no reply. Mrs. Kraus was dealing with the phone, but it didn't take her long to get back on the radio.

"Sheriff, it's Billy. He's lost Mrs. Lane and her daughter."

There was a strict code with which the federal government regulated the use of its airwaves. The sheriff's reply was a violation of that code and the Fourth Commandment.

"OK," Mrs. Kraus said, her voice crackling from the radio like a slab of bacon tossed into a hot skillet. "I got the damn phone off the hook for a couple of minutes 'cause, even if it's the kidnapper calling to tell me where he is, I got things you need to know and I need to tell them without interruption so I don't forget nothing."

"Go ahead," the sheriff said. He and Wynn were cruising the deserted streets of Buffalo Springs, looking for any sign of the perpetrator and his victim, or any living soul who might have been a witness. They were also looking for hiding places or avenues of escape, and coming up equally empty.

"All right. First, the KBI wouldn't give me much detail, even when I told them what we were working on down here, but they say Tommy Simms was back overseeing some machine shop repairs in Crawford on Saturday morning. Told the mechanics he had a lunch date, though not who with. Said he might be gone awhile. He was. Didn't come back at all. His body was discovered stuffed into a toilet in a rest stop up on the interstate about four this morning. They wouldn't give me any details, but they said what they had sounded similar to what was done to the Reverend Simms, and they did confirm that Tommy had been scalped. They would have come down to do the next of kin themselves but their investigators are holing up in Crawford because severe storm warnings have been issued for most of this part of the state. You looked at the horizon lately, Sheriff?"

Just what they needed, a thunderstorm to complicate search efforts, probably make the radios useless because of interference while it was around and maybe knock out power or phone lines and scatter the streets with the occasional downed tree or utility pole.

"No," the sheriff admitted. "I'm in the old downtown and the grain elevator's in the way. I thought the radio was picking up a lot of interference though."

"One of the KBI fellows says there's a line of monstrous thunderstorms coming our way. They've issued warnings for heavy rain, high wind, hail, and maybe some tornados. Should get here in about an hour, possibly less."

He had noticed that it was getting dark unnaturally early, though he hadn't given the matter much thought. There was too much else on his mind.

"Second, or third maybe, after the weather report," Mrs. Kraus continued. "French got Mrs. Lane and her daughter to Sourdough Ranch, only Mrs. Lane wouldn't get out of the car. Said she thought she saw somebody hanging around one of the stables and was pretty sure it was her ex. Frenchy went to see. Says he conducted a pretty thorough search and even saw somebody. That somebody ran and it took him awhile to discover it was only that kid Cody who works as a hand out there. When he finally got back to the yard, Mrs. Lane and her daughter and their car were gone. Says he thought about giving chase, only her dust was already settled and he couldn't use the radio until he got your all clear and didn't know when he'd be able to advise us she was on the loose unless he stayed right there and called in."

So much for the questions the sheriff wanted to ask. Ellen Lane's ex had made it pretty clear his wife would know how to find him, only now she wasn't available. One more avenue to recovering his daughter was closed. The Sheriff went through a string of creative expletives, but not into the radio.

"You copy that, Sheriff?" Mrs. Kraus inquired.

"Yeah, I got it." he replied, more calmly, rounding the corner at Poplar and Van Buren and noticing, to his surprise, that Mad Dog's Saab was parked in a space in front of the Buffalo Springs Antique Mall, temporarily closed—almost a year now—for remodeling. It had been the five and dime when they were boys and downtown Buffalo Springs was still a going economic concern.

"Listen, Sheriff. I saw that Lane woman, maybe fifteen, twenty minutes ago. Your crazy brother was over wandering around in the park and howling like he thought he was some kind of werewolf and he caught my attention. Anyway, as he was leaving the park Mrs. Lane was driving by the courthouse in that fancy bronze Volvo of hers. She drove off after Mad Dog and they both turned south down by Bertha's, though I don't think Mad Dog knew she was there. Far as I could tell, she was alone in the car."

"You hear that," the sheriff told Wynn. "Be on the lookout for a bronze Volvo."

"Yes sir," Wynn said, trying to remember what a Volvo looked like and whether that might have been one he'd glimpsed through an alley over on Walnut a few minutes before.

"There's more," Mrs. Kraus said. "She ain't Todd's daughter like she told you. Doc and Judy found her picture and some records over at the school. Back when she lived here, her name was Sarah Ann Simms. It's her brothers that have been murdered and her father that was scalped."

"What!" the sheriff exclaimed.

"Doc says to tell you he's still making calls, still following up on our Mrs. Lane, but she's misrepresented herself and there may be reasons to consider her a suspect. He says she could be somebody's target, too. If we don't find her, she might be our next deceased Simms."

"How does this all fit in with the nut who's got Heather?"

It was beyond Mrs. Kraus. "Look," she finally said, "I better hang up the phone and see if we don't maybe get some more information coming in. You want me to call Billy and have him high tail it back to town to help you search?"

"Yeah, Mrs. Kraus. Get him on the road and keep me posted."

"Roger, Sheriff, will do." Mrs. Kraus said, neglecting her numerical sign off.

"Sheriff," Wynn said.

"Yeah?" The sheriff didn't want to talk to Wynn, or anybody else right now. He just wanted to find his daughter.

"I think I saw something bronze parked down that alley back there."

Englishman did a u-turn that had the Chevy climbing the sidewalk in front of the old Rexall.

"Which alley?" the sheriff demanded.

The force of the turn and the brief proximity of the Rexall stole Wynn's breath away. He pointed and the sheriff and 350 cubic inches of American iron wasted no time going to investigate.

Heather English fought to come back from wherever it was she had been, an awful nightmare place. Something unnatural had taken possession of her. She was frozen, unable to move, the way you sometimes are in a bad dream, paralyzed while the demon did with you as it wished. This demon had a face and a voice and, as she gradually slipped back into consciousness, was as potentially terrible as the creature that stalked her nightmares. Worse, maybe. Dream demons couldn't really rape and kill you. Heather Lane's father could and might.

She forced her eyes open, let herself check to see if the monster was really there or if she was maybe just home, safe in her bed, and it had only been a dream.

What she saw left the question of nightmare or reality unresolved. It looked solid enough. It just wasn't like anything she'd ever seen. There was a surreal quality to it, like the work of some artist whose head wasn't on quite straight. It reminded her a little of the *Alien* movies because there were beams and pillars and braces and mechanical devices she couldn't immediately fathom surrounding her. The curious purpose of the place was made more difficult to discern because it was dimly lit. She was in a long corridor, and though it was lined with windows, not much light came through them. And the nature of that light was equally strange. It was a kind of foggy green, like the color the sky took on sometimes when a bad storm was about to hit. Behind the windows along one side of the corridor, light flashed in a random fashion, sometimes almost bright, sometimes almost invisible, a kind of strobe like effect that increased her sense of dread.

The paralysis seemed to be real. She couldn't move, at least not enough to look over her shoulder to see what was behind her. Before her was the corridor. It stretched forever. She couldn't see an end to it. It seemed to just taper off into hazy infinity. That was a scary thought. In a way, it reminded her of when she was a little girl attempting to imagine what it meant to go to heaven and have eternal life. She'd tried to picture it and what she'd come up with was similar to the corridor in the way it stretched beyond her ability to see an end. This was an uglier place, though, more brutally functional, more like hell than heaven.

She couldn't see anything through the windows. They were thickly covered with dust and grime and looked as if no one had ever cleaned them. She found no hints to help orient her there.

The floor of the corridor appeared to be concrete, as dirty as the windows and with occasional small piles of dirt or rubble or something she couldn't quite make out in the gloom. The floor was regularly interrupted by circular holes, big enough that she could easily crawl through one if she was foolish enough to want to find out what was down there, assuming she could move.

She had thought she was lying on a table, but on closer observation, she determined that it, like the corridor, was of infinite length. It was softer than a table should be, more like cloth or canvas that was fraying a little along the edges. There was a waviness to it too, where it swayed a little between regular supports.

The light seemed to be getting dimmer, the flashes brighter. Somewhere, far away, she heard a kind of rumbling, like some distant machinery, or like thunder. She didn't hear Heather Lane's father. She thought she remembered coming half-awake earlier somewhere very different, somewhere just as confusing, and hearing him talking to her, going on and on about the awful things that had been done to him. She wasn't sure whether the memory was real or just part of the dream. Whatever, she could neither see nor hear him now. If he was there, with her, he was behind her and he was being still.

She could move a little, she discovered, and in doing so, found why her movements were limited. Her hands and feet were bound with plastic restraints, similar things to the devices that locked around the mouths of garbage bags or held price tags on items in the mall. They would be easy to cut off, she knew, but impossible to break and they only pulled one way—tighter. Not that she was feeling strong enough to test them yet anyway. Her wrists were bound together, and her ankles, and there was another strip of plastic that attached wrists and ankles to each other. She was as effectively trussed as a calf that had been roped and thrown at the rodeo.

She tried swiveling her head again. This time it moved, though not far before the movement induced an awful sense of vertigo that made her moan and, for a moment, think she was going to upchuck all over herself and the table or belt or whatever it was.

The vertigo began to subside and then the belt moved and dizziness swept over her again, not quite so bad this time, but bad enough.

"It's about time you woke from your nap," a soft voice said from just behind her. It was real. This was a living hell and her demon was right here. She squeezed her eyes back down tight and wished she could go hide in unconsciousness again. Wishing didn't make it so.

Mary Ellen Chandler sat in the dark and watched as mindless strangers entered her home and brightened it a little with cheerful noises, companionable sounds in a room that rarely received guests other than those televised figures sharing their shallow plots and hollow humor. She watched, but she seldom really saw or heard them anymore.

This was a Sunday so she was wearing her robe and slippers, the same robe and slippers, if she thought about it, that she'd been wearing since Friday. On Mondays she rose and dressed. She wore stockings, jewelry, even makeup. She was always ready when the people from Hospice came, precisely at 9:00 a.m., to troop through the house to the back bedroom where her sister, Linda

Lois Chandler de la Jolla, lay perpetually dying—terminally ill, but clinging by gossamer-like threads with the tensile strength of titanium to a life that would not take her back.

Linda was always the same now. No better, no worse. She was little more than a human vegetable, fed and watered intravenously and in need of regular diaper changes. Linda hadn't talked in weeks, so it was impossible to determine whether she knew what she was doing when she soiled herself. Mary Ellen thought she did, but that she was no longer willing to waste the strength she needed to cling to life on pleasantries like speech or going to a bathroom.

Linda's consciousness responded to only one thing, now. Her eyes opened and watched when Mary Ellen brought her the morphine. The Hospice people monitored and renewed its gradually increasing dosage on their weekly Monday visits.

The visitors from Hospice were always gone by ten. Within minutes the house was dark and silent again, the TV flickering its false cheer at Mary Ellen—all dressed up and no place to go. On Tuesdays and Wednesdays she never got out of her robe either, but on Thursdays there was a brief reprieve.

There were two Hospice workers who came, a nurse and a volunteer. The nurse was the one who dispensed the morphine on Mondays. The volunteer was the one who dispensed the comfort on Thursdays. Linda appeared to be beyond the volunteer's aid, but Mary Ellen wasn't. On Thursday afternoons, the volunteer came and sat with Linda and freed Mary Ellen for a few hours away from a house where the grim reaper had already won, even if the victim had yet to concede. They were glorious hours, but too few, too far between.

Linda might not know she was dead, but Mary Ellen did. Their father's old shotgun still stood in the hall closet. Mary Ellen had taken it out several times now, checked the barrels and hammers, cleaned it, removed the shells with bird shot and replaced them with the double-ought deer loads. Linda would go easily. She was so very near her destination already. Mary Ellen knew it would be harder for herself, though if she shot her sister she knew she must shoot herself as well. She thought she could do it. Turning the weapon on herself would be awkward, but she was still limber enough to reach the trigger with her foot.

She was the middle of three daughters. The other two had both developed breast cancer. One had been dead for years. The second remained only technically alive. It ran in the family. Their female ancestors had been dying too young for generations. Mary Ellen was equally doomed. She was sure of it. She had a lump in her breast, but having witnessed the torment of surgery and treatment, as well as the futility, she had stopped seeing a doctor herself at the moment of discovery. It was another reason that, more and more, the shotgun seemed a rational alternative.

A weather bulletin was traveling across the bottom of her television screen when the phone rang. Mary Ellen hadn't been paying attention. Weather was no longer a threat to her. She always answered the phone, though it was never anything other than a salesman or someone soliciting donations for a superfluity of charities. Mary Ellen listened, politely, attentively, encouragingly, though she never bought or gave. Those brief moments when she visited with strangers nearly constituted the extent of her social contacts these days.

"Hello," Doc Jones said over a line that defied modern technology by sounding terribly remote, even more long distance than it was. "I'm sorry if this is an intrusion, but it's vitally important that I reach a Ms. Mary Ellen Chandler. This is the last number at which I have her listed and I wonder if you can tell me whether, by some chance, she still lives there, or if not, how I may be able to reach her?"

Not exactly the standard, "Our team of professional carpet cleaners will be in your neighborhood this week and can offer a twenty-percent discount on our deluxe deep-steam and shampoo treatment," or the smooth pitch of the people who wanted you to believe they were actually police or firemen and that most of your donation wouldn't go to the profit-making organization behind the request.

"This is Mary Ellen Chandler," she said. "How may I help you?"

For a man who'd been trained to defend himself, even to kill in hand-to-hand combat, the sheriff hadn't done very well against this 120 pound woman. Apparently, more than twenty years without North Vietnamese and Vietcong soldiers coming out of the jungle trying to kill you was enough to take the edge off. The kick should have been clue enough. He shouldn't have required a punch to the sternum to remind him that he was supposed to use an arm block he'd once thought his combat instructor had drilled into him as an automatic response he would never lose.

The sheriff collapsed onto the roof looking stunned. Ellen Lane didn't rip out any razor blades and rush to begin his dissection. She didn't swoop in for a *coup de grâce*. She just walked by him toward the broken windows and the trapdoor that led back into the Strand. The sheriff rolled and swept her legs out from under her and she went down and this time she was the one who looked stunned.

The sheriff was still having some trouble breathing, but he managed to complete the roll and regain his feet just as she regained hers. He'd put himself between the woman and the exit. She was watching him, gauging him, trying to decide which of them had been lucky so far and whether to try for the trapdoor or try to talk her way out of it. The sheriff must have looked more dangerous than he felt. She tried talking.

"I'm sorry, Sheriff. He was here and you let him get away. Now you're in my way and I'm in a hurry."

"He still has my daughter." The sheriff managed to make his voice sound almost normal. "I think you know where he'll go next."

"Yes," she said, "but you and your people don't make a very efficient posse. I told you about this place."

"I'm a little short-handed right now and, when he's got my Heather slung over his back, I can't shoot on sight. You didn't tell me he was a skilled climber. That might have made a difference. You haven't told me some other things. They might make a difference too."

She shifted a little and he thought she was maybe going to get physical again. The moment passed and the conversation went on.

"What things?"

"Who you really are. Why your brothers and father are dead—mutilated—and why you don't seem to care. And how you knew it and why you're out here looking for your former husband. Did you kill them? Is he next?"

She backed off a couple of paces and seemed to relax her stance a little. "Brothers? Did he get Tommy too?"

"He?"

"My loving former husband. He blames them, but he turned out to be just as sick as they are. Or were, I suppose."

"Why would he kill them? What would he blame them for? What do you mean sick?"

"It's all too complicated, Sheriff. I don't have time to explain. I thought you wanted your daughter. I thought her whereabouts would be the most important question on your mind."

"Then you do know where she is?"

"Yes," she said, looking back over her shoulder toward the approaching storm. "Yes, I know. You see, Sheriff, I used to have to run and hide often. Ben knows that. Back when I thought we were allies, I told him about all my special places. This was one. That silo on our farm was another, but it's too far if he's on foot now. There was one more. That's where he'll be, right over there. You see, Sheriff, I've always been fond of high places."

That's when Englishman understood. It wasn't the storm she was looking at. It was the grain elevator at the end of the street, towering like a reef on which the advancing wave of clouds must break before striking Buffalo Springs. His daughter was somewhere in that great white row of columns. He turned back to ask for clarification only to discover he'd been careless yet again. This was getting old.

Her kick must have knocked him out for a moment. He was lying on the roof and she was standing over him, pointing his .38 police special at him in a way that indicated she knew how to use it. "I see some handcuffs on your belt, Sheriff. I'd be obliged if you'd fasten one around a wrist and the other around your ankle. Then I'll relieve you of your key and your radio and maybe go rescue your daughter for you."

"I remember you, Dr. Jones," Mary Ellen Chandler said. "We met when you came to check on Annie at her home near the end of her illness. She thought highly of you, appreciated your honesty and your compassion. Not like Elmer who probably still blames you for not just waving your magic stethoscope and fixing everything so that he could get back to life as he expected it."

Doc had a faint recollection of sisters, pale, worried little women, hanging in the background. They had been too timid to ask him anything directly and Old Man Simms had been in a hurry to get him away from his patient, as if Doc somehow brought the disease instead of the treatment. He couldn't come up with a face.

"Yes," Doc said. "I believe I recall you as well, Ms. Chandler. I'm glad you remember me and that your sister, Mrs. Simms, thought well of me. She was a strong woman and she had great dignity."

"No, Doctor," Mary Ellen interrupted. "She was neither strong nor dignified, except on those brief occasions when the presence of outsiders made her put on that front. She was just another terrified victim."

"Ah, yes." Doc didn't want to get into a discussion about the nature of death and dying. He'd just hoped to smooth the way for the very personal and intrusive questions he needed to ask. "Listen, Ms. Chandler, I'm calling from Buffalo Springs. There've been some extremely serious developments here today. There's an ongoing situation that could prove life threatening. I'm afraid it would be inappropriate for me to disclose what those things are, but it's imperative that we have some information about your sister's family, the history behind some particularly unpleasant events."

"Oh dear," Mary Ellen said. "There've been so very many. I suppose it must be the Todd business though. The rest was so very long ago. I'm not sure whether I know enough to help you, Doctor, but ask away."

"Why yes, precisely. The Todd incident is what I need to inquire about. What can you tell me?"

"Oh my. That was all so sad and tragic. I suppose it was probably Annie's fault as much as any, because she never could accept what had happened to her and so she wasn't prepared to believe that it happened to poor Sarah either."

"Uh," Doc muttered. He wasn't quite sure how to break in and ask her to cut to the chase. Perhaps direct questions, but he knew so little he was afraid he might miss something important.

"I'm terribly sorry, Doctor. I suppose I'm rambling and whatever situation you have there requires that you get the information as quickly as possible. Since you can't tell me what's happened, I can't be sure what's relevant and what isn't, but I'll try to make this as simple as I can."

"Thank you," Doc said.

"I'm sorry, what was that? You sound so terribly distant, like you're talking down some immense pipe."

"I have you on a speaker phone, Ms. Chandler. There's a representative of the Sheriff's Office with me taking notes." Technically, Judy English had not a thing to do with the Sheriff's Office other than sharing in the parenthood of a girl who might be in terrible danger just now. That excused the exaggeration, as far as Doc was concerned. It also allowed him to keep Judy busy enough not to go running off to join the search and get in the way or endanger herself or distract the sheriff at a crucial moment. "I was just thanking you. Simple and straight forward would be great."

"Yes, then I should get on with it, shouldn't I."

This time Doc didn't risk an interruption.

"Our father molested us, Dr. Jones, all three of us. Annie Beth was the youngest and so by the time she came along my sister Linda Lois and I were able to protect her from the worst of it. And then Linda got pregnant and Mother and a few others came to realize what had been going on. After that, it stopped. Our father died three months later, while Annie was still quite young. As an adult, Annie denied it. She accused Linda and me—Linda is the oldest—of exaggerating it all, of making things up. If Linda had an illegitimate baby, she was sure it had to be someone else's. Annie blamed herself for what she could remember, and she blamed us for reminding her of it. It got so bad that the only way we could maintain a relationship was by avoiding the topic.

"Then the situation with Sarah began. Elmer always refused to see anything he didn't want to. Just like with Annie's cancer, he treated it as if it didn't exist and then expected that it wouldn't. That's how he was with Sarah. His sons could do no wrong, so long as he believed that. Therefore, his boys couldn't be sexually molesting their little sister. It was overstated, typical children's high jinks, nothing more than normal curiosity.

"Well, that may be how it started out, just normal curiosity, but there was a cruel streak in the eldest boy, Tommy, and the younger one, Peter, was such a self-centered little brat, and warped in his own way. If only Annie had handled it from the beginning, it might have been nipped in the bud, but she was in denial about her own history. She thought if these things were happening to Sarah, the girl was the one who was at fault. For boys, such things were natural, beyond their ability to control. It was up to girls to stop them. I don't know how she thought little Sarah, who was five years younger than the oldest and four years younger than the second, was supposed to take control of the situation, or even understand it since Annie refused to explain the facts of life to her.

"I'm sorry, Dr. Jones. It probably seems that I'm giving you too much detail again, but there's simply no way to understand what happened without some background.

"The Todds came to live on the farm about the time it all started. Elmer had quite a spread, but he didn't take much pleasure in sitting behind the wheel of a tractor or a combine. That's why he decided to put somebody in the tenant house on the property just across the road from the home place. That way, part of his hired hand's pay could be his rent. The Todds were a young couple with a small child of their own. Mr. Todd came from a farming family, but he was a younger son and there wasn't enough land to go around and I think maybe he'd experienced some prejudice, too. His wife, she was Hispanic you see."

She paused and sighed. Doc wondered if she was about to decide it was all too painful to talk about to a near stranger, but she'd just been composing her thoughts.

"Poor Sarah! I don't know what really happened, of course, but she must have approached Mr. Todd, made some sort of sexual advances to him. By then, she didn't know how else to react to a man. Her father was different, of course, but unapproachable. So far as she understood, she could have a male's protection and favor only by winning it with her body. This would have been when she had just turned eleven. She was becoming an adolescent. That's when it all happened, when things came undone.

"I can only guess how Mr. Todd reacted. She was a pretty little thing and I suppose some men would have taken advantage of the situation. In fact, I have reason to believe some already had. Mr. Todd, though, was made of stronger stuff.

"I think, after being properly shocked, Mr. Todd went to Annie. I don't know what Sarah told him, she'd become quite an inventive story teller by then. I think he may have suspected her father,

Elmer, and that's why he went to talk to Annie instead. Annie, of course, denied everything. It was Sarah's fault, and Mr. Todd shouldn't trouble himself, Annie would see to it that the child was punished and didn't accost him again. Well, Sarah had apparently exposed herself to Mr. Todd and there were marks and bruises and the last thing he had wanted was to cause the girl further trouble.

"What he did next should have been the right thing, but you know what Buffalo Springs is like, what a closed-in, sanctimonious, self-righteous place it can be, and it was worse then. Mr. Todd told the girl's doctor. This was before you came to Buffalo Springs. The town was bigger then, more successful, but declining. There were a number of doctors there. The others might have been all right, but this one wasn't. He was a society type. It was more important to him that he continue to be included in Elmer's and Annie's social circle than that an abused child be rescued. That meant none of the Simmses could be at fault, but he'd seen the bruises and abrasions himself. That made the molestation real, too real for Annie to deny away anymore. It also made Mr. Todd, as the accuser, the logical person to blame.

"The situation became quite messy then. Such things were never discussed in polite society. Sarah's reputation and future would be destroyed if there was even a whisper of what had happened to her in the community, though, of course, because of her behavior, there had been whispers for years. Mr. Todd was offered substantial compensation to take his family and leave, and threatened with being charged with statutory rape if he didn't. It was terribly unfair and, by all accounts, Mr. Todd was adamant in his refusal and angrier still because he'd just discovered that Sarah's brothers had begun molesting his own son, who was only just six or seven at the time. His boy had a prized stuffed toy that he carried everywhere, much like some sort of security blanket, and then one day he didn't carry it with him anymore and Mr. Todd discovered it hidden away, all encrusted with bodily fluids and what not. I gather the boys found it amusing to make the Todd child do all sorts of disgusting things with that toy.

"There was apparently a scene between Elmer and Mr. Todd in which Elmer was backed by his attorney and the doctor, and Mr. Todd was backed not at all. Young Todd stormed out, promising to fight them and saying that the children, Sarah and his boy, would testify and put things right, show where the blame truly lay. He must have gone looking for them then.

"Sarah had a number of secret places where she went to hide from her brothers, and from a world that made demands of her she couldn't understand. She only had one friend then, or perhaps ally. He was Todd's son, and as victims of the same abuse and abusers, they'd fallen into each other's company despite their age difference. They were in one of Sarah's secret hiding places that afternoon, atop the ensilage in the silo at the back of Elmer's barn.

"Doctor, I don't know what happened up there. Sarah has told all sorts of contradictory stories over the years, but judging by the way it affected her, I think she may have, in some way, caused his fall. He was a grown man, and a strong one, though, and she was just a slip of a girl. I'm confident she didn't somehow purposefully murder him.

"In any case, he fell and died. His son's sad, abused, Mickey Mouse doll was clutched in his hands. Afterwards, Sarah went into a state of perpetual hysterics and Todd's son became nearly catatonic. The powers that be decided to rule that it was suicide. Sarah was institutionalized, and when it became clear the community knew she'd been sexually abused, it was convenient to assign the cause of the suicide to Todd's fear of what would become of him when his molestation of the child was made known and charges were brought against him.

"Mrs. Todd was offered an even more substantial sum than her husband had refused. Knowing she had no support within the community, as well as no husband to feed and clothe and house herself or her child, she took it and left."

"And you took custody of Sarah?"

"Yes. It was my name on the papers, but my sister Linda and I assumed joint responsibility for her. I supplied the home. Linda provided the financial support that made it possible. It was clear Sarah could never go back to Buffalo Springs. Clear, too, that Annie would always blame her for what had happened. Annie was glad to be rid of her troublesome daughter, glad to let her sisters protect her from what she didn't want to face one more time. Elmer just wanted Annie happy and I believe he thought it was for the best and, for once, he was right.

"Sarah did well here in Wichita, and on her visits with Linda in Santa Fe. Once she was out of the hospital, though, she was inappropriately sexually active, promiscuous really. We always hoped she would out grow that. Perhaps she has."

"Ms. Chandler," Doc interrupted. He thought he had his killer now. Her motive was certainly clear. Still, there was another contestant for the role of murderer. "Can you think of any reason why Sarah's former husband might want to harm any member of the Simms family?"

"Oh my," Mary Ellen breathed. "I haven't gotten to that part yet. You see, Doctor, that's who she married. That's when we knew she wasn't really cured, nor him either for that matter. They met again at college right here in Wichita. My sister Linda and I, we tried to dissuade them but Sarah just wouldn't listen and he couldn't stay away from her. Before we knew it, she'd gone and married the boy. She was Mrs. Benjamin Todd. And Benjamin, just like Sarah, who started calling herself Ellen in my honor, had been sexually abused by her brothers and was at her side when that abuse resulted in his father's death. Oh my, Doctor. I thought you knew who Benjamin Todd was."

Getting off the roof of the Strand was simpler than Ellen Lane probably expected. The sheriff's handcuffs were more for show than use. He employed them rarely. Occasionally they went around a teenager's wrists just long enough to get his attention, and even more infrequently they helped him control a local citizen who was drunk and violent. They weren't meant to contain hardened criminals. That was part of the reason he had obliged Mrs. Lane's request and snapped them on and given her his keys and his radio. The minute her head disappeared below the roof line he was pulling his pocket knife out of his Levis and jimmying the locks. You didn't need a key to open these handcuffs. Anything pointed enough to stick in the lock would do.

The sheriff wasn't thrilled about giving up his revolver, but he did like the idea of following her. He thought she was being honest about the elevator, but she'd lied about so many things before. If he followed her unseen, she'd take him where she was going.

The sheriff gave her enough time to get off the ladder and onto the stage before he started down. He moved with all the stealth Mad Dog seemed to think their ancestry should make natural. As soon as he passed the weight-damaged rung and was certain the rest could be found at regular intervals, he turned his descent into a controlled fall. It was dark on the stage now, but for the occasional dim flash of lightning coming through shattered windows far above. The sheriff knew there was a clear path to the back door near the rear wall, though, and he followed it quickly and quietly. He was just in time to see her shoes exit into the alley. He dropped to the floor beside the door and peered carefully after her. She had seen his truck blocking her Volvo, and the shadow that was Wynn sitting in the passenger's seat. She paused at the edge of a collection of discarded cartons and considered the problem for a moment. A brilliant stroke of lightning lit the alley like a flash bulb. Wynn's head was turned to watch the approaching storm. She did what the sheriff had expected. She sprinted across the alley and slipped into a narrow vacant lot across the way.

The sheriff followed her as far as the next street. She was walking south, straight toward the Co-op store and the massive row of concrete silos behind it. The sheriff took two seconds to decide.

Wynn practically tried to claw his way through the roof of the cab when the sheriff pulled open his door. "Lord Jesus, Sheriff, you pretty near made me a candidate for diapers again."

The sheriff didn't answer. He just popped open the glove compartment and pulled out the 9 mm he'd taken out of Ellen Lane's purse at the courthouse. He dropped the magazine and checked to be sure it was loaded, then worked the slide and chambered a round while Wynn asked him what he was doing.

"Give me your radio," the sheriff answered.

"Where's yours?" Wynn complained, but he obeyed, handing over the spare the Sheriff had supplied him just before they left the courthouse.

"Stay here!" the sheriff said. "Don't leave the truck until I come tell you it's OK."

"Where you going? How long you gonna be?"

The sheriff wasn't there to answer. He was running down the alley, pounding toward Poplar Street and the dogleg that would take him over to Van Buren and put him back on her trail. The sky was filled with a celestial light show with sound effects that rumbled down the shallow man-made canyons of Buffalo Springs. A cool gust of wind reached out and teased his face and scattered leaves and crumpled paper. She was there, a block away, head raised as she studied the base of the concrete cliff. She was going to her secret place. She was going to where her husband had almost certainly taken Heather, and, unknown to her, she wasn't going alone.

"Then they seemed to have made such a positive adjustment. They were leading what appeared to be the most normal of lives. Benjamin was working for Bauman Aircraft and doing advanced studies at the University. Sarah—she was Ellen by then—was a counselor with a local mental health agency."

Judy English was taking notes like mad and Doc Jones was trying to stay with the conversation while he worked out the permutations of these convoluted relationships in his head.

"But it didn't work out, did it Ms. Chandler? Not after the baby arrived."

"No, Doctor. No, it certainly didn't. Oh, it seemed to at first and then we began to detect an over-protectiveness in Ellen, and some frustrations in Benjamin. It was like she was cutting him out of their life, hers and Heather's."

"Did he assault the child?"

There was silence for a moment as Mary Ellen Chandler considered how to answer the question.

"A court of law convicted him of the crime, then another court overturned that conviction. I don't honestly know, Doctor. If I had to choose, I'd say no. Not that she made it up, mind you. I think she firmly believes he did it, but she has a predisposition to expect betrayal or abuse from the men in her life. He was a victim too, and victims often become victimizers, but I'm afraid I think it's my niece who is the less stable of the two, or was the less stable at the time. I've no idea what a decade in jail may have done to poor Benjamin."

"So Ellen and Ben would have equal cause to blame Peter and Tommy Simms?"

"Equal, I don't know, but they certainly both despised her brothers."

"And what about her father?"

"My, does that mean something has happened to Elmer? Never mind. I don't suppose you can tell me. That's a harder question. Elmer tried to maintain a relationship with his daughter, though hardly a close one. He sent her cards and checks for her birthdays and holidays. Eventually, she stopped cashing the checks or even opening the cards. I don't think she hated him the way she hates her brothers, but there is an anger there, a sense of betrayal. In a way, I think she's angry with all of us. My sister has...health problems. When it was clear Benjamin would be released she let Ellen move into and manage her quite successful art gallery in Santa Fe, *Galería de la Jolla*. We thought it would be a good place for her in case Benjamin did come looking for her with revenge on his mind. I'm afraid Ellen took advantage of the situation. She left Santa Fe with Linda's car and quite a lot of money that doesn't rightly belong to her and without a word to my sister or me. As for Benjamin and Elmer, I never heard the boy say anything about my brother-in-law, but he must have felt that Elmer was at least partially responsible for what happened to him, and worse, what happened to his father."

"So it could be either of them," Doc muttered, "or maybe even both." Judy had stopped writing. She had her hand to her mouth and was biting the end of the pen she'd been using, a far away look in her eyes.

"De la Jolla?" Judy muttered. "Did she say her sister, Linda, is a de la Jolla?" Doc was so wrapped in thought he didn't appear to notice.

"I'm sorry," Mary Ellen Chandler said. "I couldn't quite understand."

And that was the problem, Doc decided. Even with all this new information, you couldn't quite understand what had happened, or which of them might have done it.

"**M**rs. Kraus," the sheriff said to the radio. He knew Ellen Lane couldn't hear him over the wind and thunder, and she wouldn't hear him on the radio she'd taken either. He'd thumbed it to another frequency before he climbed out onto the Strand's roof. "I think he's got Heather somewhere in the elevator, probably on the delivery floor or in the head house. Do you copy?"

"In the where? You're signal's breaking up real bad," she said around a jumble of static of her own.

"The elevator, the co-op," he repeated.

"The elevator, the grain elevator? That what you're saying Sheriff?"

"Roger, Mrs. Kraus. Get Frenchy over here to back me up. Tell him no flashing lights or siren. I don't want anyone up there to know we're coming."

"What's that you say?" Mrs. Kraus crackled and popped.

"Break, break," French's voice interrupted. "Sheriff, I copied that. No flashing lights, no siren. I'm on my way, about seven miles out, but I just hit a wall of dust and visibility's down to almost nothing. I'm not gonna be available to you quick. You copy?"

French's voice came through with surprising clarity.

"Got you Frenchy."

"Sheriff," Mrs. Kraus said. "I heard French. You need to know, Doc just called. It's too involved for me to try to explain, but either of them, Ellen Lane or her former husband, could be your killer. They both have motives. He said you should know that and take no chances with either one. Did you copy?"

The sheriff got enough to understand. He'd love to know what those motives were. They might help him figure out how to deal with the mutually hostile pair, but Mrs. Kraus was right. No time for explanations now. Ellen Lane had just disappeared into the elevator's loading shed.

"Right, I understand," the sheriff said. "I'm going in now, and that means I'm going off the air. Frenchy, they could be armed. When you come in, come in careful."

French copied but the sheriff had already shut his unit off and was sprinting for the gaping cavern of the loading shed. A wall of water hit him ten yards short of his goal.

◇◇◇

This guy was as weird as one of those psycho serial killers the good guys were always trying to track down on TV, Heather decided. Worse, the bad guys on TV were scary, but they weren't real. This guy was both.

He had talked to her virtually non-stop from the moment she woke up. Talked, but not listened. It didn't take a rocket scientist to figure that this dork had grabbed the wrong Heather. She had explained it to him quite calmly.

"You've made a mistake, sir. I'm sorry, but I'm not your daughter. That was her with me on the porch. You see, we're both named Heather. That's why I answered when you said our name. I think maybe she recognized you and was afraid and didn't say anything. Now, if you'll just let me go, maybe I can help you find her. Or maybe my father can. You see, he's the sheriff here. He might be pretty upset that you took me instead of her and this is the wild west, you know, we still string people up around here, but if you just let me go I can fix it with him and then we won't lynch you and maybe he'll help you find your daughter."

If he heard a word, he hadn't given a sign. He'd gone right on with his monologue while she was talking. Hadn't even paused when she'd tried screaming at him.

"Hey! Excuse me! Would you just listen a minute? You've got the wrong person!"

He was almost impossible to hear now over the cacophony of rain beating against the roof, the wind tearing at windows, and the constant grumble of thunder. It didn't matter. Heather had heard it from start to finish several times now.

"I wouldn't hurt you, honey" he'd said. "I loved you and your mother. I just didn't want to get shut out, and that's what she was doing. After you were born, there wasn't any room for me anymore. And I don't blame you for that, Heather. It was your mother. There were things that happened to her a long time ago. Things that happened to both of us, and seeing you, so little and helpless and all, it brought it back to her. I could tell. It was like she was shielding you from me and that wasn't necessary. I wanted to protect you too, but she wouldn't let me. God, honey, can you imagine how that hurt me, that she thought I was a danger to you. But she wouldn't leave you alone with me. If I was around, she was always there, plucking you out of my arms and finding some excuse to get you away from me. I couldn't stand it. That's why I sneaked home that time when she thought I was at work. I thought if I just once showed her I could be trusted. I crept into the house and up to your room and you had just woken up from your nap. You needed changing. I thought if I did that, got you cleaned up and dressed all neat and pretty and carried you down to where she was resting on the sofa, I could prove to her that you weren't hurt and I could be relied on and maybe we could start to be a family like we were supposed to. Only I'd never been allowed to change you before, not that it's hard or anything. It's just I hadn't seen you naked and the wonder of it all kind of swept over me and I admired you for a moment before I took a wash cloth and some soapy water and began to clean you. That's when she came in. I was trying to be so gentle and cautious but it may have looked strange or maybe it just looked strange to your mommy because of what happened to her when she was little. Maybe I shouldn't have been using that cloth I bought you with the Mickey Mouse face. She started screaming and I tried to tell her it was OK. I wasn't doing anything but changing your diaper and cleaning you up but she yelled and yelled and she picked up an iron and clubbed me with it. The next thing I knew there were policemen there and they were saying the most awful things about me. And she was telling them things I'd done to you before and how she'd been afraid of me and afraid to tell and it wasn't true, not any of it."

There was more but it all just kind of looped back around to how he wouldn't hurt her and how he loved her and how everything changed when she was born. And there was some strange stuff about Mickey Mouse and something that happened on some high place a long time ago and how it was maybe the other Heather's mother's fault. Heather English thought Mrs. Lane would do well to stay a very long way away from this guy. The family reunion he had in mind wasn't likely to end up with everyone living happily ever after.

Heather still had no idea where she was. The corridor looked even spookier now that it was lit only by sporadic lightning flashes. It wouldn't have surprised her to see one of the Borg from *Star Trek* come marching out of the columns and puzzling machinery, though she would prefer Jean Luc Picard with an away team, armed to the teeth and ready to kick butt to rescue a fan. Or her Dad. He would be looking for her, she knew that, and he was more than just Dad. He was the sheriff, he was the good guy. She hoped he'd come, but she also hoped he wouldn't because she was afraid that this fellow might be too much. This was real. Good guys didn't always win.

He reached out and touched her on the arm and scared her so bad she practically wet herself. Until that moment, the need for a bathroom hadn't occurred to her. She hadn't used one since the Hutchinson Mall, though, a very long time ago. He leaned over her and put his face close to hers and she thought he was going to do something awful now, rape her or sodomize her or kill her. Her imagination was busily supplying possibilities.

"Mommy's coming." he said, and laughed in a way that scared her even more.

◇◇◇

"Are you there, Doctor?" Mary Ellen Chandler asked the extended silence. In fact, he wasn't. He'd thrown her a quick apology and run to the office next door to use another line and call the courthouse with what they'd learned.

"Uh, no, I'm sorry, he's not back yet," Judy explained.

"I've been sitting here thinking, imagining all sorts of terrible things. Won't you tell me please, is there some possibility our Ellen is involved? Has she maybe done something awful?"

"Well...." Judy wasn't at all sure how to answer. This woman had raised Ellen Lane as if she were her own. Judy, missing her own daughter, couldn't imagine how anyone could withhold vital information from a mother. On the other hand, they really didn't know what was going on or who had done what.

"Yes," Mary Ellen continued, "I was afraid so. Well, there may be something else I should tell you then.

"The doctors told us some of what they learned about what Sarah, or Ellen if you prefer, went through. The things her brothers did to her. You see, more than a century ago one of our ancestors was said to have been a captive of the Indians for a time. She was little more than a child but she suffered some terrible things from them, maybe because they'd suffered terrible things from Whites. When they brought her back, she had two half-breed children. People blamed her, shunned her, until a rancher named Ketchum took her in and married her though he treated her more like a slave. But that's another tragedy and no point going into it. What I wanted to tell you was that Elmer loved to tell stories about the things she saw and suffered while she was a captive. He'd go into the most awful, gruesome detail, totally inappropriate for dinner conversation, let alone in front of the children. Something about that must have appealed to Tommy and Peter. You see, that's what they did with Ellen, play Indian. Not cowboys and Indians, you understand, they twisted it into cruel, diabolical, evil Indian. They called the inappropriate things they did to her counting coup, and they used to tell her, if she didn't cooperate, they would scalp her. They threatened her with razor blades and cut her a little sometimes. It traumatized her. She never forgot it. We couldn't even cut her hair for almost a year. Later, we found the most peculiar books around the house with descriptions and sometimes even photographs of scalps and people who'd been scalped.

"I hope that doesn't mean anything to you. I just thought it could be something you might need to know."

"Thank you," Judy said. "It may help. But listen, there's something really peculiar I have to ask you. Your sister...." There wasn't anyone there to hear her anymore. Just a dial tone. Mary Ellen Chandler didn't think she could help them anymore, or anyone else. She had hung up the phone in order to stare at the silent TV and the dance of meaningless images, and to think about the solution that stood, cleaned and oiled and loaded with buck shot, in the closet down the hall.

The Buffalo Springs Co-op Elevator was constructed in 1928, near the end of the community's first and only economic boom. There were nearly five thousand citizens in Buffalo Springs then. Every year since, there were fewer.

Kansas elevators are like fingerprints, no two are alike, though to the untrained eye they can seem pretty similar. They range from the old wood and metal bin type to the modern concrete tower, of which Buffalo Springs Co-op was an early example. Concrete bins may be square, round, or a variety of angular shapes optimized by the octagon. They may consist of from two bins to hundreds, with some municipal storage facilities extending more than half a mile in length.

Depending on the productivity of the soil, local elevators with two to twenty bins are usually found along railroad lines every four to fifteen miles. Buffalo Springs was flanked by four smaller elevators within a ten-mile radius. These were no more than six-bin structures. Around two of them, a small collection of homes and a filling station had sprouted. The other pair were simply lonely sentinels at otherwise insignificant crossroads serviced by rail.

Municipalities tend to have larger elevators, and it was with this hope in mind that the beast of Buffalo Springs was built. It was 408 feet in length, 48 feet wide, and 90 feet high at the roof, or 110 feet at the roof of the head house. It was a monolith, formed by one continuous pour of concrete that took almost two weeks and involved 250 workers. It contained 36 circular bins, 17 star bins and 35 outer bins, so that only one empty space between the work floor and the distributing floor was unavailable to store grain. That space contained the preferred routes for humans to travel to the head house and the distributing floor. The fastest, if not necessarily the safest, was by way of a belt elevator with steps and hand holds that rotated over a pulley in the head house and was driven by an electric motor on the work floor. On an adjacent wall there was a runged ladder, positioned in case of a power failure or failure of the mechanism. There was also a circular metal staircase in that unused bin, the safest route, but a slow and tiring one.

The fourth and last way to and from the top was an exterior fire escape at the east end of the structure. Its infinity of metal rungs was encircled by a metal cage making it unlikely that anyone could slip and fall more than a few feet without catching on something, but even at a time other than in the middle of a ferocious thunderstorm, it was hardly an attractive course. It had a rusty, weakened look to it and no one had been inclined to test its structural integrity in decades.

The sheriff chose to ride the belt. The machinery that drove it was on. That meant she had probably ridden it herself. It would take him forever to climb the ladder or the stairs and the ladder didn't have a safety cage. It was there in case the belt failed and there were places, about every ten feet, where you could transfer over to the relative safety of the spiral staircase.

Riding the belt had about as much appeal to the sheriff as a proctological exam, but a pair of lunatics could be fighting to death over his daughter up there. He caught a loop, found a place for his feet, and held on tight.

Even the belt took forever. Riding nearly a hundred feet in pitch darkness made him doubt that the belt was moving, though it continued to sway and vibrate. That tiny square of flickering light far above didn't seem to get any nearer. He listened for the sound of hard breathing that she must surely be making if she had taken the ladder or the stairs and heard nothing, nothing but his own hard breathing, caused only by tension, and above that, the almost constant rumble of approaching thunder.

The sheriff had planned to step off onto the ladder and climb onto the stairs a little below the delivery floor so that he could arrive a bit less precipitously than the belt would bring him, but he found he just couldn't make himself let go of the loop and trust his weight to a rung hanging somewhere out there in the darkness that he couldn't even see. While he was still trying to convince himself to take the risk, he arrived. That tiny square suddenly expanded and surrounded him. He had the option of bailing out onto the delivery floor or going on up to the head house where he would either get off or follow the belt over its uppermost pulley and, if he could hold on and reverse himself without falling, begin the long, long journey back down.

He dived between a pair of semicircular safety railings and rolled under a delivery tube, muscles tensed for a blow or a bullet, eyes searching wildly for some sign of his daughter or the loony twosome. Nothing. Just a short corridor to the east end of the elevator, rows of cloudy windows that hinted at the ferocity of the storm just beyond but providing no more than a translucent view of flashes that seemed to come from every direction including down.

The machinery under the head house blocked his view of the delivery floor to the west, but this end seemed clear of killers, kidnappers, and kidnappees. As he maneuvered around the belt and the stairs he spent a bad moment wondering if she might have sent him up here as part of some elaborate hoax, started the belt running to the top for no other reason than to convince him that she'd come here, when, in fact, she was bound for some other place instead.

He found them, then, just beyond the head house. Two figures, facing each other, motionless, poised in tense postures from which deadly strikes might be launched, but safely out of each other's reach. The sheriff recognized the dull gleam of his service revolver in her hand. Her husband stood just beyond, looming over another figure that appeared to lie on the grain delivery belt. There was something bright in his hand too, poised threateningly near the form that the sheriff was sure was his Heather.

The sheriff brought the 9 mm up, sighted on the farther figure, confident he could bring the man down and still have time to get the woman, in case she should prove to be a threat to his daughter as well. He even began to squeeze before it occurred to him that part of the translucence from the explosive light show beyond the windows was dust, the grain dust that hung in the air from the recent transfer of grain out of these bins to make room for this year's harvest. It reminded him of why the place had all those windows. When men were working here, they opened them so the wind could carry that dust away. The dust was a danger, and not just to allergy sufferers. The stuff was as hazardous as a natural gas leak. All it took was a spark, like the one a 9 mm might produce when its hammer fell on a percussion cap and exploded the powder behind a lead projectile. Pull that trigger, the sheriff suddenly realized, and he and his daughter might be dead long before he had a chance to see whether he'd hit what he aimed at.

The cemetery was, just as he'd been told, a small, sad place with little evidence it was even there. A few old hardwood trees that wouldn't normally stand in the middle of a field were about the only outward indication. When Professor Bowen left his car he'd discovered a few other hints. Here and there an ancient marker lay, or occasionally even stood, weathered far beyond his ability to read its inscription. There was a broken cross atop a pile of boulders, large rock cobbles that someone had brought up from one of the Kansaw's tributaries. Someone had labored long and hard to etch a message in the stone at the top. "Here they found freedom," it proclaimed. And hardships beyond counting, Professor Bowen knew, but hardships they would have thought worth bearing as the price for that other cherished institution.

The sky had gone ominously black and threatening in the southwest as Neil Bowen made his way back to his car and, for a reason he couldn't explain to himself, set out south. He wanted to see their country, this homeland they'd briefly shared with the Indians and the pioneers before those hardships drove them elsewhere. It was flat land, gently sloping down to the wood-lined creeks that meandered through green-gold wheat fields toward that increasingly angry looking horizon. Finally, Neil Bowen had decided he needed to turn back, but the urge to explore, to see more of what he had not seen still compelled him. He turned west. He should intersect the blacktop that ran north and south through the edge of Buffalo Springs by going that direction. Within a few miles, he was beginning to regret his choice. That mountainous range of clouds was advancing at a troubling rate, flashing warning signals along an immense stretch of horizon. He had to put on his lights long before sunset was due and he could see that a great brown wave of dust was rushing his way like some memento of dirty-thirties Kansas. He was starting to get concerned about actually finding that blacktop when he found the girl instead.

She was a lanky teenager with short dark hair. She was wearing jeans and a cotton blouse. She looked as scared and lost as he was beginning to feel. There weren't any farm houses close by and even though he wasn't too thrilled at the idea of how a black man offering a ride to a young White girl might look to the locals—especially after his earlier encounter with Wynn—he couldn't go past and leave her to face the storm alone and unprotected. He slowed as he pulled alongside her and rolled down his window just as the first blast of wind and dust rocked the car and nearly knocked her off her feet.

"Hi," he said, finally recognizing the girl who'd been brought to the courthouse on a stretcher. "Are you all right? Do you need a ride?"

"Do I," she agreed fervently as she scrambled in the passenger side door. "You're a life saver."

"What on earth are you doing out here?" he asked. The car rocked with another blast of wind and reverberated with the echo of the sand blasting it was receiving. Bowen could see only a few yards ahead of his front bumper. "Does your mother know where you are?"

"She's such a dweeb!" the girl said. "She's the one who stuck me out here."

Neil Bowen had visions of getting involved in a child abuse case. Just what he needed to top off a day in which he'd already spent too much of his time in the company of law enforcement officers. "What, she dropped you off out here in the middle of nowhere?"

"Like practically," the girl replied as they began easing along the road again, headed west toward that hypothetical strip of macadam. "She's been acting so weird. I mean like totally flipped out. She took me to this deserted farm and told me to climb up this ladder at the back of an old barn and wait for her in a silo. Of all the crazy things! She said it was a safe place and she'd come back for me. That was before the storm was so near so I went back where she said. The ladder was like all flimsy, you know, but that's what she'd told me I should do. I climbed up there and got clear to the top and there wasn't anything inside, just this big empty hole with no way in and no way out and, like what was I supposed to do? Wait up there for the ladder to give out? I came back down and hung around the barn for a while, then I went up and knocked at the door to the house but there wasn't anybody home and the storm was starting to look pretty bad. I thought maybe I could walk to another farm or find a ride into Buffalo Springs. I have friends at the Sheriff's Office. Could you take me there?"

If Neil Bowen could, he would. He wondered, though, how Wynn or whoever happened to be at the courthouse would feel about their former black murder suspect bringing in this unescorted teenage White girl. Freedom might have been won, he mused, but some hardships remained.

Mad Dog was in his speedos and body paint again. He had given a lot of thought to the metaphysics of the thing and had begun to realize that costume and location were not necessary, other than for helping him achieve the right state of mind to do what he had to do. He was enough of a neophyte, he decided, that the props, though irrelevant, helped him focus his powers on the forces he planned to summon and manipulate. It was kind of like golf. No grown man in his right mind would wear knickers and knee socks out where other folks could see him unless he was walking onto a golf course. The clothes didn't make him shoot a better game, unless they helped him feel like one of the pros on TV. In the same way that a golfing costume might lead to a near par round, Mad Dog's war paint helped put him in the mood to impose his will on the evil he'd inadvertently summoned.

He didn't go for quite the same patterns this time, though. There was a tube of glow-in-the-dark opalescent blue in the pack. It felt right to him. On the basic black that covered his body he streaked lightning bolts down arms and legs and, for a reason he couldn't explain, drew finger wide, horizontal stripes across his ribs. Black didn't seem right for his hands and his head, except around his eyes and mouth and over most of his nose. For the rest, he used the florescent blue. As storm-induced, premature darkness settled over Buffalo Springs and the place Mad Dog had chosen to confront the forces of malevolence, his body disappeared and became one with the night. Only a pair of apparently detached hands and a glowing skull linked by lightning streaks of sex-shop body paint remained. He finished by tying the leather thong around his temple and inserting the eagle feather. He was ready. Mad Dog watched the flickering horizon and began to chant, words as unnecessary as the paint, but words that helped his mind concentrate on its task.

"*Maheo*, I ask your blessing. Spirits of the four directions, I ask your blessing. Spirits of the sky world, I ask your blessing. Spirits of the underworld, I ask your blessing. Spirits of the surface world, I ask your blessing. Spirits who bless me, help me put things back in harmony. Spirits of evil, I summon you. Spirits of evil, you must go back where you came from. Hear me, I, and the spirits who bless me, we command you."

He went on like that for a long time, sitting in the lotus position on the old rug he'd spread, earlier in the day, on the grass of the Veteran's Memorial Park. Now, he sat as close to the upper world as he could, on a flat white roof not far from a metal tower on which a blinking red light stood to alert air traffic to the existence of a monumental cliff of white concrete. He could feel them coming. He could feel that ancient, terrible evil drawing nearer, just as the storm also drew nearer and the heavens flashed and roared and opened.

The rain soaked him and the wind buffeted him. There was something about the awesome power of the storm that was gratifying, a physical manifestation of all the metaphysical forces on which he called. But there was something troubling about it too. His body might only be painted with lightning bolts, but the sky was filled with them. Jagged flashes of raw energy split the heavens and crashed into trees and roofs and fields below. Below, that was the key here. Lightning sought the easiest path from sky to ground, or vice versa, and the shortest path was where he sat, on the roof of the head house of the Buffalo Springs Co-operative Grain Elevator, more than forty feet above the highest tree or building nearby. Considering that made it harder to concentrate on being a shaman. Surely, though, he could control the lightning just as he could control the evil. Metaphysically speaking, he was convinced of it. But somewhere inside was the little boy who'd marveled at the split and burned tree trunks he'd seen result from such storms, and the scattered bodies of the animals—marked with eerie fern-like, arborescent discolorations—lying where they had gone to seek shelter under the branches. Doubt is the enemy, he told himself, and tried not to think about that. Then the world flamed and a white light engulfed the pole and the flashing beacon and something picked Mad Dog up and flung him backwards until there was no longer a roof under him and he began to fall.

"I knew you'd come," he said. "I thought about meeting you at the belt elevator, but I knew you'd have to come to me, wherever I was."

Heather could hardly hear him over the roar of the storm, and she couldn't turn her head far enough to see who he was talking to. At first she thought it was just more gibberish aimed at her, but this time another voice answered. It spoke in a higher register, a feminine voice, but not a soft one.

"You were right," she said, "but you were wrong, too."

The voice sounded familiar, but Heather wasn't certain. He'd moved closer to her just before the woman arrived and there was a long sharp blade in his hand near her throat, something home-made with razor blades bound to a steel shaft. It curbed her curiosity and persuaded her not to ask who was there, but to wait and listen instead.

"I knew you'd come because you had to. I'm a threat to the only thing you love more than yourself...or you think I am." To Heather it sounded like a variation on the things he'd been telling her since she first started to regain consciousness. It was like he wasn't listening to what this woman was saying to him any more than he'd listened to her. Like he'd played this scene out in his mind so many times that he knew it by heart. He knew everyone's lines and it didn't matter if someone else got theirs wrong. He simply carried on.

"I used to think we were allies against them, that if we just circled our wagons the Indians couldn't hurt us. They still could, of course, and they did, but we found each other and helped each other heal. Or so I thought until Daddy found Mickey. Even then, I thought you were trying to take Mickey away from him so you could give him back to me, but you threw Mickey and Daddy couldn't quite reach and then you tripped him and he fell down.

"Still, I was willing to forgive you and love you because that stopped our Indians and we'd both suffered so very much, but then our daughter came along. That's when I found out I wasn't your partner. I couldn't believe it. You thought I was like them, like our Indians. You shut me out, and then you had me locked up like an animal."

"You are an animal. It was you who tripped your father, not me, and worse, I know what you did to our little girl." Heather recognized the voice now. It was Ellen Lane, the other Heather's mother. What was she doing here? Where was Dad? Heather Lane's disastrous family history had stopped being fascinating. Heather English just wanted to go home.

"I wasn't an animal, but you may have turned me into one. Look what you've made me do to her just to get you here. Just to get you to come to me this one last time."

"That's the part you don't understand, Ben. You screwed up. You haven't lured me into a trap, I've hunted you down. You're not in control here. I am."

He moved closer, slipped between Heather and the endless windowed corridor, held the blade to her throat with a gentle intensity that made it all the more terrifying.

"Do you think I'm surprised to see that you've brought a gun? What good does that do you? You're not that good a shot. If you don't kill me instantly, my knife's at our daughter's throat. Even if I don't try to hurt her intentionally, the way you expect, even if you just wound me, I might jerk and kill her by accident. Put the gun down, my love. Put the gun down and I promise you she'll be safe. I'll let her go. I'll make you a trade, your life for hers. That's fair, isn't it. That's what you want. Put the gun down and give me your hand. I'll cut her loose and she can run for it. You can tell her where to go, how to get away and I won't interfere. Take my hand. Then you and I'll go through those windows over there and it'll be like it should again, just the two of us, together, going to join Daddy and Mickey, free of Indians forever."

"No!"

"You don't have a choice, my love," he said clasping Heather's hair with one hand and putting the knife to her carotid artery with the other. "Do it now."

Heather couldn't see it, but she could hear the sneer in Ellen Lane's reply. "I do have a choice, Ben. You blew it. You grabbed the wrong girl. Our daughter's a long way from here in a safe place and this time that makes me the predator and you the victim."

Heather heard another noise she recognized. She'd been around her dad and guns long enough to know what it sounded like when a revolver was cocked.

"This is Heather," he said, but for the first time there was just a hint of doubt, the tiniest indication that he wasn't sure and the plot of his tragedy might not end the way he'd pictured it.

"Yes, but she's somebody else's Heather, not yours and mine."

"You're trying to trick me but it won't work. Even if this isn't our daughter, you wouldn't take a chance on hurting some innocent girl just to get at me. Even you aren't that cruel."

"I'll do what I have to in order to protect my child, Ben. You can bet your life on it," the other Heather's mother said. Heather could tell the man was still considering it, weighing the implications and making up his mind, but she didn't have any doubts. Ellen Lane was about to take out her husband and God help Heather English if she was in the way.

The sheriff came at them on the far side of the belt that delivered grain the length of the elevator, the belt on which Benjamin Todd had deposited Heather English's trussed form. He wasn't worried about Ellen Lane shooting anyone with his pistol. He'd loaded it with blanks before climbing to the top of the Strand. The sheriff always had a pouch of blanks on his belt because firing a couple of shots in the air worked wonders when he was breaking up the occasional drunken brawl at the Bisonte Bar. Using blanks insured nobody got hurt and he didn't have to squabble with the management over the cost of patching holes in their ceiling. Since they were available, letting Ellen Lane have a harmless pistol and a head start had seemed like a great idea—a way to make sure she would lead him where he wanted to go, then be unable to cause any harm once she got there. Of course that was before the sheriff encountered the grain dust in the Co-op. The dust changed everything. Blanks could ignite dust, blow the top off the elevator, just as surely as normal bullets. It wouldn't matter that nobody got hit by flying lead.

It wasn't an easy approach and the sheriff didn't manage it quietly. He'd had to clamber over and under tubes and machinery he only dimly understood. It was impossible to see clearly in the flickering translucence that penetrated the elevator's windows and Englishman painfully banged into unseen metal supports and pipes and rails the deceptive lighting had hidden or made him think stood elsewhere. The clamor he was making didn't give him away though, not over the almost constant roar of wind sucking at windows or the staccato rattle of rain driven just this side of hard enough to shatter glass. And there was the thunder, never quieter than the rumbling of an adjacent megasaurian belly, more often crashing with end-of-the-world violence that shook even this monstrous structure of concrete and steel rebar and made it impossible for him to hear any of the words Heather Lane's parents were exchanging.

The sheriff, whose relationship with God centered on mutual disbelief, found himself hedging bets and asking favors. If only he could get close enough to jump her and knock the gun away.... Well, then he'd still have the problem of what to do about the man with the knife and his daughter, but at least they all might live long enough for him, and any God who cared to lend a hand, to begin solving the next stage of this endless series of life and death situations.

He was almost there when he tripped over a discarded wrench, lost his balance and nearly fell into the gaping circular mouth of one of the eighty-eight bins. An inch or two and he'd have plunged through seventy feet of darkness onto a conical floor that would have ensured his shattered pulp flowed into the chute at its base.

He lost enough skin off one shin to make it hard not to add his voice to the din, but shifted his balance in mid air so that he fell with more of his weight outside the hole than in it. He lost his radio, though, and never heard it hit bottom. This fresh and unexpected brush with mortality was enough to raise a non-existent ruff of hair along the sheriff's spine, but there was still a damsel in distress here, his daughter. Limping instead of running, watching the floor more carefully than he had, he worked his way nearer.

He was close. He could hear their voices, make out words. "You can bet your life on it," she was saying. Just a few more feet and....

The world ended in a flash of white-hot brilliance and a roar that tore the air from the sheriff's chest and knocked him off his feet. She'd pulled the trigger and the dust had ignited and they were all dead...only that couldn't be, he realized, not if he had the time to think it. Blinded, deafened, stunned, the sheriff knelt on the dusty floor among piles of spilled grain and tried to comprehend that it had been a lightning strike that dropped him, not death. Victory still might be salvaged if he could only make himself see and think and move again. He found an angled support beam and used it to pull himself back to his feet. He blinked his eyes in an effort to clear away the after images of that blinding flash, gradually discovering that he could distinguish the outlines of the distant windows again, strobing just as furiously as before. The grain distribution belt was only a few feet away. He stumbled toward it, avoided the mouth to yet another bottomless pit and found the belt's frayed canvas edge. The crumpled shape of his daughter lay on it only a few feet away, but there were other crumpled shapes as well and one of them still held a pistol, still pointed it at the other, and the sheriff knew there wasn't time to do anything but try to stop that shot. He grabbed the belt, took hold of its edge, and launched himself across it as the world ended yet again.

It ended differently this time, with less light, but every bit as much confusion. There was a distant crash, the whine of far off electric motors, and suddenly the sheriff was blinded by wind and dust, knocked off balance as the belt began to move beneath him. He tumbled to the floor, collided with a support column he hadn't seen, saw stars instead, and felt blood begin to flow down his temple again. He wiped the blood and dust and dirt from his eyes. It was the same place he'd occupied moments before, but different. Those endless rows of windows that had allowed only a blurry glare to pierce them were open now, all of them, driven out into the storm at a 45 degree angle that kept out most of the rain but admitted a howling gale that cleansed the air of explosive dust at the expense of sandblasting his eyes. The wind raised plumes of debris and pelted him with a shotgun-like rain of grain kernels. She could shoot now. It wouldn't matter. She was very close, blinking her own eyes clear. She must be as confused as he was because she seemed to have lost track of her husband who was lying just to the sheriff's west. The gun was centered on the sheriff. He felt the wad from the blank bounce off his stomach when she fired. She looked surprised when he didn't fall down, and then she looked elsewhere.

Maybe it was because of the otherworldly apparition that suddenly burst from the door to the stair leading to the head house. It was tall and skeletal, little more than a ribbed stick figure supporting a grinning skull and grasping talons, glowing an unnatural hue. It looked like something from a fever dream, or a secret warehouse in Roswell, or a dead-teenager movie. It howled and moaned and it came straight for Ellen Lane, who watched it, frozen, the gun still pointed at the sheriff as the wind and the nightmare reached for her.

The man who should have been most shocked (in every sense of the word) by the arrival of the lightning bolt, was the one who was most expecting it, or, if not lightning, some other manifestation of the evil forces he intended to face or the benevolent ones whose help he was soliciting. The blast could have interfered with every electrical impulse inside Mad Dog's body, but it didn't. Instead, it sent him somersaulting backwards through the door that led down into the head house. That could have killed him too, only he didn't fight it. He was waiting for something big to happen. When it did he left his body out of the equation and tried to grapple with it only mentally. He went down the metal rungs loose limbed, rolling like a drunk. At the base, he bounced off a wall, slamming against a row of switches, two of which were activated by his passing, before he went windmilling down the second set of stairs toward the delivery floor still relatively uninjured—bumped, scratched, and bruised, but functional. He arrived at the top of that second stairway feet first and decided something wanted him to stay that way. He still wasn't sure whether the lightning had been an assault or an assist, but he suddenly felt certain that the evil he must banish waited for him just beyond the door at the bottom of those stairs. He hit it like he'd hit those linemen when he was a football hero for the Buffalo Springs Bisons, bellowing like a mad bull, forearms extended, with all the speed and weight and strength that was in him.

The door didn't stop him any better than opposing players had. He exploded into a whirlwind of confusion, dust and grain and bodies everywhere. One of them had a gun. He saw it, knew somehow that the person behind it intended to do harm with it, and so he charged. He didn't know it was a woman until later. All he saw was a thing, a destructive force, an ancient evil he had loosed and helped to find physical form. It watched him come, frozen, unwilling to believe that he was here in all his power and in the company of the spirit keepers on *Maheo's* business. At the last instant it tried to bring the gun around but not before he was on it. He knocked the weapon out of its hand and kicked it toward the windows, then tossed the evil thing off into the darkness too. That was when he realized the thing hadn't come alone. There were two of them, not allies except perhaps against him and the prison to which he intended to condemn them once again. He found one, bent and lifted it struggling from the floor. It was a creature of the underworld. It drew its strength out of the earth and already, at this elevation, it was weakened. Out of contact with the floor, it was nearly powerless. The second one wasn't though, not yet.

The second one came at him cautiously, confused by his appearance, confused, perhaps, by his presence on both physical and metaphysical planes. Mad Dog still couldn't see very well, but it didn't matter. Their physical forms weren't important. This was a battle of spirits. The thing circled him for a moment, assessing him and then it pounced. It danced at him, feinted, reached out and slapped him with something bright and cold and sharp.

"One," a voice seemed to whisper in Mad Dog's ear. He couldn't have actually heard it over the wind and the thunder and his own mad howl.

He felt it, though, a sudden sharp afterimage of agony along his ribs, and as something warm and wet that trickled down his side and dripped onto the floor. He was right. This would be more than a spiritual contest. They would fight him on the physical plane as well. The battle, Mad Dog decided, was going to be just as challenging as he'd expected.

The sheriff didn't have time to stay and watch. Somewhere, a motor had come on to open the windows. At the same time, a second motor had started the grain belt moving. His daughter was on it and the sheriff didn't have a clue what other machinery might lie along its path to crush or mangle or chew her. In fact, there was nothing but the belt, and an occasional delivery tube she would simply brush aside. When she reached the end it would just have dumped her on the concrete floor and done her no harm. The sheriff didn't know that. This had been a day with too many frying pans and too many fires. Where Heather was concerned, he was beyond the ability to take even the tiniest chance.

The sheriff threw himself aboard the belt. No one, not even the spectral being that was almost certainly his brother, tried to stop him.

If there hadn't been all those support beams and feeder tubes and those frightening holes into empty darkness, the sheriff could have made better time off the belt than on it. Instead, he crawled along the rolling, bouncing surface, like a kid caught on a nightmare carnival ride. They were nearly to the end before the sheriff grabbed her and yanked her off and onto a relatively open spot between a stack of disassembled tubes and a cross hatching of pillars supporting the roof. He found his pocket knife and freed her hands and ankles, crushed her to him in an ecstasy of love and relief.

"Oh, Dad, not so hard," she said, and he released her almost instantly, terrified of the awful injuries his touch must have nudged from painful to agonizing.

"Heather, what is it? Where are you hurt?"

"I'm OK, Dad. Just don't squeeze me. I've really, really gotta pee."

◇◇◇

"Two," the voice whispered again. This time it was the figure he held over his head. It had managed to reach down behind him and run something sharp across his left shoulder blade. The cut wasn't deep enough to sever anything vital because his muscles were still working well enough to keep it up there, but it was harder now and the other one was still out there circling, looking for an opening. He didn't know how many more times he could afford to be tagged.

Mad Dog turned and located that second shadowy tormenter. It gamboled among the machinery and pillars, watching him, waiting for the right moment to strike. It would be so easy to surrender to the demands of the physical world and counterattack, but Mad Dog reminded himself that he was fighting on two planes. He shifted the one above his head and ducked a swipe from its steel talon while he watched the other dance, but he made his mind watch for the rhythm of it too. As one demon came for him again out of the darkness, he pivoted and dropped and interposed the other between himself and the place he knew the blade would be.

"That's three," he heard faintly echo through his head, but it wasn't. The one he held dropped its talon and let out a shriek as it began to writhe and fight him even harder than before.

A new noise competed for his attention. The sound was something Mad Dog sensed both as a rumbling in his ear and a tugging at his essence. Above the maelstrom he thought he heard a run-away train bearing down on Buffalo Springs. Mad Dog had lived in Kansas long enough to know what it was. He was also learning to understand another world view, one that let him see it as a weapon he might wield.

Mad Dog felt that the one still with a blade was behind him, ducking under beams and looking for a clear avenue from which to come slashing once more. Mad Dog didn't have to look to know it. Their relative positions were clear to him. He looked, instead, toward the windows where the wind and rain had slackened but a primal roaring indicated that yet another monster stalked the world. A jagged bolt of lustrous blue, matching Mad Dog's body paint where it wasn't covered with his blood or that of the flailing figure he still pressed toward the ceiling, lit the flatlands to the southwest and revealed a twisting rope of unsuppressed violence snaking across the fields of ripening wheat toward their battlefield. Mad Dog understood this wasn't just any tornado. It was a spirit wind. It had come to claim the loser.

Mad Dog knew what to do with the demon he already held. He sidestepped a pillar to block the blade wielder's slash at his back and began to jog toward the windows. He cut left, then right, weaving among a forest of metal braces and feeder tubes. The windows weren't far, but the demon with the razor's touch wasn't far either. It wasn't easy, not with the burden he carried and not with the frenzied thrashing and wailing it made as it realized where Mad Dog was taking it.

Lightning flashed again. The funnel was nearly on them. Mad Dog looked for a place to plant his feet for the throw. His feet were invisible, hidden by the blizzard of dust and grain being sucked across the delivery room floor and out the windows into the whirling maw that waited to carry him, or them, to another dimension. To join Dorothy in Oz maybe? Random thoughts suddenly reeled through his mind. It was the wrong moment to lose concentration, trapped as he was between forces equally willing to steal his life. He tried not to doubt.

Mad Dog steeled himself, adjusted his load, took two more steps, and hopped to the spot from which he would plant his feet and use every bit of the strength in his arms and legs to throw the first of these evils through a window open on infinity. There wasn't any floor where Mad Dog landed. His feet came down squarely in the middle of an opening onto seventy feet of empty grain bin. He had just enough time to realize what was happening to him as he began to fall. Just enough time to understand that a momentary lapse was about to cost him his life, and, worse, let the demons go free.

The sheriff knew trains only came to Buffalo Springs to collect the bounty of Benteen County's harvest. Regular freights hadn't passed through in decades. The moment he heard what sounded like an approaching locomotive, he knew what it was.

"Heather," he said, "we've got to get out of here."

Heather was around behind the nearest support pillar relieving her bladder. If there were proper facilities available up here, they were likely (and appropriately) in the head house. She was too desperate to care.

The train was approaching faster than seemed possible. Why not, the sheriff thought, throwing mental hands into the air. It had been that kind of day. Now, just when it seemed like he might find a light at the end of his tunnel it turned out to be an onrushing train—or a tornado that sounded like one.

"What's that noise, Dad?" Heather fastened her jeans as she reappeared at his side.

"Tornado, I think. We need to get off this floor, find shelter. And we need to get past a bunch of crazy people between us and the way down."

He grabbed her hand and began leading her beside the belt, still rolling ever westward. There was a time that a single lightning strike inside the county would have shut down the power to everyone for hours. The sheriff was grateful for the technological improvements that had prevented a similar failure tonight. Somehow, that was why the windows had opened, and part of why they remained alive. Still, it would have been nice if whoever turned on the belt and opened the windows had taken the time to switch on the lights as well. All those open holes over gaping pits made this trip across the dark loading floor more of an adventure than he cared for.

The rain was falling outside all those windows more gently now, lightning exploded less often, and the bellowing thunder was diminishing and growing more distant. The moan from the approaching vortex was another matter. It was very close.

The wind was picking up again, not slashing this way and that as it had. Now it was coming straight through the north windows, gathering dust and grain and flinging it across the loading floor toward the opposite bank of glass. The sheriff was afraid he knew why. It was like a black hole had formed over there, drawing everything into it. As he watched, wisps of torn cloud began to stream through the north windows and rush across the floor like a crowd of misty ghosts hurrying, lemming like, toward the nearest drop. The sheriff recalled the movie *Twister* and wondered if he should expect the clouds to be followed by cows. Probably not, he decided, up here atop the elevator. The wisps became streams and their pace became frantic. It was a special effect the movie could have used—eerie, terrifying because of what it signified.

"Oh Daddy, look," Heather shouted and the sheriff didn't want to because he could hear the awed panic in her voice and he remembered how long it had been since she'd felt the need to call him Daddy.

It was just beyond the windows across the way, poised like some whirling viper hanging from a curdled sky. It coiled, its spinning jaws grinning at them as it searched the concrete wall for weakness, tasted the air for lives to swallow. The sheriff saw a pair of running figures hurrying toward it. The first was actually two, a giant carrying a smaller form above its head. The second was smaller and trailing, but bringing something bright and metallic in its hand.

The wind was an almost physical force that ripped at the sheriff and his daughter and demanded they follow it, go out and feed heaven's serpent. The sheriff took hold of his daughter and pushed her down against the base of the nearest pillar.

"Grab it," he shouted. "Lock your hands. Hold on with all your strength and don't let go for anything."

The sheriff couldn't tell whether she heard him or simply obeyed out of an instinct for survival. He fumbled at his belt and found the 9 mm. The wind rocked him and wouldn't let him steady himself but he couldn't just let the one with the blade chase his brother into the waiting vortex. He aimed, squeezed, fired. A flash of blinding white lit the sky and showed him the whirlwind was growing impatient and had begun tearing steel window frames from their foundations as casually as a cruel child might pick the wings from a butterfly. It showed him, too, that his brother had disappeared, was suddenly and completely gone, leaving behind the bouncing, rolling form he had carried and a second, stumbling form at which the sheriff had just fired. Whether the one with the blade had been hit or affected by whatever had plucked Mad Dog out of thin air, the sheriff couldn't tell and wasn't given time to find out. A window exploded behind him, showering him with shards of broken glass and scraps of metal. Something huge and dark and tumbling slammed against his shoulder and knocked him under the belt, wedging him against its supports. A red mist rose up behind his eyes and claimed him and took him where even his daughter's terrified screams couldn't reach.

It was a tight fit, but Mad Dog's body paint, along with the blood from his wounds and that of the being he was carrying, had proved a good lubricant. Mad Dog lost a little more skin on the way into the bin, but the extra weight of the form held above his head had been just enough to pop him through the opening like a cork shoved into a bottle. He'd been a little slow to realize what was happening, release his hold on the first evil, and grab for the lip of the hole as he descended through it. There'd been just enough time to see the one he'd dropped hit and roll and show surprising resiliency in springing back to its feet. And to watch as the second one slammed through the space Mad Dog would have occupied if there hadn't been an opening to a grain bin at exactly this spot.

"That's four," Mad Dog had thought he heard as it sailed past and the first one somehow twisted to avoid its claw and instead got tangled with the second and the two of them spun a few steps closer to the windows. The sky serpent chose that moment to strike. One instant they were there, the next, they weren't, and then Mad Dog felt the lip of the opening slip from his fingers as he began to plunge into seventy feet of emptiness. Yet what he felt wasn't terror, but relief. The twin evils were gone, sucked off this plane of existence as suddenly and cleanly as Dorothy and Toto, hurled back into their spiritual prison until they might, somehow, sometime, find peace and harmony within themselves or encounter a spirit kind and powerful enough to heal them.

Mad Dog fell and heaven's serpent reached for him, pulled the air from the empty container and, with it, Mad Dog, until his hands felt the rim again, grabbed it, and hung on. From outside, the wind blew across its mouth and produced a deep harmonic tone that vibrated like a massive pipe organ and shook Mad Dog like the reed of a colossal wind instrument. The wind and the serpent made a flute of the grain elevator. They played a brief song that Mad Dog had never heard before, and yet recognized. He would make himself a flute, he thought, and try to reproduce that melody.

If he lived.

Something had happened to his right hand. He could hardly feel his fingers anymore. It made keeping his grip that much harder, especially because the cut on his back had damaged some muscles and weakened his arm. Mad Dog, who could normally still manage twenty chin-ups, couldn't do even one. More important, he wasn't that confident of simply holding on either. He could feel the blood running down his legs and dripping into the pit. That blood was carrying his strength with it and, he sensed, there wasn't that much left. He'd used it all, mentally and physically. He hung in the dark and silence and contemplated his mortality.

It had turned comparatively silent. The tornado had gone somewhere else now and the storm was going with it. There was still the rumble of distant thunder out there, still the steady fall of a gentler rain. The sounds penetrated the grain bin and echoed softly back from the distant floor.

If this was where he was going to die, Mad Dog thought, it wasn't a bad place. Though this particular cavern stood above the ground, he thought it still qualified as a part of the World Below. That made this *Esceheman's* place, Our Grandmother's, and if his spiritual form was about to be separated from his physical one, he would be happy to trust his soul to her safe keeping. She would guide him to the place he was supposed to wait until he and the world were ready for another cycle. He felt himself slipping, his blood soaked fingers just didn't have the strength. If they managed to find his body and get it out of here, he would have liked to tell someone to put his remains out on the plains, raised above them on a scaffold in the way his people had done it long ago. He would have liked to explain to Englishman what had happened here, and to the little historian from Fort Hays State. Over a rare steak and fries and a long cool beer at Bertha's he decided, as the weight on his hands shifted, someone grasped his wrists, and a voice came echoing strangely from above, taking a long time to penetrate mental wanderings complicated by blood loss.

"Mad Dog, is that you?" the sheriff asked.

Mad Dog didn't answer and Englishman spoke again. "I can't think who else would be crazy enough to paint himself up like some Halloween skeleton and run around on top of a grain elevator in the middle of a thunderstorm, but I'm gonna be real upset if I pull you out of there and you turn out to be a psychotic murderer instead."

"Hey, little brother," Mad Dog said. "This round's on me." And then he didn't remember anything for a while.

The sheriff's legs were so weak that they would hardly hold him upright anymore. That's what came of supporting more than two hundred pounds of makeshift-bandaged half-brother down a spiral metal staircase from the top of the Buffalo Springs grain elevator while your badly shaken preteen daughter lit the way with a failing flashlight. At least it had been down. And every step of the way had been accompanied by an explanation of the events of the day as seen by a recent but thorough convert to Cheyenne theology—versions physical and metaphysical. By the time he got to the bottom of those steps, the sheriff was almost tired and dizzy enough to believe it. He was also too exhausted to go for his truck, not that it mattered since Frenchy had finally arrived.

They went, lights-and-siren, back to the courthouse through a town that was surprisingly untouched by the furry of the storm as Mrs. Kraus filled him in on details over Frency's radio from out of the ether and Mad Dog offered equally ethereal interpretations. There were some branches down and hail had shattered a few windows along Aspen in storefronts that were mostly abandoned anyway. A few more sheets of plywood weren't going to make the street look much sadder and more forsaken than it already was.

The occasional street light still burned, as did flickering lights in the homes they passed. The sheriff glanced at his watch and was surprised that it was only a little after ten. He felt like the day had gone on forever, more like forty-eight or seventy-two hours than the eighteen he'd been up. Buffalo Springians were glued to their TVs watching the evening news, curious to see if somewhere else had been hit harder by the storm and whether tomorrow would bring more of the same. In Kansas, the local weather report was as riveting as global events like wars and revolutions. Even at the height of the cold war, a Kansan had felt more threatened by the weather than Soviet nuclear weapons. Take a year of the state's weather damage and pile it in one place and the destruction was probably comparable to a missile strike. After the equivalent of one nuke a year, the sheriff decided, it wasn't too surprising that the folks who stayed here were a pretty hardy and independent lot. And after listening to Mad Dog's dissertation on shamanism and ancient evil, he decided, they were maybe a little peculiar, too.

Mrs. Kraus had told them that Doc and Judy were back at the courthouse with their collection of evidence. That was what made the courthouse their immediate destination. The sooner they got Mad Dog to Doc and received an evaluation of wounds and blood loss, the sooner they'd know whether they had to call in a medevac and get Mad Dog to whatever hospital in an adjoining county wasn't socked in by the storm. From the way he continued raving, the sheriff thought things probably weren't too serious. Most of it didn't sound like Mad Dog was any more out of his head than usual.

The sheriff supposed they would find the bodies soon. Most likely tomorrow, though where was anyone's guess. Tornados were funny that way. They might be dangling from power lines or the branches of a tree. They could have been slammed up against the side of a building or dumped into one of the nearby creeks. Most likely, though, they'd simply be cast aside from hundreds or thousands of feet above the endless plain and allowed to drift back to earth about as gently as if they'd stepped in front of a speeding grain truck and been turned into instant roadkill.

Mad Dog didn't think they'd find bodies. He thought both their physical and spiritual forms had been plucked away from this existence and imprisoned "elsewhen or at some other where." Time and space would be completely flexible for them now, according to his world view.

A quick glance down one of the cross streets convinced the sheriff that even the mobile homes—nah, what did they call them now (premanufactured or something)—even the half dozen or so of those that had sprung up on the west side were still firmly attached to their tie downs, trusting the next storm would be as gentle to them as this one. That they were still there, he supposed, was just one more Kansas miracle.

Mad Dog's theology linked them, Ellen Lane and Ben Todd. To him, they were just two parts of the same madness, the Ketchums, perhaps, revisited. The sheriff could appreciate his opinion. The couple had obviously been linked by an ancient evil—the molestation of two children by those who were bigger

and stronger and crueler. They'd been bound to the abuses of
previous generations as well, and their tragic aftermath, and learned
some sort of distorted need and loathing, each for the other. Still,
the sheriff couldn't help but wonder which of them had done the
murders. There probably wasn't going to be any way to tell now.
From what Mrs. Kraus said, the KBI had remarkably little physical
evidence to link anyone to their dead Simms. His own best clues,
those footprints under the reverend's fuse box and across the back
yard, were gone by now, erased by the storm as surely as the couple
themselves. The sheriff found he favored the woman because of
the savagery of the vengeance that had been visited on her brothers
and the comparatively gentle attentions to her father. On the basis
of pure physical strength, and it had taken a lot of muscle to cram
a pair of Simmses into a pair of public toilets, he had to think it
was the man. Rage could raise a lot of adrenaline, though, or more
than a decade of false imprisonment could inspire a really twisted
and brutal retribution.

Just as Mad Dog was sure they wouldn't find the bodies, the
sheriff was sure they'd never know which of them had been the
killer, or if they'd conspired in the deeds or just accidently meshed
in some improbable fashion. Just now, he was too tired to care.
His daughter was curled up on the seat next to him, snuggled into
his chest under the protective crook of his arm in a way that wasn't
likely to happen between them very often anymore. That, along
with the presence of his rambling, but beloved, elder brother, was
enough to make him feel like the winner, no matter how little he
might have had to do with resolving the day's events.

Frenchy brought them around the corner by Bertha's in a
controlled skid and targeted an empty slot directly before the front
steps to the courthouse. They had hardly come to a stop before
Doc was in the car with a stethoscope and a blood pressure cuff
and Judy was hauling Heather out of his arms. Mrs. Kraus greeted
him with the kind of fond hug he wouldn't have believed was in her.
She offered him a cigarette and a light and he accepted before it
occurred to him that he'd quit smoking more than twenty years ago.

"Jesus, Sheriff," she was saying. "Are you all right? You look
like you been rode hard and put away wet. There's blood and
scrapes all over you. Should I get Doc to come take a take a look
at you when he's done with Mad Dog?"

"Nah, I'm all right," he lied, the tough guy in the John Wayne role, reassuring folks that his wounds weren't mortal. This was how Kansas sheriffs were supposed to act wasn't it? Sort of a "shucks, t'wern't nothin, ma'am," school of pain management. The place where the horn had grazed his back hurt like sin, almost as bad as his legs. Heather had checked it, though, and the wound wasn't deep.

There he'd been, looking for cows to start blowing across the loading floor atop the elevator and he'd almost gotten his wish. It wasn't a cow that crashed through the window behind him though, it was a buffalo with an arrow through it that had been part of a sign directing traffic on the highway to stop for a Buffalo Burger. It was peculiar, too, how it had come to rest with that arrow pointing straight down into the grain bin in which his brother was hanging. The sheriff had been out of it for a minute, in no shape to determine just where Mad Dog might have gone if that stupid sign hadn't been sitting there, demanding that he examine it and then look where it was pointing. Maybe, he thought for just a second, there was something to this metaphysical stuff after all.

"The twister took 'em? Lord!" Mrs. Kraus said. "Ain't that something. Them storms do the craziest things. You know, after the tornado hopped the elevator it come right across town, headed straight for the courthouse. Wynn called me from a pay phone downtown when he heard Frenchy's siren. Told me he saw the funnel and was sure it was going to take the courthouse right out."

Wynn, the sheriff had forgotten all about him. "Where is Wynn?" he asked. "Is he OK?"

"Oh yeah. He's fine. He's walking in. Wanted to know if I thought it would be all right if he drove your truck over and I told him to leave it set right were it was. Wrecking one car a day is enough. Besides, the exercise'll do him good.

"Anyway, we were all in your office, waiting by the phone and the radio and hoping to hear some good news out of one of them any minute and, instead, we all of a sudden heard it coming. Sounded like God had brought a big Hoover to suck up the sinners. We never had time to even think about heading for the basement before it came and went. I ran outside to see if there was any damage, and, you know, it was the damnedest thing...."

She paused, waiting for the sheriff to ask just what that damnedest thing could be. It took him a moment to recognize his cue. He'd encountered enough damnedest things that day for a lifetime.

"What was it, Mrs. Kraus?" he finally managed.

"The rose garden. That damn, forever expanding rose garden. It's gone. Every single plant, roots and all, best I could see, and not a tad of damage to Mr. York's house or the back of the courthouse either. It just set down right on those roses and it huffed and it puffed and it blowed 'em all away. And those metal posts he filled with concrete and set back there, it took them too. And the pile of metal poles he was fixing to set, along with his bag of concrete and his pile of sand and even his damned wheel barrow and tools. He came wandering around his house about a minute after I got out there. Stood, shaking his head and saying 'Enough's enough. I give up. No more roses.' I tell you Sheriff, it makes you think maybe the Lord's on our side."

The sheriff let her euphoria wash over him and pick him up and carry him along for a minute, until he saw Doc's posterior come backing out of Frenchy's car.

"How is he, Doc?"

"Frenchy and I are going to take him over to the office and I'm going to give him a few stitches and some fancier bandages and drip a pint of plasma into him. He's telling me he wants to take you over to Bertha's for a steak and fries and a long tall cold one. After I'm done, I think that'd be about the best thing in the world for him, but maybe you should go find him some regular clothes to get into first. Then somebody better call Bertha and let her know this is a prescription visit and that Frenchy and I'll be coming along too, and maybe some of these other folks from the courthouse as well. You know Bertha. She'll open up anytime if there's enough business.

"We'll be about an hour and a half," Doc said. "That'll give you time to handle what you've got to." He nodded toward the front steps of the courthouse where another Heather stood beside the professor from Fort Hays and looked frightened.

The sheriff had managed to avoid thinking about her. His happy ending was someone else's tragedy. He turned and started walking toward her. Like his daughter, she was almost as tall as her mother, filling out too, beginning to look almost like a woman. Except in her eyes. The eyes that watched him approach belonged to a scared little girl.

"Just a second," Judy was keyed up and breathless when she caught the sheriff as he walked toward the courthouse steps. "We've got to talk."

Her intensity frightened him. "No," she said reading the incipient panic in his eyes. "Everybody's still OK. There's just something we need to discuss before you start making arrangements for Heather Lane."

He was exhausted and the thought of taking on that chore was more than he wanted to bear. Anything that put it off was welcome. He let her guide him toward the seldom used concrete bench at the southeast corner of the building, out of everyone's hearing.

"Oh Englishman, have you thought about what's to become of her?"

Former spouses aren't noted for recognizing each other's best qualities. The sheriff knew Judy could be a remarkably empathetic woman, once you got past her me-and-mine-first approach to human relations, but this surprised him. He hadn't expected her to be able to give more than a passing thought to anyone other than their daughter for days.

"Well, I'll contact her family. From what Doc said, they're elderly aunts, not healthy. I don't know whether they'll be up to taking on a teen. If not, since there are no other immediate relatives, she'll be turned over to the state."

"And end up in some foster home," Judy made it sound the sort of cruel fate that Oliver Twist faced in a nineteenth century orphan asylum. "We can't let that happen to her, Englishman. She should stay with us. I was thinking, maybe we could adopt her."

"What?" The world tilted with the absurdity of her suggestion and the sheriff mentally stumbled and fought for his balance before answering with all the compassion that had become typical of their discussions. "Are you nuts. The state's not going to let a divorced couple keep her just because she happens to share the same name, age, and looks as our daughter."

"We could get married again," Judy said, and this time he actually had to reach out and grab the back of the bench to keep from pitching over in astonishment. "And there's another reason we should keep her. You know I've been doing genealogical research?"

The sheriff was having trouble following the conversation. Still, this seemed safer to respond to than her previous statement.

"Ah, sure. You told me Mad Dog and I are probably only one sixteenth Cheyenne, instead of the quarter Mom always thought."

Judy seemed almost apologetic about that. "I thought, if it was true and I could prove it, our daughter might be eligible for some college scholarships, or that it might make it easier for her to get into a good university. But it didn't work. That's the way it is with genealogy. You don't always find what you expect, though what you do find is usually interesting."

The wind whipped her auburn hair and blended the scent of wet earth with Judy's perfume. The Kansas wind—it was back, blowing again the way it always did. Knowing that helped the sheriff steady his world a little.

It was absurd, but the idea of getting back together with Judy, of being a full-time father to his daughter and maybe helping a child in need, was intriguing. Though wisdom dictated he avoid the topics, the sheriff found he had to ask.

"Judy, didn't you tell me once you never really loved me? Was that true, or did you say it just to hurt me?"

A familiar look of calculation flickered across her face until he reached out and took her hands in his. "You've got to be honest here, Judy. This is too serious for anything else."

"Some of each," she admitted. Her eyes dropped for a moment, then defiantly flashed back and locked on his. "But most of the time I still love you, Englishman. So listen. This is really important.

"After I ran out of records to follow for the generations back of Grandma Sadie, and hit a brick wall looking for your father, I started on my side of the family. Did you know my mother was adopted?"

"Sure. I remember Mom telling me that when you and I started getting serious."

"She knew?" Judy's astonishment could probably be heard clear to Bertha's. "I didn't know! Why didn't you tell me?"

"Hey, I just assumed you knew. And I never thought it was important. I remember telling Mom I didn't care, and didn't really want to know about it unless there was some reason you and I shouldn't get married and have children."

She pulled away from him. "No one ever told me," she said, quieter now, but beginning to pace back and forth, too upset and frustrated to stand still. "I had to find out for myself. I was going through some old family files and I discovered the adoption papers. Mom, my grandparents, they're all gone. I asked Dad, but you know how his memory has failed. If he knew, he can't recall, or won't tell me. So I went hunting on my own and I finally did it. I came up with her birth certificate. My Mom was born in Albuquerque. Most of the spots where my real grandmother filled out information about who she was or where she and her family were from are blank. She put her name down as Lois Lane. A joke, I thought. And a dead end. I was sure I'd never trace her, but, Englishman...she was just thirteen and she wasn't married. She wrote down the father's name as Osuna de la Jolla. There was a girls' school near Albuquerque in the '30s, when my mother was born, a place that specialized in situations like this. It was the de la Jolla Academy for Young Women, and it used to be on Osuna Road."

Judy grabbed the sheriff's arm and pulled him around to face the courthouse steps where Heather Lane huddled beside the professor from Fort Hays State. "That little girl over there, she has an aunt whose name is Linda Lois Chandler de la Jolla. Her Linda Chandler came from right outside Buffalo Springs. She was molested by her father, had a baby. Heather just told me Ellen Lane chose that surname because her aunt used the same alias when she was young and in trouble. Don't you understand, Englishman. She and my mother were cousins. Heather, our Heather, and I are related to that Heather. By whatever Byzantine twists of fate, we're her family."

"Whoa, Judy, you lost me."

"Englishman, the Chandlers were a prominent family here. They had three daughters, Linda Lois, Mary Ellen, and Annie Beth. All of them were sexually abused by their father. Linda had a child by him. My mother. Somehow, my grandparents adopted the baby and brought her back to Buffalo Springs. Linda probably never knew where her daughter went. She and Mary Ellen left the county as soon as they could, but Annie stayed and married Elmer Simms. They had three kids too, Tommy and Peter, who both got cut up and stuffed in toilets today, and the woman who picked her alias from the aunts who raised her, Ellen Lane, the other Heather's mother.

The sheriff shook his head. "Can you prove all this?"

"I don't know. Maybe, with time."

They didn't have time. Even if Judy was right, knowing was different from proving. They could remarry. It was a curiously appealing idea, but, he feared the plight of this second Heather was a fragile cause on which to pin a cure for all the failures that had doomed their relationship. They could start the proceedings next morning, hire the best lawyers and pay whatever they asked, and it would still take years. More years, probably, than this Heather had left before she was old enough to choose her own family. She needed someone now.

"Hello." It wasn't a very good connection. Lots of snaps, crackles and pops, as if a breakfast food company had taken over the long distance service.

"Yes, hello. Is this Mary Ellen Chandler?" the sheriff asked.

"Yes," she said. She wasn't quite sure why she'd bothered answering. A habit of boredom, she supposed.

"I hope it isn't too late," he said.

Nearly, she thought, looking at the shotgun, neatly polished and oiled and loaded. "No, not quite."

She sat on the chair at her sister's bedside, the gun propped against the adjacent dresser. She had a lovely little Victorian writer's box in her lap. She had chosen a piece of her favorite stationery. On it was neatly printed her list of reasons and apologies, her bequests and benedictions. It had taken only half a page, and though it seemed such an inadequate attempt at summing up two lives, she found that she couldn't think of anything else to say.

"My name's English," he said. "I'm the Sheriff of Benteen County. I'm afraid I have some difficult news for you."

"Yes," she said, wondering what remained that could seem difficult at this stage. She rather supposed something terrible had happened regarding Ellen or Ben or the Simms family. The doctor she'd spoken to earlier had hinted as much.

"It's about your brother-in-law and your nephews. It's about your niece, too, Sarah, or Ellen, the girl you raised, and her former husband as well, I'm afraid."

"I thought it might be," she said without emotion. "Dr. Jones called earlier with a number of questions. I couldn't help putting together some conclusions of my own. What's happened, Sheriff? Have any of them survived." Not that it mattered much, except that she might want to rewrite the suicide note and revise some of her bequests.

"No," he said. At least he wasn't the kind to beat around the bush and waste her time...though time was all she had now— seconds, minutes, hours—it depended on this call. "No," he said again, "I'm sorry. None of them survived."

"May I ask what happened to them?" She thought she knew, and it was just one more reason to go ahead with her plans, but she found that she was still curious. It still mattered to her. She wanted to know just how totally she had failed in her obligation to Ellen, and what that failure might have cost others.

"Mr. Simms died of heart failure, sometime Friday we believe. Both his sons were murdered, maybe last night or early this morning. Then Ellen and Benjamin Todd were killed tonight."

"I suppose it was Ellen or Ben who killed the boys, or the two of them together. Did Ellen and Ben murder each other then? Some kind of suicide pact," she asked, "or did the one kill the other and then take the coward's way out alone?" Her phrasing surprised her. Did she really consider herself a coward too? Well, she supposed so. What was one more failing?

"No, not exactly. They were done in by a tornado, plucked right out of a building and, technically speaking, we don't know that they're dead yet because no one has found their bodies, but someone saw the funnel cloud take them. There's really no doubt."

"A tornado?" It was impossible to keep the amazement out of her voice. "They were together and they were alive and a tornado swooped down and carried them away?"

"Yes ma'am. If it makes more sense to you, it seems likely they were trying to kill each other at the time."

She found herself smiling a little. "Yes, I'm afraid it does. It's tragic, of course, but then they were each tragic figures, as everyone in our extended family seems to be, so I suppose the result is for the best. I do hope, though, that they didn't hurt anyone else along the way."

"No ma'am, not seriously, though there's still one pending."

"Well, I'm terribly sorry. I do hope that person will be all right. I wish I could have done more to prevent it, but then there are so very many things I wish I could have done."

"There's nothing left to do for this generation, or their predecessors," he said, "but there's still a way that you can help."

"Of course, Sheriff." She glanced at the shotgun. It would wait a few minutes more and the note needed editing now. She supposed there was still something he didn't understand. She didn't mind trying to explain, she just didn't think she could accept the responsibility anymore. "What would you like to know?"

"Well ma'am, it's not me really. There's a young lady here who, all of a sudden, doesn't have any parents. She wants to know if she can maybe come stay with her Aunts Mary Ellen and Linda for a while."

"Oh my God!" Mary Ellen said. "Heather? I thought Ellen had left her safely behind in that New Mexico convent. Poor dear Heather was involved in all these new tragedies? Is she all right?"

"Physically she's fine. As for the rest, I suppose it'll take awhile to tell. All her life maybe, and the answer might depend on whether you can take her in."

"Us? You want us to take Heather?" It was unthinkable, even if there wasn't that lump in her breast and a loaded shotgun waiting beside her, both prepared to put severe limits on her ability to interact with yet another damaged child. "No, I don't think that would be possible. We just couldn't...."

"Yes, I suppose I understand," the Sheriff was saying.

"My God, we can't take care of ourselves, how can we take care of a teenage girl. It's too much responsibility." Mary Ellen said it to the phone, but she wasn't really justifying things to the sheriff. She was trying to convince herself.

"Yes ma'am," he was saying over that distant telephone line. "I'll tell her."

It wasn't right. She knew that. She should try. She was still responsible, and that's exactly what this was all about. Who knew what this experience had done to Heather. Who knew what Ellen had put her daughter through already, and Annie to Ellen before that, and her parents to her sisters and herself, and so on and so on. One generation failing another. And every time, that failure perpetuated itself. And would just go on perpetuating itself until someone took responsibility and stopped it. Mary Ellen wasn't foolish enough to think she was the one who could do that. But maybe, just maybe, Heather could find a way to assume the responsibility for herself, take charge of her own fate...if only she had help.

"Sheriff, I'm sorry," she said. "You just don't understand. I'm seventy-two years old. I.... I think I have cancer. My sister, Linda, is seventy-four. She does have cancer. They say it's spread throughout her body, terminal, just a matter of time. I know we should do something for poor Heather, but how can we...two old ladies, one practically dead, the other following hard on her heels. If only we weren't alone. If only we had help, some family left who was willing to pitch in."

"Ms. Chandler," he interrupted. "What if I told you that you have that family? What if I told you your sister's granddaughter is right here in Buffalo Springs and wants desperately to help?"

"Linda has a granddaughter?" She couldn't believe it. And more, she couldn't believe that Linda, who had not responded to anything but the morphine for weeks, had her eyes open and was staring at her. Linda's lips were moving, trying to form words. She'd been so sure everything that was Linda was already gone, but something was left, enough was still there to whisper a faint and hopeful question.

"I have a granddaughter? May I see her, please? " Linda had so little breath, she was only able to whisper the first sentence. Her mouth merely formed the words of the second, but Mary Ellen recognized them, and how terribly important they were to the spark inside Linda that refused to let the cancer win.

"Your family here will help all they can, but you have to let us. You'll have to accept custody and then help us prove the relationship," the sheriff was saying. "Will you do that? Can I bring her?"

Mary Ellen picked up the shotgun. It could solve everything so quickly. Heather and an unexpected family would make things terribly complicated. Linda wasn't up to it. Mary Ellen wasn't sure she was up to it either. Linda watched her and waited. Mary Ellen opened the breech, removed the shells, and deposited them in the waste paper basket beside Linda's bed. She folded the note she'd so painstakingly transcribed and let it follow. Linda smiled and Mary Ellen realized there were tears on both their cheeks. She answered the distant voice at the other end of the telephone line, and she answered Linda, too.

"Yes," she said. "Yes you may."

Afterword & Acknowledgements

I was born on the exotic flat earth where this novel is set. Most Americans never see it, except from an airplane or an interstate. Should you search for it now, it will prove illusive. The rural experience and the family farm seem bound for extinction. They will outlast my generation, but not, unless we salvage them, by much.

Benteen County and Buffalo Springs aren't real. They're the product of my imagination, though Benteen bears a striking resemblance to Reno County and Buffalo Springs is much like an exaggerated amalgam of Hutchinson, the city where I was born, and Partridge, the village where I attended school from third through twelfth grade.

None of the characters exist in fact either. I know people like them, some in Kansas and some elsewhere. Hicks, for instance, are hard to find in Kansas (except, occasionally, on the board of education). Schooling alone is not a disqualifier, but all of my own hick-free rural high school class of twenty-four continued their educations. Seventeen graduated college and seven of those earned advanced degrees. The only hick in Benteen County, "Wynn some, lose some," is based more on characters I met in that same urban bureaucracy where I first encountered a must-hire system.

Kansas has its share of eccentrics, but an oddball like Mad Dog could exist anywhere. And Mad Dog is neither a nut case nor a fool. The Cheyenne philosophy which he espouses, with the assistance of Professor Neil Bowen, is as accurately depicted as possible. For that, thanks to Dr. Karl H. Schlesier and my training in anthropology at Wichita State University and the University of Arizona. Karl has been teacher, mentor, and friend. I conceived of Mad Dog as a result of his book, *The Wolves of Heaven*, then clarified many elements of *Tsistsistas* Shamanism through conversations with the author. Mad Dog wasn't raised as a Cheyenne and, therefore, if he has made mistakes or misrepresentations, it is because of that limitation which I share. Neither he nor I have anything but the deepest respect for those beliefs.

There are so many people to thank for so many things that the task seems impossible. Failing to do so, however, would be unforgivable. Mom and Dad read to me and told me stories and otherwise encouraged career choices that profit the soul rather than the bank account. Them first, then, before all others.

Mad Dog & Englishman began as something to fool with until I chose the topic for my important novel—the one still collecting rejections. From that first partial incarnation, thanks to Martye, Peter, and David. Thanks too, to Tom. I wish you could have stayed to see how it ends.

Special thanks, this go around, to my agent, Paige Wheeler, and the patient guidance and thoughtful editing of Barbara Peters, as well as Louis Silverstein and Robert Rosenwald and the other fine folk at Poisoned Pen Press.

In between, some contributors are gone too soon. Thanks, Don and Steve, great friends and constant supporters, sorely missed.

Thanks to Jodi, Kita, and Charlie, three sisters to an only child. John Stewart scored the novel without knowing. And to Alex, one more Barbara, Bills, Bloodlines, Bob, Bruce, Charlene, Chris, Claire, Claudia, Clues, Dave, Dennis, a different Don, Donna, Douglas, Elaine, Frank, Gary, Gayle, Hillary, Jacquie, Jims, Jessica, Joe, John, Julie, June, Kansas-L, Karen, Kate, Lee, Lyn, Lynn, Mani, Margaret, Mark, mat, Marty, multiple Mikes, Nadine, a pair of Pats, Paul, Rebecca, Robert, Ron, Sallie, Sandy, Sharon, some Susans, Tania, Terrie, Tina, Tom, and Tony: the novel and I owe so much. Without my wife, Barbara, it simply wouldn't exist. For flaws, or failing to acknowledge someone who deserved it, only I am responsible.

JMH
Tucson, by way of Hutchinson, Darlow,
Partridge, Manhattan, Wichita, Sedna
Creek, et Tabun, Albuquerque, and a
yellow brick road

To receive a free catalog of other Poisoned Pen Press titles, please contact us in one of the following ways:

Phone: 1-800-421-3976
Facsimile: 1-480-949-1707
Email: info@poisonedpenpress.com
Website: www.poisonedpenpress.com

Poisoned Pen Press
6962 E. First Ave. Ste 103
Scottsdale, AZ 85251